MIGUEL'S GIFT

D1015228

MIGUEL'S GIFT

BRUCE KADING

ACADEMY

CHICAGO

Copyright © 2017 by Bruce Kading
All rights reserved
First edition
Published by Academy Chicago Publishers
An imprint of Chicago Review Press Incorporated
814 North Franklin Street
Chicago, Illinois 60610
ISBN 978-1-61373-625-8

Library of Congress Cataloging-in-Publication Data
Names: Kading, Bruce, author.
Title: Miguel's gift / Bruce Kading.
Description: Chicago: Chicago Review Press Incorporated, 2017.
Identifiers: LCCN 2016029766 (print) | LCCN 2016036244 (ebook) | ISBN
 9781613736258 (pbk.: alk. paper) | ISBN 9781613736272 (pdf) | ISBN
 9781613736289 (epub) | ISBN 9781613736265 (kindle)
Subjects: LCSH: United States. Immigration and Naturalization
 Service—Employees—Fiction. | Homicide investigation—Fiction. | Illegal
 aliens—Fiction. | Fraud investigation—Fiction. | United
 States—Emigration and immigration—Fiction. | GSAFD: Mystery fiction.
Classification: LCC PS3611.A3285 M54 2017 (print) | LCC PS3611.
 A3285 (ebook) | DDC 813/.6—dc23
LC record available at https://lccn.loc.gov/2016029766

Cover design: Rebecca Lown
Cover image: Shutterstock/IVASHstudio
Typesetting: Nord Compo

Printed in the United States of America
5 4 3 2 1

Whoso would be a man must be a nonconformist.

—Ralph Waldo Emerson

PROLOGUE

Chicago, 1974

Dusk came early that day. The clouds had rolled in, cloaking the streets in a wintry gloom. Alarmed by a forecast of snow, commuters fled the city like an army in retreat.

Agent Michael Landau pulled into heavy traffic on North Clark Street while his partner, Frank Kelso, casually scanned the pedestrians who hurried along, their shoulders hunched against the cold, damp air. Landau checked his rearview mirror as they crossed Foster Avenue. "We just lost Tatum at the light," he said evenly.

"It's OK. He knows where we're going," replied Kelso.

"You said mainly Peruvians at this place?"

"Yeah, the foreman's Peruvian. Takes care of his own."

They drove on silently for a few moments, and then Kelso said, "Hey, pull over. That guy's wet." He was looking at a scruffy young man wearing a faded leather jacket, who was leaning with his back against the brick facade of a bookstore. The man had long, unruly blond hair, and there was a sullen, almost angry look on his face.

Landau edged the car over and studied the man. "Looks like an addict. What makes you think he's illegal?"

"I'm not sure," said Kelso, already stepping out of the car. "Tell Buck."

Landau grabbed the mic. "Buck, we're going to talk to a guy—half a block north of Foster, east side."

"Be right there," said Tatum, shaking his head. It was vintage Kelso—never willing to ignore a suspected illegal, even if it was inconvenient. When the light changed, Tatum accelerated briefly and then slowed. There was Kelso, talking to a man whose glazed eyes were darting in every direction, looking for a way out. This could be trouble, thought Tatum. As he slid the transmission into park, a quick movement caught his eye—Kelso and the man now struggling, Landau running toward them. Tatum flew out of the car and reached for the handcuffs on his belt. Sharp commands and curses echoed down the street, a tangle of three bodies pitching back and forth, the glint of metal at the center of desperately flexed arms and hands. Tatum dropped the cuffs and pulled the .357 revolver from his shoulder holster—too late. A flash of orange and the dry crack of gunfire. Kelso letting out a deep, wavering moan and falling away.

Tatum leaned forward, his arms extended, elbows locked, and fired. At such close range the shot smoked a ring of black powder into the man's forehead, the hollow-point bullet expanding like a grenade on contact—a deadly explosion into vital brain tissue. The man instantly crumpled against the brick wall, his head falling limply to his shoulder, eyes open but lifeless.

As they waited for the ambulance, Landau held Kelso around his shoulders and tried to comfort him. A nearby shopkeeper offered a towel, and Landau used it to slow the blood surging from Kelso's chest. Tatum stood over them, waving onlookers away and repeating over and over, "Yer gonna be fine, Frank." But Tatum couldn't pull his eyes away from the young man he'd fatally shot. Though he couldn't place it, the face was hauntingly familiar.

Frank Kelso lost consciousness and died before the ambulance arrived, just five minutes after the bullet pierced his heart—a bullet fired from his own gun.

Part I

1

Chicago, 1987

They were to meet outside the pawnshop on the south edge of the Loop. "I'll pick you up early, around five thirty," Willis had grumbled. "I'm not gonna wait around if you're not there."

Nick Hayden stood alone in the darkness, feeling a bit lopsided from the unfamiliar weight of the .38-caliber Smith & Wesson revolver on his right hip. Wearing a sport coat and tie, he held his arms across his chest against the cool morning air and listened to the city—the echo of traffic, the squeak and clatter of the elevated train. A patrol car rolled by, shined its spotlight on him, and continued on. Now and then a shabbily clad wino would stumble in or out of the three-story flophouse next to the pawnshop and look Nick over suspiciously. Glancing at his watch, he saw that it was nearly six o'clock and was seized by a moment of panic—perhaps he'd gotten the location wrong.

Seconds later a battered green van, its tailpipe coughing a trail of black smoke, came to a stop at the curb. Hayden at first ignored it—no way could that wreck be an official

Immigration Service vehicle—but the loud honks got his attention. He stepped closer and could make out the stern visage of Joe Willis behind the wheel, puffing a cigarette. Nick slid into the passenger seat.

"Morning, sir," he said.

Saying nothing, Willis jerked away from the curb, took a sharp right turn at the corner, and pulled into the four-lane westbound expressway. The van shuddered and teetered from side to side, while Hayden gripped the armrest for support.

A crosshatched metal screen separated the front seats from the cargo area, where wooden bench seats ran the length of each side. Peering through the screen, Nick spotted a reddish stain on the metal floor, but in the faint light he couldn't tell if it was dried blood, vomit, or salsa. He sniffed the air, thick with the fetid vapors of sweaty prisoners who'd ridden there.

"You'll get used to the smell," Willis said. "The openings in the screen are the real problem. Last month one of the wets pissed all over a detention officer's shoulder."

Willis wore a brown polyester suit with leather patches on the elbows. His head was completely bald, and his nose was covered with an intricate network of blue and scarlet veins. Thirty years of unfiltered Lucky Strikes had taken their toll: his voice was gravelly, his teeth heavily stained. Though he appeared older than his fifty-four years, a feral energy pulsed through his wiry frame.

"Sometimes we cram twenty wets in there and they're pressed up against the screen," said Willis. "Farting, belching, upchucking huevos rancheros—you name it."

"You always drive this vehicle?" asked Hayden.

"No, but detention claimed they were shorthanded today. Been happening more and more lately." Willis took a final drag on the Lucky, flicked it through the open window, and glanced at his sandy-haired new partner. Though Hayden appeared physically capable, Willis saw callowness in the young man's brown eyes.

"I hear you didn't go through the Patrol," said Willis.

"No."

"Figures. Those geniuses at headquarters don't have a fucking clue."

The sun rose in a dramatic burst, unfurling like an amber carpet over the city. Willis weaved through the traffic, cutting off several vehicles as he skipped from lane to lane. Whenever they honked or flashed their lights in protest, he let out a chuckle, as if provoking a reaction was cause for celebration. They soon passed the city's tightly packed office and apartment buildings, exited the expressway, and entered a vast, partially developed industrial park, where most of the warehouses were two-story brick structures separated by fields of prairie grass.

The fuzzy snap of the police radio came through the speaker on the floorboard, followed by the amused voice of Sam Payton. "We're almost there, Joe. Seems like we had a little problem last time."

Willis grabbed the mic from under the dash. "You've got a gift for understatement, Payton. I've still got boot prints on my face. Maybe you can do better this time."

"If thirty wets come at us, it's gonna be the same thing," said Payton. "We'll do what we can."

Nick listened intently, hoping to glean something useful. He still had no clear idea what to expect during this, his first field operation, or how to respond if things went awry. Though he'd been given a badge and assigned to area control— the unit responsible for rounding up illegals in the Chicago area—he'd not yet gone to the academy for training. The day before, after a fifteen-minute orientation session with the district firearms officer and half an hour of firing off practice rounds in the basement range, he'd somehow managed to shoot a qualifying score and been issued a .38-caliber revolver. Journeymen officers who, like Willis, had started their INS careers as Border Patrol agents had offered a frosty reception, many of them barely willing to acknowledge Hayden's presence. Now he was hoping his crusty partner would fill him in on what to expect, but Willis's attitude toward Hayden seemed to fluctuate between indifference and outright hostility.

"This is my first field operation, Mr. Willis," Hayden finally ventured. "What do you want me to do?"

"You'd like that, wouldn't you? For me to tell you exactly what to do, so you don't have to think for yourself. Well, it doesn't work that way. In this job you have to think on your feet, and there's no book that tells you how to do it."

There were a few moments of stony silence before Willis spoke again: "How many sets of cuffs they give you?" he asked, softening his tone a bit.

"They said you'd have some."

Willis grunted and pulled his jacket back to reveal five sets on his belt.

"Here, you can have two of mine. Just start grabbing bodies when they take off and wet 'em down."

"Wet 'em down?"

"Get 'em to admit they're illegal—mostly Mexicans at this place."

"What if—" he began, but Willis cut him off.

"It's the place with the loading dock in front," he said, pointing to a warehouse about a hundred yards away. Seconds later a dozen or more brown-skinned men wearing T-shirts could be seen running from the rear of the building into the surrounding fields.

"Shit, somebody saw us and called the plant," hissed Willis. He grabbed the mic. "Payton, head off the wets flying out the back!"

As Willis brought the van to a skidding stop beneath the front loading dock, a large metal door opened and about ten men exploded from inside, jumping from the dock to the pavement. One of them sailed from the dock onto the top of the van, clomped across the roof, and jumped off the back. Willis swung his door open as a runner was passing by, striking the man's arm and sending him flying to the ground.

His heart pounding, Nick leaped from the van in pursuit of two panic-stricken young men racing toward an adjoining field. They were slender and fast but were soon slowed by the tall, wet grass. One peeled off to the right, but Hayden stayed locked on the other.

The Mexican thrashed desperately through the waist-high grass and cattails, while Hayden steadily gained ground until they both sank into a shallow, muddy ditch. Holding him by the shirt, Nick clumsily pulled out his badge. "*Soy de Inmigración. ¿Tiene papeles?*" Hayden gasped. "You got papers?"

The Mexican, winded and disheveled, shook his head and looked down at the mud covering his shoes and pants. Hayden took a moment to catch his breath before cuffing the man's wrists together. He then walked him back to the parking lot, pleased that he wasn't returning empty-handed. Willis and the other agents were gathered next to the van with a dozen handcuffed Mexicans.

"When I told you to wet 'em down, I didn't mean throw him into a fucking lagoon," crowed Willis. The other agents laughed but not with the relish of Joe Willis. Hayden managed a sheepish grin, knowing he'd passed a minor test.

"All right, get 'em into the van. Let's get outa here," said Willis.

The van hung low under the weight of the prisoners as it sped toward the office. The Mexicans laughed and talked cheerfully among themselves as though nothing much had happened. Surprised that the Spanish he'd learned in school and while traveling abroad was holding up pretty well, Hayden listened as one of the Mexicans regaled the others with stories of his previous arrests along the border and in Chicago.

Ten minutes later they pulled into the basement of the Federal Building, where agents were transferring prisoners to green-uniformed detention officers. The Mexicans found themselves dwarfed by fourteen burly Poles, arrested at a construction site. Hayden and a detention officer escorted the illegals into an elevator equipped with a large compartment behind metal bars and another smaller space for the accompanying officers.

It was quiet except for the sound of breathing and a low mechanical hum as they were whisked up to the third floor. The tight quarters and metal bars had sobered the prisoners, and there was a palpable feeling of defeat among them, their plans and dreams at least temporarily obliterated. They stared at Hayden with looks of resignation, sadness, and something else—a measure of respect, the kind of respect that borders on fear. Nobody had ever looked at him that way before. A curiously pleasant feeling of power swept over him.

A steady procession of vehicles continued through the morning, agents unloading their prisoners like fishermen unloading their catch.

———

The atmosphere of the area control squad room was grim but functional. Thirty gunmetal-gray desks were arranged in tight rows, each with a vintage Smith-Corona typewriter and a straight-backed chair. There were no dividers for privacy, no family photos or other personal items, and no wall decorations. Even when sunlight penetrated the grime on the floor-to-ceiling windows, the room had a dingy, impersonal feel that was vaguely depressing. Black metal filing cabinets lined the pale green walls and an earthy scent, reminiscent of a men's locker room, permeated the air.

A corpulent young woman, smacking gum and looking bored, listened to the scratchy radio transmissions from agents announcing their arrest totals, destinations, and estimated times of arrival. In response, she repeatedly muttered "ten-four" into the desktop microphone, while making entries on a log sheet.

Hayden led the young Mexican he'd arrested toward an empty desk next to Willis amid the chatter of typewriters and buzz of conversations. Several agents interviewed a group of young men from Pakistan, who had entered the country as students and were found working as cabdrivers. The "Pakis" were dark-skinned and thin, their eyes roaming nervously around the room. The Mexicans sat quietly, their hands folded between their legs, responding softly to agents' questions.

Standing out like flashing neon signs were five transvestites from Central and South America, arrested the night before at a club where they did impersonations of well-known female entertainers. They all had fake eyelashes, flaming red lipstick, and long, brightly colored nails. The hulking Poles on the opposite side of the room grunted terse responses via interpreters and stared at the transvestites, as if trying to decide whether they were repelled or attracted by them.

There was a sense of urgency in the air because buses would be leaving that night with those Mexicans who could be persuaded to sign "voluntary departure" agreements. A Greyhound bus destined for Juárez was already waiting in the basement.

Hayden rolled the standard report form into the typewriter and began collecting biographical information, but he found the pandemonium distracting. Willis, unfazed, methodically rapped out the forms using his index fingers, hardly acknowledging the silent figure seated next to him. After thousands of arrests and interviews, there was little need for talk. He already knew the answers.

Willis noticed that Nick had stopped typing and was watching the little dramas playing out around him. "We don't have all day, Hayden," he snapped. "Get moving."

"Yes, sir."

"And don't call me 'sir.' I'm not a supervisor, thank God."

Only a few of the agents noticed that Lou Moretti's door had swung open at the far corner of the room. Moretti, chief of area control, had a thin layer of oily hair combed over his large head and a red, alcohol-ravaged nose. He wore a cheap, snap-on tie, and his shirtsleeves were rolled up to his elbows. Moretti, who rarely left his office when things were going well, stalked out with an angry gleam in his eyes.

"OK. Everybody stop what you're doing," he roared, and the room fell instantly silent. Moretti began pacing back and forth like a sentry guarding a checkpoint. "I don't care if the wets hear this. They can be my witnesses if the shit hits the fan. I've got a list here with eighteen names on it." He lifted a pair of glasses to his eyes. "We've got Nigerians, Jamaicans, Guatemalans, Colombians, Chinese, a Laotian . . .

all arrested early yesterday. But what *else* do you suppose they have in common?"

He continued pacing, knowing nobody would answer.

"They all pose a threat to *my* financial well-being because they've been sitting in lockup for twenty-three hours and haven't been served with a formal notice as to why they're being deported. This presents a bit of a problem because the ACL fucking U would love nothing more than to sue the shit out of . . . guess who?"

Moretti stopped pacing and faced his audience. He paused for emphasis, then bent forward and spoke with exaggerated gentleness, as if addressing schoolchildren.

"Yeah, *me*, that's who. And anybody else they can shake down. They're going for personal assets these days, ladies and gentlemen, not just the government's. They have this crazy idea that I am somehow responsible for everything you guys do. And I find that very frightening." He straightened and his voice deepened. "So whichever of you is responsible, I want something on my desk within the hour."

There were several moments of silence as Moretti scanned the room with tired, cynical eyes. He stopped when he noticed one of the prettier transvestites and the agent sitting next to her in the middle of the room.

"Wickberg, I don't care if you bring in fake women, as long as they're deportable," he said. "But there's no reason to take two hours to process each one. People are starting to talk."

Leticia Boyer, the Hispanic Judy Garland, fluttered her fake eyelashes at agent Adam Wickberg. "Adam, I didn't know you took more time with us. That's so cute," cooed Boyer as she reached over to pat his hand.

Wickberg's face turned crimson as the squad room erupted in laughter. Moretti rolled his eyes and shook his head. "OK,

OK. Remember, I want that paperwork within the hour." The office buzz quickly resumed.

Hayden turned to the Mexican sitting next to him. "Bad luck today, no?" he asked in Spanish.

"Yes, sir. You run very fast," said the Mexican.

"The mud slowed you down."

Willis observed the exchange with visible irritation. "What the hell are you doing, Hayden?"

"Just trying to be civil," Hayden responded.

"We don't have time for fuckin' civility," said Willis. "This guy ran you through a mud pit, remember? Collect the information and ship his ass."

At that moment a tall, heavyset man in a tweed jacket appeared next to Hayden's desk. Charlie McCloud had wavy brown hair, his eyebrows and mustache flecked with hints of red.

"You upset again, Joe?" said McCloud with a patient smile. "Let your blood pressure skyrocket and you won't make retirement."

"Mind your own business. Besides, I don't wanna retire," Willis said, with a wearied look, as if he'd been through this before with McCloud.

"Young fella was just exercising his Spanish a little," said McCloud. "No harm in that, is there?"

"We don't have time for idle chitchat," said Willis sharply, getting up from his desk. "I'm going for coffee. Watch my guy, Hayden."

McCloud chuckled softly and turned to Hayden. "Nick Hayden?"

"Yes, sir," said Hayden. He stood and shook McCloud's hand.

"Charlie McCloud, your training officer. I've been out of the office for a few days. How things going so far?" There was a trace of sympathy in McCloud's eyes. "OK. I'm sure I can learn a lot from Mr. Willis." "Yeah, Joe's been around—knows the street. Listen, when you get a break here, stop by my office. No rush—I'll be in all afternoon."

After Nick finished the paperwork, he interviewed and processed two more of the Mexicans they'd captured outside the factory. Willis had caustically informed him that the only way to remove dozens of illegals in a single day was to convince them to give up their right to a deportation hearing and return voluntarily to their homeland. The court system would collapse if they all demanded a hearing before an immigration judge, and it would delay their departures for several days. But each of the three Mexicans Hayden interviewed had readily agreed to return to his country immediately. Altogether, fifty-eight Mexicans had been arrested that day by area control units in Chicago, and almost all of them would be on the bus headed for Juárez later that night. After being released on the other side of the border, many would quickly return, often to the same jobs they'd left behind. Clearly, the merry-go-round of capture, removal, and reentry satisfied everybody, even those temporarily caught in the net. Delays orchestrated by the bureaucracy were a relatively small price to pay.

It was late afternoon before things quieted down and Willis allowed Hayden to leave the unit. Nick stopped in the washroom on his way to McCloud's office. Tired but exhilarated, he splashed cold water on his face and took a moment to reflect. This was going to be more of a challenge than he'd anticipated—thrown into the fire without formal training and partnered with a guy who seemed like a character out of a Dickens novel. He could see that the job's physical and emotional demands were such that his clandestine mission could not be his top priority, at least for now. Still, he was confident that in time he would find answers to the questions that had been preying on his mind all these years. Keep your eyes and ears open and trust nobody, he told himself. He patted his face dry, brushed the remaining bits of dried mud from the sleeves of his sport coat, and began the short walk to McCloud's office.

———

Charlie McCloud picked his way through Nick Hayden's personnel file with growing interest. Hayden had earned a degree in English literature from the University of Illinois and spent almost two years traveling and working odd jobs in Spain and Germany. Then he'd successfully completed a year of law school before dropping out and signing on with INS—a rather curious sequence of events, McCloud thought. Why would he give up the prospect of a lucrative career as a lawyer in favor of employment with a relatively obscure federal agency?

McCloud had arrived at the INS Investigations Division in Chicago by a more traditional route. Born and raised in central Michigan, he'd been hired by the Border Patrol upon graduation from college and been dispatched, along with his young wife, to Yuma, Arizona. But after two years on the job he'd begun to find the work tedious; and his wife, never excited about her husband's career choice, felt marooned in the heat, wind, and isolation of the desert. Encouraged by his wife, McCloud had applied and been accepted into the graduate program in political science at UCLA. Almost simultaneously he'd been selected for a criminal investigator position at the

Chicago INS office, a job he'd applied for on a whim. He ultimately convinced his wife that the job would pay for his education and he could attend night school at DePaul University. The job would be temporary, he'd told her, until he could transition into the world of academia.

On reporting for duty at his new post, McCloud was assigned to area control but was soon transferred into the fraud investigations unit where he began working criminal cases—setting up complex undercover operations that targeted organizers of immigration fraud schemes and traffickers in counterfeit green cards, social security cards, visas, and birth certificates. In the process, McCloud discovered that life as an investigator in a large city, particularly one as riddled with crime as Chicago, was far more interesting than tracking illegals in the desert.

McCloud was soon hooked. The cases were like novels crammed with vivid characters, and *he* was orchestrating the storyline. Within a few years he'd posted more convictions than anybody else in the office and had become an acknowledged expert in the immigration fraud cases that abounded in the Chicago area. Prosecuting attorneys could rely on McCloud to deliver cases that were so well documented that there was little or no question about their outcome. And when the defendants received prison sentences, nothing could match the feeling of accomplishment—knowing that he'd helped bring at least a small measure of justice to society.

To his wife's chagrin, he'd never gotten around to enrolling at DePaul, and she began to observe unwelcome changes in her now remote and distracted husband. His warm, vulnerable side seemed to have disappeared, and he'd developed a blunt, condescending way of communicating that made her feel cut off and alone. Five years after their move to Chicago, and feeling as though she was living with a stranger, she took their two girls and left him. On reflection years later, McCloud couldn't blame her. For reasons he didn't grasp at the time, he'd become self-absorbed, begun drinking heavily, and devoted most of his energy to his beloved investigations. Only in retrospect was he able to see that in his zeal to succeed professionally, people had become as impersonal to him as chess pieces on a board. Perhaps unavoidably, it had spilled over into his personal life.

Finally, after more than nineteen years on the job, his forays into criminal investigations began to lack the urgency that had sustained him for so long. He lived in a small one-bedroom apartment and did his best to hide the fact that he was very lonely. He put in long hours at the office, hoping a new case would reignite the old magic, and secretly feared what appeared to be the barren landscape of retirement.

When the training officer position opened up, McCloud jumped on it, keenly aware that if he didn't take the job, some young, ambitious agent hoping to pad his résumé would happily parrot the company line to new agents, who had no idea of what they were getting into. McCloud knew things—not just how to conduct investigations—and he wanted to share them.

McCloud worked out of a small, windowless room—"the bunker," he called it—the walls lined with bookcases. When Hayden arrived, the door was open, and McCloud had him take a seat while he finished reviewing his file. Hayden noticed that among the manuals and law books on the shelves were several volumes by Steinbeck and Hemingway.

"Everybody knows the first year of law school is the hardest," said McCloud finally, peering at Hayden over reading glasses that sat on the tip of his nose. "You made it through and then walked away. That's pretty unusual."

"I was tired of school and wasn't looking forward to two more years," said Hayden. "Besides, this job sounded fascinating—being around people from other cultures . . . a different kind of learning opportunity."

McCloud raised his eyebrows. "That sounds pretty esoteric, Hayden. This isn't some human laboratory where you go around in a white coat and make notes on a clipboard. If you keep talking like that, they'll call you 'the professor.' And that ain't good." McCloud nodded toward the squad room down the hall. "They want you to be good backup, not a student of local anthropology."

"No, of course not," Hayden replied stiffly.

"Most of these guys aren't impressed with degrees or higher education. In fact, having a degree can work against you and create suspicion. It's like in Cambodia when the Commies took over—Pol Pot wanted to kill anybody who wore glasses because he thought they were intellectuals and couldn't be trusted. Your law school experience won't help. If anything, it'll create distrust."

"I never expected it to give me any special status," said Hayden.

"Well, don't get me wrong. I think it's good that we're hiring guys who are educated and creative, because the cases we're working in other units are becoming more complex."

"What kind of cases?"

"Smuggling, counterfeit documents, fraud schemes to get papers. There are great cases out there, hanging like ripe fruit. But for now, as a trainee, area control is the best place to learn the street."

"How long will I be there?"

"At least two or three years. Area control is the equivalent of being a uniformed beat cop but without the uniform. Eventually you'll get a chance to work criminal cases in another unit, which is like being promoted to detective."

"I don't have any problem with picking up illegals for a couple years."

"Good, because you have no say in it. You go where they want you to go and do what they want you to do." McCloud paused momentarily for a reaction.

Hayden nodded respectfully.

"You'll go to the academy in a couple of weeks," McCloud continued. "Then we'll have training classes for you and other guys who are in their first couple of years on the job. You'll have to go before the retention panel after a year to find out if you've made it through probation."

"Yes, they told me."

"I'm surprised with your background you didn't go with one of the pretty-boy agencies—the FBI or Secret Service. They would have taken you."

"This opened up first and . . . it looked like a good opportunity."

McCloud leaned back, webbed his hands behind his head, and studied Hayden for a moment. "I don't know if anybody's mentioned it, but the bosses have decided to be aggressive again in picking up wets, at least for a while, so things can get pretty dicey in area control. When you're arresting hundreds of people every week there are going to be some bad apples in the mix, so be prepared for anything. Stay alert. And regardless of what Willis or anybody else tells you, don't forget that you're dealing with human beings out there. You have a lot of power in this job, and even though you have to enforce the law and arrest people, they deserve respect. It's part of being a true professional. Some of these guys have forgotten about that."

"Yes, sir. I'll remember that," said Hayden. McCloud seemed to have finished, but his penetrating stare made Hayden uneasy. Nick nodded toward the bookcase. "I see you like Hemingway. I've read almost everything he's written." "The short stories in particular are great," said McCloud. "Hemingway's books are even more interesting after you've read his biographies." McCloud gazed distractedly at the bookcase for a moment. "He was a genius, but he wouldn't have been any good at this job."

"Why's that?"

"Because he was an artist, and artists are looking for transcendent truths. Where could he find that around here? Plus, he had internal demons and was always trying to prove something. That can be dangerous in this line of work. Hell of a writer though." McCloud paused briefly. "Anyway, we're done here for the moment. I'll let you know about your training schedule in the next few days."

"OK."

Hayden stood up to leave and was reaching for the door when McCloud thought of something. "You know, the name Hayden sounds kind of familiar. Can't place it, but I know I've heard it before."

"It's a pretty common name. Everybody's run into a Hayden at some point, I guess."

With a grimace and shake of his head, McCloud shoved the file into his desk drawer. "OK, I'm here if you need anything."

"Thank you, sir." Hayden closed the door and stood in the hallway, his heart galloping. He drew a deep breath and let it out slowly. Perhaps McCloud had come across some other Hayden and his curiosity meant nothing. But Nick had known all along that he was vulnerable, that it was entirely possible that McCloud or another veteran agent could make the connection. It was as if he were straddling the rim of a deep canyon. Even a small gust of wind could send him tumbling off the edge.

———

Tom Kane drove the Plymouth Fury through the bright morning sunshine that streamed between abandoned warehouses on South Halsted Street. Many of their large windows had been shattered by vandals' rocks, and flocks of sparrows soared through the openings like fleets of tiny warplanes. The sweet aroma of bread from a commercial bakery filled the air. As Hayden took in the scenery from the passenger seat, they entered an area of decaying apartment buildings and small businesses, some of which were boarded up.

"Ten years ago this area was thriving," said Kane, playing the role of tour guide. "A lot of the businesses moved to the suburbs where it's safer. But there are still a lot of wets down here in these roach-infested buildings." Kane waved dismissively toward a bus stop where several Hispanic-looking men were huddled. "Hell, we shouldn't even bother with factories. We could fill up our cars right here."

Kane was wearing his usual charcoal-colored suit, the elbows shiny from wear, a narrow black tie over a white shirt, and dark sunglasses. If you gave him a black fedora, he could pass for one of the Blues Brothers. Kane had a rangy, powerful build and thick, dark brown hair that flowed over the tops of his ears. When he flashed one of his infrequent smiles, it came off anywhere from mischievous to menacing.

Though women considered him handsome, they also found him gruff, remote, and a bit frightening.

Kane had never thought that growing up in a working-class Irish family on the southwest side of Chicago had prepared him for much of anything. But sharing close quarters with five brothers and four sisters in an atmosphere of nonstop bedlam seemed to have girded him for his future profession. From the start, he brought to his work an almost manic energy and an instinct for taking charge of fast-moving events in the field. His confidence, often drifting into arrogance, sent a warning to anybody who might challenge him and kept most people on the defensive. He thought of the job as his salvation, a crusade that filled the emptiness, though he never spoke of it in those terms. Instead, he adopted the more typical agent's pose of the grim and bemused cynic.

Kane was apprehensive when told he'd be partnered for the day with Hayden, who had been to the academy for training and was now four months into his first year. Though Kane, like Hayden, had not come through the Patrol, he sensed the new guy was a "thinker." Too much thinking and analyzing, the theory went, creates confusion, hesitation. Hayden also had an independent streak, and unlike most young agents who sought the approval of senior officers like obedient lapdogs, he didn't follow his superiors to their favorite watering holes at the end of the day, keeping his distance as if he didn't want anybody to get to know him. Aside from being irritated with having to buy their own drinks, Kane and many of the journeymen resented what they saw as aloofness.

Still, Hayden had shown that he was equal to the physical challenges of the job. Most recently he'd sprinted a quarter mile to chase down a massive Greek ship-jumper, who'd thrown an agent off a tannery loading dock and fled with a wild look on his face. Hayden had used a wrestling technique he'd picked up in high school to drop the man to the ground with a dramatic thud and, after a struggle, had somehow been able to get cuffs around the Greek's huge wrists before backup arrived. As the Greek outweighed Hayden by seventy pounds, it had meant something to Kane and the other agents.

They continued south on Halsted Street, the heavy, boat-like Fury rising and dipping as though absorbing swells on Lake Michigan.

"It would be easier to just pick them off the street than going to the job sites," said Hayden, nodding at yet another bus stop cubicle filled with young Hispanic men.

"Yeah, but headquarters wants us to go to factories so we can show we're opening up jobs for Americans. Most of the wets on the street are working someplace, though, so in reality it doesn't make any difference," said Kane. "The whole enforcement program is a mess."

"What would you do to fix it?"

"Simple. You need to prevent them from getting jobs by making them produce valid immigration documents—not the phony ones they use now. The law passed last year requires employers to check the documents of their employees, but it *doesn't* require verification. If the documents and numbers are checked through INS before they're hired, there'd be no way for them to work, and bingo!—the game's over. If you cut off the jobs, you cut off the wets. They wouldn't come. But the powers that be won't do it because they know it would work. They want everybody to think it's really complicated and almost impossible to resolve. The Republicans want cheap labor, and the Dems want the votes of the tonks who will eventually vote Democratic. All the new law did was lay the groundwork for a booming counterfeit document industry that everybody ignores. We're stuck in the middle—you, me, and the tonks."

"What about the argument that they only take jobs nobody else wants?"

"That's bullshit. Sure, the restaurant workers, but look at the people we pick up. Meat-cutters and drywall workers are making good money. They get jobs in the trades—teamsters, construction workers. The wets are easier to control than American workers."

Judy Svoboda, one of only two female agents at the Chicago office, was leading this morning's raid of a furniture factory on the South Side. Kane, following Svoboda and four other vehicles, turned off Halsted Street into an area of small, dreary-looking factories. A smoky discharge clouded the sky, and the pungent odor of industrial chemicals came through the car window. Kane grabbed the transmitter off the dash.

"Where do you want us, Judy?"

"Cover the back parking lot and the alley," she said.

Kane pointed up the street to an old brick warehouse. "That's the place—usually loaded with Jamaicans."

As Svoboda and the other units pulled in front of the building, Kane drove through a side alley and parked in the nearly empty rear lot, where they could clearly view the only door at the back of the building. It was quiet, and the summer air was hot and gritty.

"We'll give them a few minutes," said Kane. "They usually dig in here instead of trying to leave the premises."

Hayden was just as wary of working with Kane as the other way around. Like Willis, Kane had a giant chip on his shoulder, which Nick assumed was a defensive measure designed to conceal vulnerability. In fact, it seemed to him that many of his new colleagues had insecurities they chose to bury because it would be devastating to acknowledge doubts or inner turmoil that might be construed as weakness, and weakness could not be tolerated in this line of work.

"How long have you been in this unit?" asked Hayden.

"Four years. They like me here because I produce. But I wouldn't mind a permanent assignment to Stark's unit."

Hayden had heard a lot about Richard Stark's fraud investigations unit, considered the most prestigious in investigations. The agents in fraud and the antismuggling unit were often seen moving purposefully through the hallway in sweatshirts and jeans, some of them sporting beards and long hair. They worked undercover criminal cases, using informants and sting operations to set up their targets. Almost all agents aspired to join the unit, if only to position themselves for a higher grade. But it was difficult to break into the unit because senior agents filled most of the positions.

"You married?" asked Hayden.

"Nope. You almost can't be married and do the job right. You try to do both and you'll be like a wad of silly putty—stretched in every direction. If you look at the real producers, they're all single, or they're headed in that direction. Better just to have girlfriends and don't get trapped." Kane spoke in a clipped staccato as if reciting indisputable facts.

They sat quietly for several moments, and then Kane spoke. "Judy is probably going through the song and dance with the manager. He always stalls around to give the Jamaicans a chance to dig in. Let's go." He yanked the keys from the ignition.

"Don't we need to wait for her to give us the OK?"

Kane glanced at Hayden with a playful look in his eye. "We saw a guy come out, see us, and run back inside. He

was wearing braids to his shoulders and a T-shirt that said I
Love Jamaica. There's our probable cause."

They left the vehicle and advanced toward the building.
Kane opened the back door, looked inside, and motioned with
his head for Hayden to follow. Hayden went in, shut the door
behind him, and engaged the heavy chain lock.

The two agents found themselves in a large room with
brick walls, which was connected to the rest of the warehouse
by an open gangway. The room was lit softly by lights high
in the rafters and appeared to have been suddenly deserted,
as music was playing on a portable radio at a large table and
several workstations were strewn with tools and wrapping
materials. Kane turned off the radio, and it became eerily
quiet. Set back from the table were rows of cardboard boxes
on pallets, stacked about fifteen feet high.

"They're probably hiding inside the boxes at the top," said
Kane, heading down one of the aisles. "I've found them here
before." He pulled a long, black metal flashlight from his belt.

Hayden went down another aisle and began climbing a
column of boxes, using the openings in the pallets as a ladder. He had almost reached the top when he heard a crash,
the clatter of the flashlight, and Kane cursing loudly. Hayden
jumped to the ground, raced toward Kane's voice, and saw
a black man with dreadlocks, clad in a blue work shirt and
jeans, dashing toward the rear exit. The man had just disengaged the door's chain lock when Hayden took hold of his
shirt collar and pulled him back.

"I want no trouble, man," the Jamaican shouted. He held
his hands out in front of him to show that he had no weapon.

"OK, just get your hands up on the wall," said Hayden,
gripping the man's arm.

Before the man could turn around, the large hand of Tom Kane was pushing Hayden aside to grab the Jamaican by the throat. He flung the man against the brick wall and drove his fist into the man's mouth. The back of the Jamaican's head struck the wall, and he let out a groan.

Hayden instinctively grabbed Kane's arm and shoved him, sending him backpedaling awkwardly.

"What the hell are you doing?" shouted Hayden, and then caught himself. He was on probation and had openly defied a senior officer.

Kane quickly righted himself and was glaring at the exit door, which now stood open, a mild wind blowing through it—the Jamaican nowhere in sight. Hayden ran outside into the parking lot and scanned the area, but there was no sign of the man. He ran to the edge of the building and looked down the alley, but all was quiet there as well. He stood silently for several seconds, hoping to see or hear something that would give away the Jamaican's escape route, but there was nothing. Finally Hayden turned back toward the factory door to find Kane leaning his elbow against the doorway, still breathing heavily.

"Nice going, Chief," said Kane, his eyes aflame.

"The guy was scared. He wasn't going anywhere," said Hayden calmly.

"He knocked me to the floor and you're worried about *him*?"

Kane clenched his fists and strode toward Hayden. Just then Charlie McCloud appeared in the doorway behind Kane.

"You guys all right out here?" asked McCloud.

Kane stopped and spun toward McCloud.

"Yeah, we're fine," said Hayden, who relaxed his defensive posture.

"We just lost a runner, that's all," said Kane, whose rumpled shirt was pulled out in front over his belt.

McCloud paused and looked at them, waiting for the real story, but neither spoke. "OK," he said finally, "we could use your help inside. They've got eleven Jamaicans in the lunchroom."

"Sure, Charlie," said Hayden, walking past McCloud and through the door.

McCloud, who was familiar with Kane's unorthodox methods, looked at him suspiciously.

"I'll pull our car around front," Kane said.

"Yeah, you do that," said McCloud. As Kane turned toward his car, McCloud shook his head and walked back into the factory.

———

It was a cool autumn morning, still a bit dark outside the Polish restaurant. Willis sat rigidly at the table, coffee cup in hand, engrossed in the newspaper. Hayden perused the sports page and looked up the aisle whenever the waitress with nice legs rushed by. Occasionally he would check on Willis, observing him as a person might watch a tropical fish, more a curiosity than a threat.

All the senior agents had plenty of Joe Willis stories, like the time Willis "arrested" a new agent, Arturo Santos, who'd been sitting innocently in area control on his first day on the job. Willis had unceremoniously thrown Santos into the crowded lockup, ignoring Santos's claim that he had not yet been issued a badge and identification. When the truth emerged, instead of apologizing, Willis excoriated local management for not warning everybody that they'd hired a new agent who looked wet. "They should have put his mug shot on the damn bulletin board," he declared angrily.

Though Willis was entertaining in his way, Hayden had hoped for a new partner when he returned from the academy. Unfortunately, nobody other than a trainee would put up with Willis, so they were stuck with each other for the time being.

"This so-called war on drugs is a loser," muttered Willis, staring down at a *Chicago Tribune* story about the mountains of federal money spent to fight drug lords.

"I suppose it can't really be controlled," Hayden offered blandly.

"You want to legalize drugs, is that it?" grumbled Willis, without looking up from the paper. "What a charming idea."

It didn't matter how hard Hayden tried. Willis seemed to enjoy twisting anything Nick said to spark an argument or emphasize the gulf between them. Hayden knew it wasn't really personal, that he would give *any* trainee a hard time, especially one who hadn't been in the Patrol.

Willis himself had gone through rough times when he'd started with the Patrol thirty years earlier in Brownsville, Texas. Born and raised in a lower-middle-class suburb of Chicago, Willis, with his strange accent and fast-talking intensity, had been treated as an outsider, especially during his first year on the border. If *he'd* had to go through it, so should everybody else.

After finishing his fifth cup of coffee, Willis looked at his watch, winked at the waitress, and threw a dollar bill on the table. "Let's go to work, trainee," he said coolly. Willis pulled sunglasses from the pocket of his sport coat and marched into the emerging sunshine as if he didn't care whether Hayden followed him or not.

As Hayden pulled the Ford Torino onto the Stevenson Expressway, Willis rifled through the glove compartment as though looking for something to read, wiped an undetectable layer of grime from the inside of the front windshield, and spent several minutes on the radio making important-sounding but thoroughly unnecessary calls to other agents involved in the day's operation. Finally he settled down and began a lecture on the true merits of various federal law enforcement agencies as opposed to their public images.

Hayden had already heard several versions of this narrative from Willis, and his mind drifted. Peering out the window, he wondered whether the white cloud that hung over the sleepy town of McCook was mist rising from the nearby canal or pollution from smokestacks that stood inelegantly in the distance. He recalled playing a baseball game in McCook as a teenager and losing a fly ball in the opaque, misty sky. His mind fell deeper into the past, until a name jolted him like a strong whiff of ammonia.

"Buck Tatum," declared Willis, who tilted his head up as if scouring his memory for an image of Tatum. "Only federal agent in Chicago to smoke a guy in the last fifteen years. FBI in Chicago hasn't in years, even with thirty times the number of agents we have. The average citizen thinks FBI agents are out there risking life and limb on a daily basis. Hell, most of 'em never make arrests. How can you develop any street smarts if you're not out there making arrests and getting into fights and all the shit we have to do?"

"So Tatum was an immigration agent?"

"Yeah—an INS agent, not FBI, not DEA," sputtered Willis.

"Were you there when it went down—the shooting?"

"No, I wasn't there. But we lost a good man because of the trainee."

"What happened?"

Willis sighed and paused a moment to pull up the details in his mind. "Well, a guy named Frank Kelso was working with this rookie . . . Landau, I think was his name. Smart kid, but not cut out for police work—had no Patrol experience. Kelso and the trainee were riding together somewhere on the North Side, Tatum following them."

Willis picked bits of lint from his polyester slacks as he continued.

"Kelso had a great nose for wets—could pick 'em out of a crowd as well as anybody I ever knew. He sees a guy who looks suspicious—a big guy from Argentina it turned out. So Kelso jumps out of the car and he's talking to him, but before he can cuff him, the guy starts fighting."

Joe lit a fresh Lucky and cracked the window open. Hayden had become rigid behind the wheel.

"So they're both struggling with the wet, trying to get him under control. But the wet goes for Kelso's gun and manages to fire a round—right into Kelso's heart. He's dead, or will be in a few minutes. Tatum shoots the guy in the head, killing him. But Landau never gets a shot off—never even gets his gun out. If he'd reacted like he should have, Kelso would still be here. Guess he didn't have it in him to kill a guy, even when his partner's life was threatened."

"Is that what Tatum said?"

"Tatum was pretty closemouthed about it. Whole thing upset him—wouldn't talk to anyone. But they did an investigation and that's what came out."

"What kind of a guy was Buck Tatum?"

"He was in the Patrol for sixteen years. Good man, until the shooting. Then he was different." Willis took a long drag from the cigarette and sent a billow of smoke out the window.

"Different how?"

"Shooting seemed to hollow him out—walked around like a fucking ghost. He retired about a year later. Disappeared. Might be dead, for all I know." Willis paused a moment and then turned toward Hayden. "Why you so interested in Tatum?" Hayden had to concentrate to prevent a shake in his voice. "It's not Tatum. It's the shooting. You don't hear about stuff like that very often. Maybe I can learn something from it." Willis spit out a piece of loose tobacco. "One thing you can learn is if your partner's life is threatened, you act without hesitation."

"Right," said Hayden. His heart was thumping and perspiration covered his forehead. He was grateful when a garbled radio transmission came through the speaker. Willis grabbed the mic and bent over to listen to the scratchy voice—somebody asking for their location and ETA. Hayden used the distraction to take a deep breath and wipe the sweat from his forehead. Willis gave a lengthy response and put the microphone back in its holder on the dash.

"To get back to my point, the bureau would have us believe that Efrem Zimbalist Jr., who shot a guy every week on television, is a realistic portrait. That's what they tell them at Quantico, and like a bunch of Boy Scouts, they believe it."

By now they had left the scented mist over McCook behind and the sky had cleared, but Hayden had retreated deep into his thoughts and was oblivious of his surroundings. Though Willis spoke with authority about the shooting, how reliable was his account, no doubt tainted by personal prejudice and the passage of time? Willis had seen nothing himself, so anything he said was suspect, and crucial details were missing. That calmed Nick a bit. He took another deep breath and tried to push it from his mind. He had no choice. In a few minutes, they would begin another roundup of wets.

2

He often shambled down Twenty-Sixth Street, smiling at everybody as if he were running for political office. Standing six feet two and weighing over two hundred and fifty pounds, Marcos Ortega was a commanding presence. His large, round face was dominated by a hooked nose and a thick, black mustache that curved around his mouth bandito-style. Some were drawn to him by his sunny disposition; others were intimidated by his size.

Mesmerized by stories of unlimited opportunities in America, Marcos had left his remote Mexican village at the age of twenty-five, slipped across the Rio Grande, and headed straight to Chicago, where he'd been welcomed into his uncle's home in the largely Hispanic Pilsen area on the South Side. Ambitious by nature, he'd taken an English course for Spanish-speaking immigrants, augmenting what he'd already learned at his Catholic school in Mexico. Without legal papers or connections, he'd not been averse to starting at the bottom of the economic ladder, and took a job as a dishwasher at a busy Mexican restaurant on Eighteenth Street. There he'd met a waitress by the name of Connie Salinas.

Connie was so quiet and efficient that she was seldom noticed amid the noise and bustle of the restaurant. She kept her dull, black hair pulled back in a ponytail, wore no makeup, and had a pudgy figure that was virtually devoid of feminine curves. Connie was not pretty and had never thought of herself as pretty, but she was a superb waitress, driven by fear of a complaint or a look of disapproval—the lingering effect of a demanding and temperamental father. She didn't live so much as react, meekly following the path of least resistance. Aside from a perfunctory nod or greeting as they passed in the kitchen, Marcos paid no attention to her.

One day Marcos was unloading dishes into a basin of hot water, steam rising all around, when he looked up to find Connie standing at the far end of the kitchen staring at him.

"Is first time I see you without stack of plates," said Marcos, flashing a big smile. He spoke English clearly but with an accent. "You are always busy, no?"

Connie froze. She nervously pushed away strands of hair that had fallen across her eyes. "Oh, yes. It is very busy," she mumbled.

"Come see me if you get break. Is lonely back here," said Marcos, instantly recognizing the possibilities. Though ostensibly a Catholic, he saw his faith less as a deterrent to committing sinful acts than as a means for absolving them.

"Yes, well . . . I better get back to work," said Connie with a shaky smile, grateful she'd been able to speak at all.

Two days later Marcos asked her to go out with him. Connie was so surprised that she lost her grip on a plate of chicken mole and it crashed noisily on the kitchen floor. Omar Garcia, the restaurant owner, rushed back from the cash register.

"I'm so sorry, Señor Garcia," Connie said, dropping to the floor to clean up the mess.

"Hey, you," Garcia shouted angrily at Marcos, "get back to your dishes and don't be bothering the waitresses." When the dust settled, Connie was smiling and conversing with customers as though a new person had been born.

Connie lived with her parents in a small bungalow in the Pilsen neighborhood. Her father, Ray Salinas, who had worked for twenty-three years at an auto repair shop on Ashland Avenue, had forbidden her to date until she was eighteen, and then only if he approved. He saw all men as predatory by nature and was therefore fiercely protective. Ray was a short, stocky man with massive forearms and hands that had grown incredibly strong from his work at the shop. Over the years, he'd been arrested many times for instigating liquor-fueled brawls at the local bar. Though Connie was now nineteen, she knew her father would be suspicious of Marcos, so she told her parents that she was going out with "a friend from work."

They had dinner at an unpretentious little restaurant on Damen Avenue. Marcos chose a table in a quiet corner and ordered a bottle of inexpensive wine to go with their steak burritos. He said little, listened respectfully to everything Connie said, and treated her with great courtesy. She felt comfortable talking with him and thought this was quite remarkable—an indication of a special relationship.

Marcos provided Connie with few details of his past, but that was how her father was, and apparently the way most men were. He was too shy, she thought, to kiss her on their first date or the next one. But on the evening of their third date, as they were standing outside a movie theater on Cermak Road, Marcos placed his hands gently on her shoulders and looked at her very seriously.

"Connie, would you do me honor of being my wife?"

Shocked but overjoyed, she threw her arms around his neck and kissed him. Marcos smiled down at her as one smiles when giving a child a birthday present.

"Of course I'll marry you! We'll have the most beautiful wedding!"

"But not yet, my dear. That cost money, and I no want to go to your father until I have better job. I hear about your father. We go to city hall to get married first. Later I tell your parents, and we plan big wedding. We no live together or say anything now. Is important we no say nothing." She, too, feared her father's reaction to the news, so agreed to keep it a secret for the moment.

Connie and Marcos applied for a license and were married at city hall by a judge who absently muttered the vows. It wasn't the wedding she'd dreamed of, but there was something romantic about doing it secretly, and she consoled herself with thoughts of the real wedding to come. In lieu of a honeymoon, they went out to lunch at a greasy spoon, where Marcos told her they should say nothing to Omar or anybody else at the restaurant for fear word would get back to her parents. He again stated that he didn't want to present himself to her father as a mere dishwasher and that her parents would be hurt and angry for not having been invited to the marriage ceremony.

The surprising news emerged at the end of their meal. "I almost forget," Marcos said. "We must go to immigration office. I no can go to your father unless I have green card."

Connie was momentarily speechless. She'd assumed he was a legal immigrant. He spoke English so well and carried himself with ease and confidence, unlike the other illegal Mexicans at the restaurant, who rarely spoke and were almost invisible.

"Why didn't you say anything about that?" she asked softly.

"I thought you know this—from others at restaurant." He paused. "I no do this for the papers. You must no think this, my dear."

"No, of course not," she said with a nervous smile.

"We have wedding in church in few months," he declared. "I save money so we have nice apartment."

As Marcos talked enthusiastically about their plans, Connie felt somewhat reassured, though it was now even more important that her father not learn of the relationship until her husband had secured his immigration papers.

Two days later they submitted a petition at the INS office and were told they would be called in for an interview. In the weeks that followed, Connie's life resumed its old rhythm—as if she weren't married at all. Marcos had made it clear that he took his Catholic faith seriously, and they could not consummate the marriage or live together until it was sanctified by a church ceremony. She would continue to live with her parents and Marcos with his uncle. Connie, like Marcos, had been raised Catholic and, though she was burning with sexual passion, was grateful that her husband was a man of faith. They would wait for everything to be right in the eyes of God.

Connie had begun to run out of patience when, eight weeks after they married, Marcos told her that he had good news. "I get new job at tortilla factory. I will be foreman and make more money. And we have interview at immigration office next week and if goes well, I get green card."

On a cold December morning they appeared at the INS office and were interviewed by a young man wearing wire-rimmed glasses. Since Marcos claimed to have entered the country on a temporary visa at a border crossing, he was eligible to obtain permanent status without returning to Mexico.

The examiner asked a few questions about how they met and seemed impressed with the couple's apparent happiness about being newly married. With numerous other couples waiting to be interviewed, the officer stamped the application APPROVED and informed Marcos he would receive his green card in the mail within a month or so. He was now a legal resident and was given a piece of paper emblazoned with a stamp to prove it. When they left the building, Marcos was so pleased that he kissed Connie with a passion he'd not shown before.

"I start at tortilla factory day after tomorrow," said Marcos. "Then we tell your parents our plans. No say anything now. We surprise them together. Tomorrow will be last day at restaurant."

But Connie's elation over this news was short lived as Marcos did not show up at the restaurant the next day. She repeatedly called his uncle's house, but there was no answer. That evening, after distractedly eating dinner with her parents, she hurried through the dark streets to the uncle's house, about a mile away. But the lights weren't on, there was no response when she rang the doorbell, and Marcos's car was nowhere to be seen in the neighborhood. She returned home but was barely able to sleep that night.

At the restaurant the next morning, she found that Marcos had been replaced by a short Mexican who blended seamlessly into the background. After her shift, she took the bus to Twenty-Sixth Street to inquire at the tortilla factory. Encouraged to see Marcos's car parked outside, she went into the office and asked to speak to her husband. The receptionist looked at her curiously and said the workers could not be disturbed during working hours, but agreed to deliver a message. Connie scratched out a note saying she was worried about him and asking him to call her.

But Marcos did not call, and the cold reality began to set in. She had been duped—abandoned by her husband before they had even spent a minute together in the same house. There was no question in her mind that this had been his intention from the beginning. He had used her and discarded her like a piece of trash. That night, tears welled up in Connie's eyes as she lay in bed, staring at the ceiling, embarrassed and ashamed for having been so easily taken advantage of. After she'd had a long cry, she began to feel something unfamiliar: a deep-seated loathing of another human being.

A few days later she went back to the INS office to tell them of Marcos's misdeeds and was referred to the same man who had conducted their interview. She immediately informed him that she wanted to withdraw the petition she had filed for her husband.

"No, it's too late for that," he said, explaining that the petition had already been approved—that Marcos had been accorded legal status. He listened gloomily as Connie told him of Marcos's deception.

"Well, even if I can't withdraw the petition, you can deport him, can't you?"

"No, it's not that simple."

"After what he did, you can't deport him?" She'd been rather calm up to that moment but now felt a surge of anger. "Why not?"

"We would have to revoke his legal status first. It's a very difficult process, and the courts have ruled that living together or consummating the relationship is not really required. Once he receives permanent status, the burden of proof shifts dramatically. You two dated before getting married, so there was a relationship of some kind. It is highly unlikely we could prove that from the beginning he only married you to get his card. He'll just say you had a fight and realized you weren't right for each other."

Connie stared at him in disbelief.

"It's what we call a one-sided fraud," he offered feebly. "They're very hard to prove, and we have limited resources."

Before leaving the building, Connie took a seat in the reception area and tried to gather herself. The realization that Marcos had deceived her had already been emotionally devastating. Now the shock set in that he was going to get away with it. She looked around at couples waiting to be interviewed and wondered how many of the women were being victimized, their worlds about to fall apart. After a few minutes she staggered out and made her way down State Street.

Though the temperature was below freezing, the city was adorned with brilliant sunlight. It was the week before Christmas, and crowds of people bustled happily past Salvation Army bell-ringers and colorful decorations. But Connie found the gaiety intolerable. She trudged heavily down the steps into the darkness of the subway.

As she arrived at the platform a train was pulling away, its red lights growing smaller as it disappeared in the tunnel. Alone in the cold, dimly lit station, Connie waited for the next train home.

———

Marcos, bored and distracted, watched his crew of illegal Mexicans bag warm tortillas on the line, mulling the risks and rewards of his latest idea. Aside from the tedium and endless paperwork of his job, he knew it would never provide him with the financial independence he desired. The only way to make serious money, he'd concluded, was to run his own business—something he could manage without giving up the steady income and respectability of his job.

When a newly hired worker walked by, Marcos reached out and playfully spun him around by the shoulder. "Let me see that card of yours, my friend—the one I made a copy of this morning," said Marcos in Spanish. When the young man looked up suspiciously, Marcos quickly reassured him. "I know they're all phony. Do you think I give a damn?"

The man fumbled through his wallet, removed the laminated card, and handed it to Marcos.

"How much you pay for this?" inquired Marcos.

"Two hundred fifty, for that and the social security," said the man, looking around nervously. Hair-netted Mexican workers were watching tortillas coming at them along a perforated stainless steel assembly line. Several of them turned to look but couldn't hear the exchange because of the drone of the machinery.

"You got it from one of those *cholos* at a bar?"

The man nodded and looked away. Marcos pulled his own card from his wallet, the good one given to him for marrying Connie Salinas, and examined them both. The man's card looked bad by comparison, the printing not as sharp, but it was good enough to serve its purpose.

"OK, get back to work," Marcos said, returning the card and patting the man on the shoulder. Marcos headed to his office in a state of building excitement. For the love of God, why hadn't he thought of it earlier?

Marcos always made a great show of cooperating when INS agents arrived to check the workforce at the tortilla plant. One of the lead agents, a funny, bald-headed man named Willis, even seemed to view him as a partner in weeding out illegals. During his last visit, Willis had commented about the problem of counterfeit documents.

"Nobody is working those cases. Not a high-enough priority with the front office or the clowns at headquarters," Willis had said casually, after finding almost all of the workers at the tortilla factory in possession of counterfeits. "I can't remember the last time anybody got busted for selling phony documents. It's a damn outrage. I'm not even allowed to tell you how to detect one."

"Yes, it is shame, Mr. Willis," Marcos had replied sympathetically. "I not know they were bad cards. What can I do? They all look good to me."

A week later, Marcos talked it over with Sixto Montoya, a truck driver who made regular deliveries of flour to the tortilla plant. Like Marcos, Sixto had secured legal status through a sham marriage to an unsuspecting woman. The two men had become friends, Sixto often lingering in Marcos's dusty little office over coffee and donuts. Physically, they were a study in contrasts. Sixto, thin and wiry, had sharp features and a permanently serious facial expression.

The men spoke in their native Spanish. "We are sitting on top of a gold mine, my friend," said Marcos with a coy grin.

"What are you talking about?"

"Let me show you something." Marcos opened his desk drawer and pulled out a manila folder. He removed a single sheet of paper on which an image of a green card had been copied. He pushed the copy across his desk.

Sixto surveyed the page. "Yes, I've seen plenty of these. What about it?" He spoke quickly, spitting the words out as if they were bitter in his mouth.

"I've got forty of those in this folder from just the past two weeks. I always have to make a copy to prove we checked documents before hiring to comply with the new law. But they are all phony. And we don't even have to check them through the government to see if they're good."

"Yes, I've heard about it," said Sixto. "There's no need to show a good document, so they all want the fake ones. It's a joke."

"Yes, a joke with a big payoff! Look at those who sell the documents—drunks, drug users, and lowlifes who hang around the bars. They get arrested, go on binges. Whoever brings order to it will make a lot of money."

Sixto was looking past Marcos, thinking it through. His eyes shifted back to Marcos. "What do you have in mind?"

"The key is buying in quantity and selling at a reasonable price. We could drive the small operators out of business in a very short time. I can get some money from my uncle. The blank cards can be purchased cheaply across the border in Tijuana. That's where the printing presses are. My uncle even has a contact there. The Mexican cops let them operate freely because of bribes. I'm taking a trip down there. When I get back I'll need somebody to take control of things in your area on the North Side. I'll take care of things on the South Side. I thought you might be interested."

"Of course I'm interested," said Sixto, who lived in an area thick with immigrants of every nationality. He pulled a cigarette from the open pack in his shirt pocket and held it between his fingers. "What sort of profit could we expect?"

"The blank documents can be purchased for very little, a few dollars per document—green cards and social securities. They can be sold easily on the street for at least a hundred fifty for a set. The equipment needed to put the cards together is very cheap. We can be the wholesalers and sell to the guys who will work the street and make the cards. The more vendors we have, the more we make. We'll have them do business quietly, behind the scenes. I'll give you a good price on the blanks, and you'll be free to distribute them as you see fit."

Sixto lit his cigarette and dropped the match to the cement floor. "This is risky, no? What about the feds?"

"That's the beauty of it. I have spoken with an immigration official. He tells me they don't have the manpower to go after the counterfeiters. They're leaving it wide open."

Sixto blew out a long cloud of smoke before speaking. "I'm sure I could find people to help us on the North Side. It should not be difficult."

"I'm leaving for Tijuana on Friday. Just be careful who you talk to about this."

"Yes, of course," said Sixto.

Though making decent money at the factory, Marcos had begun to feel pressure to develop other income. He had already paid for a divorce from Connie, who had gone along with it on the promise that he would pay her two thousand dollars within the next few months, though he knew there was little chance he would make good on that.

Now that the divorce was final, he would have to go through the charade of remarrying his young wife in Mexico so that he could file the necessary papers for her and their two children. It would look suspicious, but he would claim they had lived together common-law and never married. To prove otherwise, *la migra* would have to find the tiny church in the remote Mexican countryside and dig up the marriage certificate. It seemed clear that they didn't have the resources to check such things. Even if they did, he knew people in Durango—records could be destroyed.

The restaurant was quiet, aside from the distant clinking of glasses in the kitchen. The lunchtime customers had cleared out, except for an old man, who sat in a booth nursing a bottle of Corona. Two waitresses sat at the counter lazily counting tips. The owner, Felix Vasquez, a thin, nervous Panamanian, sat in a rear booth, staring at the entrance.

Marcos lumbered into the restaurant and stood heavily inside the door, like a gunslinger entering a saloon. He was wearing a short-sleeved, embroidered white shirt that hung down over his belt, and a pair of cowboy boots, so that he appeared even more imposing than usual. Marcos smiled at the waitresses, nodded at the old man, and did a visual sweep of the restaurant, his eyes stopping to admire the colorful paintings of bullfighters that lined the walls.

Vasquez, speaking Spanish, greeted him as if he were royalty, escorted him to a booth in the back, and had a waitress deliver coffee. "My friend should be here shortly, Mr. Ortega. In the meantime, can I offer you something to eat?"

"Perhaps some of your delicious flan," said Marcos with a smile and a twinkle in his eye.

"Of course," said Vasquez, who snapped his fingers and gestured to one of the waitresses. "Rita, some flan over here right away."

Marcos was amused by the hubbub his arrival had caused. His status in the community had clearly grown over the past six months, particularly with small business owners whose employees were illegals and needed phony identification. Through subtle intimidation and by offering lower prices, Marcos had already succeeded in driving most of his competitors out of business.

"I should come by more often," he said. "Everybody knows you have the best enchiladas in the barrio." He stirred several teaspoons of sugar into his coffee, and the waitress delivered a dish of flan covered with caramel sauce. Marcos divided the flan into two pieces and shoveled one of them into his mouth. He winked at Vasquez appreciatively, sipped the coffee, and set the cup down. "When you called, you said this friend of yours could be of service to me in some way."

"Yes, perhaps he can," Vasquez began. "He arrived two weeks ago from Panama. You understand how it is, getting started here. He is living on the North Side. I think he would be good at this kind of work . . . with the documents. It could mean more money for you, Mr. Ortega."

Marcos's face hardened. "I'm busy enough as it is," he said coldly. He didn't care to have Vasquez giving him business advice. "Most of my people start by working regular jobs. I don't like them depending on this to get by. Even I keep a regular job at the tortilla plant."

Vasquez, realizing he'd been inept, tried to repair the damage. "You know better than I about such things. I'm sure he will find other work, as you suggest. He is an intelligent man and would do as you say if you took him on."

"Of course he would do as I say," said Marcos indignantly. "What sort of business do you think I'm running?"

Vasquez was momentarily speechless—searching for words that would placate his irritable guest—when Salvador Rico entered the restaurant.

"Here he is!" said Vasquez.

A solidly built man of medium height, Rico was wearing drab, loose-fitting work clothes. He stepped up to the table, a tight smile on his face, and held out his hand to Marcos. Vasquez made the introductions.

"It is an honor to meet you, sir," said Rico.

Saying nothing, Marcos remained seated and reluctantly shook Rico's hand. He nodded curtly for Rico to sit next to Vasquez and absently punched little creases into the flan with his spoon.

"So, Felix tells me you arrived not long ago from Panama," said Marcos.

"Yes, we are from the same neighborhood in the capital," said Rico, who had small eyes with lids that looked almost oriental and a wide, flat nose. A scar cut across his upper lip, upsetting the normal curve of his mouth. But Marcos could see nothing remarkable, nothing particularly revealing of character. His manner was respectful. "You are not working yet?" he asked.

"No, but I talked to a man yesterday about working in his photo shop."

Marcos sipped his coffee and thought it over. Although he was initially unreceptive, what would it hurt to take on another vendor? This Rico would be in Sixto's area on the North Side, so he wouldn't have to deal with him. It would make Vasquez look like a man of influence and he would be indebted to Marcos—more complimentary flan and free meals. He motioned with his spoon toward Vasquez. "It is only because of this man that I will allow you to work for me. Don't forget that you owe him a debt of gratitude."

"Yes, of course I am very grateful," said Rico, with a quick nod at Vasquez.

"You will need other income and a legitimate job as cover," said Marcos, and he slid the remaining half of the flan down his throat like a pelican swallowing a fish. "I have a man up on the North Side—Sixto Montoya. Give me a phone number and he will call. If he tells you to do something, imagine it is me talking. He will give you an area—show you what equipment is needed to get started. You will have to buy the equipment and documents yourself."

"Of course. That will be no problem."

"Sixto will show you the ropes," continued Marcos. "We don't charge more than a hundred and fifty dollars for both the green card and social security card. It would be easy to take advantage because many of them don't have any idea what a fair price is. We make money, but we don't gouge them. If I hear of any vendors charging more, they are cut off. Do you understand?" There was a resonant edge to his voice, suggesting that anyone who defied him would be dealt with harshly.

"Of course, Mr. Ortega," said Rico softly. "You can count on me to do as you wish."

3

It was cold, and a thin layer of new snow powdered the streets. Though the snow provided faint illumination, it was still quite dark. The cars advanced like a slow-moving funeral procession, the snow absorbing their sounds. Hayden could see the GETTY'S MEATS sign at the top of the three-story brick building and soft yellow light through hazy windows. The odor of freshly slaughtered meat was seeping in through the partially open car window.

"Hey, Joe, buy your pork chops at the store like everybody else," said Sam Payton over the radio. During their last visit, he'd spotted Willis stuffing a bag of freshly cut ribs into his coat pocket and had been needling him ever since.

"They were throwin' 'em out," barked Willis. "Mind your own business, Payton."

It was one of the few remaining slaughterhouses on the South Side of Chicago. The pigs, fatted to bursting, were trucked in, emptied into a large pen, and then, squealing mightily, herded into a narrow chute that led them to workers who would stun the animals with an electronic prod. They were then hoisted onto a hook that sent them toward an army of butchers—men dressed in blood-spattered white coats and plastic helmets, who would slit the pigs' throats and carve them into parts. Wielding long, razor-sharp knives, the men were strong and had large, powerful hands. They did their work without speaking, without thinking, concentrating only on the relentless parade of flesh and bone. Most of them were from Poland, many having entered the States on tourist visas before melting into the vast Polish community in Chicago.

As several tan Plymouths pulled into the parking lot and others took up positions around the perimeter of the building, the secretary, sitting near the front window, immediately recognized them. She called back to her boss, who was in the adjoining office with his door open.

"Mr. Getty, it's those jerks from INS again."

Without hesitation, George Getty, a rotund, middle-aged man with dark bushy hair, picked up the phone and pushed the speaker button that sent his voice out to the plant. He said simply: "INS is here." While the agents were still getting out of their cars, the reaction inside the plant was immediate and well rehearsed. Eighty percent of the workers dropped their knives and left their workstations.

Getty knew he could legally refuse to allow INS to enter, but that could lead to a search warrant operation that would shut the plant down for several hours and likely generate a blizzard of unfavorable publicity, as INS would sometimes bring the press and TV media along to spotlight the problem of undocumented workers. Hoping that some of his Polish workers would hide while he stalled, Getty spent five minutes in a half-hearted effort to reach his attorney before allowing the agents to enter the plant.

Once inside, the agents split into pairs and spread out. One of them, Milos Jankowicz, who spoke Polish fluently, would assist other agents in interviews as needed. The question of their alien status was usually answered, however, by the fact that they were fleeing or hiding.

Hayden went with Judy Svoboda to search the third floor. They found it deserted, but there was a thin metal stairway leading to a skylight that opened to the roof. Svoboda climbed up to check it out. The skylight was not properly latched, and there was moisture on the steps at the top of the stairway.

"Looks like they've been up here," she said.

She pushed open the skylight, and a block of cold air came through, along with a sprinkling of dry snow. She poked her head above roof level and looked around. There was enough light reflecting off the snow to see the area clearly. Observing no movement, she stepped up onto the roof, Hayden behind her. They stood next to the skylight, listening. About thirty feet away, a massive gray metal generator produced a deep hum and belched out plumes of steam. Svoboda pointed to footprints in the snow leading away from the skylight toward the edge of the roof. They followed the footprints to a fire escape ladder that curved over the tile parapet. Hayden looked over the edge at Agent Tim Reynolds, who was standing in the alley below.

"Hey, Tim, any activity from up here?" Hayden called out.

"I heard something up there a few minutes ago," said Reynolds. "But some guy ran out through the dock in front, so I wasn't here for a while. Looks like somebody came down here while I was gone." Reynolds was peering at the snow and a line of messy footprints that indicated that at least one person had escaped down the alley.

Hayden looked at the snow on the roof. There was another fresh path between the parapet and the generator, but it was impossible to tell from the muddled footprints whether somebody had come to the parapet from that direction or the other way around. Hayden gestured for Svoboda to follow him, and they walked toward the generator. As they drew near he noticed a suspicious puff of condensation drift skyward from around the corner.

"OK, buddy, let's go," said Hayden as he turned the corner. Hayden saw the flash of the carving knife and instinctively reached up with both hands to grab a wrist the size of his own arm. He swung it away, twisting the man's arm and shoulder at such a severe angle that the knife slipped from his grasp and the Pole cried out in pain, both of them tumbling to the snow-covered roof. Svoboda dropped her knee into the man's back so that he was splayed out on his stomach. As Hayden stood up, he could see him better—a stocky young man wearing a long white butcher's coat. Hayden kicked the knife away through the snow, grabbed a set of cuffs from his belt, and pulled the man's arms behind his back, as Svoboda continued to apply pressure. The man was weeping and spewing Polish but made no effort to resist Hayden, who quickly closed the cuffs on his massive wrists.

"Are you crazy?" cried Svoboda at the Pole. She then glanced up at Hayden and registered a look of concern.

Hayden felt the coolness on his forehead but not the line of blood that flowed past his ear and down his jaw. He could see from Svoboda's expression that something must look bad, and he reached his hand up to feel the wetness. Seeing the blood on his hand and in the snow, he pulled a glove from his jacket pocket and pressed it against his forehead.

"Let me take a look at that," said Svoboda, who reached over to lift the glove off the wound long enough to get a sense of it. "It's not as bad as I thought. Not too deep. He just grazed you."

"I can go to the clinic downtown if I need a few stitches," said Hayden, breathing heavily. He looked at the Pole, who lay crying on the roof.

"That was a pretty good move you put on this guy," said Svoboda, who'd retrieved the bloody carving knife. "I'll have Reynolds come up and take some photos. I'm sure they'll prosecute on this."

Ten minutes later, after a dozen other Poles had been arrested and loaded into vehicles, Hayden sat in the passenger seat, looking at the snow falling and melting against the windshield. Svoboda had fished a bandage from a first-aid kit and pasted it across Hayden's forehead. If he thought about it, Nick could feel a subtle throbbing, but he knew it wasn't serious, and a strangely pleasant torpidity had swept over him, as though he'd been given a mild anesthetic.

The Pole was in the backseat with Jankowicz next to him as Willis, uncharacteristically silent, pulled slowly away from the slaughterhouse and headed toward the office. The Pole was sitting forward, unable to sit comfortably because of the handcuffs behind his back. The tears had dried on his cheeks, but his eyes were shining with emotion. Every few seconds he sniffled back the discharge from his runny nose. He looked pleadingly toward Hayden, who stared vacantly out the front window. The big Pole seemed to think his fate now rested solely in Hayden's hands. Finally he could contain himself no longer and began speaking rapidly, spraying Jankowicz with foamy spit.

"He says he is more sorry than he can express in words," said Jankowicz, who translated in a dry monotone. "He says he has never done anything like this before—that he panicked with the thought of having to go back to Poland so soon after coming here. He just arrived two weeks ago. He says he's not a criminal, has no criminal record. He is here only for his family, to take care of them."

Hayden felt numb and was barely listening. It was too complicated, he thought, trying to discern who was a threat and who wasn't. This man had a story to explain it, of course. Everybody had reasons or excuses, even for committing acts of violence. Maybe the Pole was telling the truth. Then again, maybe he'd murdered his wife, fled Poland, and this explained his desperation. Either way, it didn't matter. They were all threats, and they were everywhere. It was the only way to think about it if you were going to survive. He felt neither hatred nor empathy, just a weary recognition of how things were.

The Pole was muttering quietly to Jankowicz.

"He says he wants to know if you can forgive him for what he has done today. He will always be ashamed of this," said Jankowicz.

"Tell him to shut up," said Willis. "We've heard enough."

There was silence as Hayden gazed out the window. The Pole was leaning forward, tensed, waiting for some response, but Hayden said nothing. After a moment Jankowicz raised his hand and shook his head at the Pole, who leaned back awkwardly, his shoulder blades pressed low against the seat back. It was very quiet as the vehicle rolled smoothly through the snow.

———

"Other people punch their time card and go to work," said McCloud. "You punch in and walk into the middle of a tornado. And that's why you like it."

In contrast to the bedlam that reigned every afternoon on the third floor in area control, it was serenely quiet on the twenty-second floor. The small conference room, just across the hall from a US District Court, offered expansive views of the Chicago skyline. As he spoke, McCloud paced slowly in front of the floor-to-ceiling windows. Hayden and the two other agents attending the lecture, who were both in their second year on the job, were intrigued with this departure from the ordinary curriculum, which was usually a discussion of some tedious aspect of immigration law or procedure.

"By his third year on the job, the typical agent in Chicago has arrested over a thousand illegals. You're dealing with people en masse—moving them like herds of cattle. Over time you can't help but think of them as objects—cargo to be processed and shipped. It all happens gradually so you don't notice it, but inevitably the awareness of your impact on other human beings begins to deteriorate. Psychologists call it 'emotional erosion'—when the daily requirements and stress of the job force you to erect a firewall around your emotions. And when that happens you're in danger of falling into what I call the 'gladiator syndrome.'

"The gladiator, caught up in his heroic mission, sees that the problem of illegal immigration is huge and his ability to deal with it is very limited. It's not just the countless wets, but the criminal activity that inevitably follows. His powers of recognition have sharpened to the point where he can detect wets and criminal activity everywhere. Since he takes his job seriously, this creates intense frustration and imposes a psychological burden. So the gladiator tries to level the playing field by overstepping his legal authority. And initially he gets away with stuff, whether it's an illegal search, manufacturing probable cause, whatever. Naturally, this strengthens a false sense of invulnerability. He thinks he's Superman and doesn't know there's kryptonite out there.

"Out on the street doing the job, he's dynamic, in control, ordering people around, and taking charge. People listen to him and usually defer to his authority. When he gets home, he puts his gun away, but the armor remains. Other people's feelings and thoughts have begun to splatter like insects on a windshield. Not

surprisingly, the wife or girlfriend isn't going to like this new attitude. And as the gulf between them grows, he gradually spends
less time at home. The tavern becomes his refuge—a place where
he can be himself and commiserate with other agents.

"Believe me, this gladiator syndrome is unsustainable. Reality will eventually intervene and knock him off his pedestal.
He will take risks on the job that are foolish, and outside of
work he'll push people away so that he becomes more and
more isolated. A bunker mentality takes over.

"But it doesn't have to reach that point. When you see the
warning signs, you need to pull back and put some emotional
distance between yourself and the job. You can choose to
be a philosopher instead of a gladiator. You won't see things
in such black-and-white terms. A more mature, thoughtful
attitude will emerge, so you won't take your job or yourself
so seriously. And that's a *good* thing."

McCloud paused a moment before continuing. "You may
even develop a vague sort of kinship with the wets because
they're caught up in the same mess you are."

———

Seven months into his first year, Nick Hayden caught a break.
An extra car became available, and Willis, due to his seniority,
was allowed to ride alone. Hayden was more than a little
relieved, as dealing with his partner's mood swings and auto-
cratic style was emotionally draining, and though Hayden had
performed well, Willis still hadn't fully accepted him.

Nick realized it wasn't personal—that Willis had difficulty
getting along with everyone, particularly trainees who hadn't
been in the Border Patrol. Though eccentric, Joe was a competent, dedicated agent whose world had become defined by

the job's physical and emotional demands—a kind of low-level warfare he'd grown to cherish. Chicago, a city of gruff characters, patiently tolerated him, as did his professional colleagues.

As they drove toward the office on their last day together, Hayden made a final peace offering: "Thanks for putting up with me, Joe. I learned a lot from you."

This caught Willis off guard, and he seemed at a loss for how to respond. Finally, he said, "Well, buttering me up ain't going to do you no good. You've still got plenty to learn."

Hayden smiled. What else could he have expected from Willis?

Hayden's next partner was Vince Kozlowski. Born and raised on the southwest side of Chicago, Kozlowski had a lopsided nose, a wry smile, and a calm manner that instantly put others at ease. Though tough and capable, Kozlowski didn't have a nasty bone in his body, nor did he lust for higher office.

Kozlowski hadn't been in the Patrol and was far more accepting of Hayden than most of the other journeymen agents. He was in many ways Joe Willis's opposite—free of ego, not taking anything personally, and wanting only to get the job done so he could go home to the domestic bliss he shared with his wife and three young children. Having grown up amid the corruption and inefficiencies that were a normal part of life in Chicago, Vince was patient with government policies, no matter how incoherent or perverse. Resistance to these forces was, in his mind, both futile and self-destructive. Whenever Hayden voiced frustrations over the disarray of immigration policy, Vince would gently chide him.

"Look at it this way," Kozlowski would say with a knowing smile. "It's great job security. There will never be a shortage of wets. If the government wanted to stop illegal immigration, they'd make employers check the phony documents the wets use to get work. But they don't wanna do that because it would work. Obviously, if the wets don't think they can get jobs, they won't come—and we'd be out of a job. Just go along with it, take your paycheck, and try to enjoy life." Earlier than most of his colleagues, Kozlowski had embraced the "philosopher" mindset. Hayden thought he was one of the most uncomplicated and emotionally healthy people he'd ever met.

Meanwhile, it was a wild time out in the field. Under pressure from headquarters, Moretti ordered agents to keep hitting businesses until they'd corralled at least a hundred illegals every day. "Don't bother coming into the office until your cars are fully loaded," he warned.

Setting out before dawn in caravans of up to twenty vehicles and a detention van or two following along, they invaded one factory after another, many of them housed in crumbling warehouses that violated every city code imaginable. Agents grew accustomed to working around physical hazards: asbestos hanging from warehouse pipes, open vats of foul-smelling toxic waste, and assembly lines choked with smoke and deafening noise.

The agents' arrival typically led to pandemonium—large segments of the workforce scattering in every direction. Fights and altercations of one kind or another became daily occurrences. Among the notable injuries sustained by agents that spring, Al Winfield was struck in the back of the head by a Nicaraguan, who came out of a tool shed wielding a long piece of metal tubing as if it were a samurai sword. At the office it was discovered that the Nicaraguan had been deported three times before, had assaulted an INS agent in Newark, and was wanted for armed robbery.

Jack Hibbert got into a brawl with a Mexican on the roof of a factory. The Mexican slashed Hibbert in the arm with a switchblade but was captured when he jumped off the roof and broke his ankle.

Coming to the aid of a fellow agent outside a scrap yard, Judy Svoboda was attacked by a snarling Doberman and had to shoot it down. The same day a group of El Salvadorans fled a factory and ran onto a nearby freeway, dodging high-speed traffic. A car skidded into one young man, sending him flying onto an embankment, breaking both of his legs.

If apprehensions were running low, agents would pretend to have information on whatever business they happened to be passing. Those were often the most productive operations. Agents were very adept at implying that owners had no choice but to allow them to take over their properties and interrogate the entire workforce. Confronted with a team of ten or more federal officers glaring at them with righteous indignation, few had the temerity to turn them away.

The more daring illegals would resist the flight instinct during raids, hiding in plain sight, but their poses of casual indifference were often dead giveaways. When questioned, some would claim to have been born in Texas or California, but they had difficulty explaining why they could speak no English. Others, insisting they were born in Puerto Rico, had no idea where the island was or knew nothing about its history or customs. Nevertheless, agents were keenly aware that arresting someone who turned out to be a citizen would lead to lawsuits and depositions, so they proceeded with caution.

The mere presence of the INS caravans in ethnic neighborhoods aroused fear and panic, as immigrants of all nationalities had become familiar with the INS fleet, most of them clunky, tan Plymouth Furies with antennas poking from their roofs. Fleeing illegals scurried in front of traffic and down side streets, and the Furies would roar off in pursuit. The chases often led to enclaves of illegals in stores or apartment buildings, and the backseats of the Furies steadily filled up.

Agents made so many arrests every day that pat-downs got sloppy, and sometimes weapons weren't found until illegals were admitted into lockup. Moretti would dump a boxful of undetected knives and switchblades on a table in the middle of the squad room. "This is what you guys are missing," he'd bellow. "I won't tolerate an agent being killed on my watch because of negligence. When you throw your borders open, some bad people are going to come in with the average wet who is just looking for work to support his family. Do I have to remind you of the agents we've already lost around the country?"

Amid the stress of field operations, personal animosities between agents sometimes came to a boil. Once that summer, Hayden entered a parking lot outside a factory to find two men grappling on the oily ground. He jumped in to assist in the anticipated arrest, only to find they were both journeymen agents, pummeling each other over some perceived slight.

As illegals often concealed themselves in the dirtiest and most remote sections of warehouses, agents frequently ended the day covered with layers of soot and grime. Yet the dress code required a jacket and tie, so each agent had a collection that was frayed and soiled.

McGinty's Tavern, just around the corner from the office, became a decompression chamber at the conclusion of the day's field operations. Agents, especially the older ones, would pause to fortify themselves with beers and shots of Irish. Then they would grab a sandwich and head up to the office for the hectic drudgery of writing up illegals for deportation, which often took all afternoon and well into the evening.

Hayden found that he thrived on the excitement, challenges, and unpredictability of field work. While some agents would lose their composure amid the chaos, he would often arrive at a state of inner calm, particularly when things were spinning most out of control. Eventually his coolness under pressure drew quiet compliments from senior agents.

Meanwhile, twelve-hour workdays left little time for outside activities. Hayden usually returned exhausted to his spare studio apartment near DePaul University. He sometimes forced himself to go for a short run before wolfing down a dinner of pizza or canned soup. If he had any energy left, he would study immigration law manuals in preparation for the written exams he would have to pass. Then he would sleep hard and get up early. It was a demanding schedule, but he didn't mind because it was more interesting than anything he'd ever done in his life, and he was convinced it was important work.

Still, knowing he could be fired without cause during the first year, Hayden was apprehensive about his upcoming appearance before the probationary review panel. Despite having earned a reputation as a hard worker and doing well academically, he felt like an outsider—tolerated, perhaps, but not embraced by his colleagues. He wondered whether the incident with Tom Kane and the Jamaican had something to do with it. But the issue that caused the greatest concern was his reason for taking the job in the first place. If it were discovered, he would certainly be fired. He'd asked senior agents a lot of questions about the shooting, and that may have raised suspicions. McCloud had been curious about his name, and though they'd since developed a good relationship, he could have referred the matter to the regional office for further investigation. Anything seemed possible.

When Hayden found out that the head of investigations at the Minneapolis field office would be part of the panel, he had a sinking feeling. Victor Bolton, a hardliner with an enormous

ego, didn't like agents hired "off the street." A number of proba-
tioners at the Minneapolis office who hadn't been in the Border
Patrol had been fired in recent years for no legitimate reason,
and Bolton had purportedly enjoyed letting the guillotine fall.
Then there was Jack Connelly, director of investigations at
the Chicago office. With his carefully combed white hair, pencil
mustache, frequent scowl, and horn-rimmed glasses, Connelly
was a distant figure, not one to engage personally with the
younger agents, and he tended to shift with the wind, which
could be dangerous. Connelly would be in charge of the panel,
and his opinion would be crucial. It would be Connelly, Bolton,
and somebody from the regional office to render final judgment.

On the morning of the hearing, Hayden sat at his desk in
the empty squad room and tried to remain calm as he waited
to be called into Connelly's office. He was wearing the only
suit he had that hadn't been torn or otherwise damaged during
a field operation—a gray pinstripe, crisply pressed, accompa-
nied by a white shirt and a red silk tie. He hadn't slept well
the night before and noticed in the office lavatory that he
had dark circles under his eyes. The suit at least made him
look respectable, he told himself.

Moretti had earlier informed him that Earl Fasco, a regional
investigator, had been selected as the third person on the
panel, and that Fasco had spent most of his career doing
internal investigations, cases in which agents had taken bribes
or engaged in other improper conduct. Nick suddenly felt
they *had* to know something.

He had been told to be ready at nine o'clock. It was already
ten, and still they hadn't sent for him. Feeling edgy, he took
a stroll down the hall past Connelly's office to the drinking
fountain. Through the frosted glass windows, he could see
three blurry figures sitting behind Connelly's desk and a fourth

in a chair in the middle of the room facing them. That had to be Lou Moretti. It was normal for them to talk to his supervisors, but why for so long? A few moments later, Moretti emerged from Connelly's office and approached Hayden.

"They want you in there now," said Moretti. Hayden studied Moretti's face, but his eyes were flat and expressionless. Hayden buttoned the jacket of his coat, took a deep breath, and walked into Connelly's office.

All three of the men were sitting rigidly behind Connelly's large desk, glaring suspiciously at Hayden. Connelly was in the middle. Without standing, he introduced Fasco and Bolton. Hayden stepped forward to shake their hands. Bolton shook his hand with exaggerated firmness and offered an icy smile. Fasco, a swarthy man of about fifty, leaned forward, allowed a weak shake, and sank back into his chair, looking down at the file materials in front of him. Hayden glanced at the papers and could make out what looked like his original application for employment, which sent his mind racing. Why would Fasco be studying a document that had nothing to do with his performance during the past year?

Hayden sat in the chair vacated by Moretti. The room felt stuffy and warm. All three of the men were now silently looking down at the papers in front of them and occasionally glanced up at Hayden as if to reconcile what they had read with the person sitting before them. This went on for what seemed like several minutes, while Hayden's temperature rose around his shirt collar.

Then Bolton, a square-jawed, middle-aged man with a receding hairline and a deadly serious manner, plunged forward before Connelly had a chance to say anything—a clear breach of protocol.

"Hayden, we've reviewed your evaluations and your academic record. Is there anything you want to tell us that you think is important to this proceeding?" said Bolton in a deep, sonorous voice. Though now certain they knew something, Hayden decided there was no point in admitting anything. He wasn't going to break, not without being confronted with specific evidence. "No. I'm willing to let the record speak for itself." He was pleased that his voice sounded calm and steady.

Bolton was sitting with his large hands folded in front of him on the desk, looking at Hayden intently, as though he could look through his eyes and into his soul. He examined Hayden silently for several moments in an apparent effort to unsettle him. Nick noted an impish grin on the face of Jack Connelly, apparently amused by Bolton and the situation. He didn't know what to make of that, but took minor comfort from the fact that Earl Fasco looked utterly bored.

"I see you weren't in the Patrol," said Bolton, who made it sound like an accusation.

"No, I wasn't."

"That's unfortunate." Bolton paused before continuing. "You know, a number of years ago an agent from this office was killed—shot dead by an illegal alien. Were you aware of that?"

Though growing increasingly nervous, Hayden maintained his surface composure. "Yes, I've heard about it."

"It was found that an officer, a trainee like you, didn't have what it took to shoot a man before that man killed his partner," said Bolton, who let the statement hang in the air. Hayden said nothing, and Bolton continued. "It ended up costing the life of a good agent. I knew the agent who was killed, Frank Kelso. He was a fine man. So I'm going to ask you an important question."

Hayden noticed that Fasco and Connelly were now fully engaged in the exchange, staring at him as though they knew what was coming.

Bolton continued: "If you had to pull that trigger to save yourself or your partner, would you hesitate?"

"No, of course not," said Nick, as Bolton studied him doubtfully.

Hayden was still girding himself for an extended interrogation when, to his surprise, Jack Connelly stepped in. "Well, Hayden, you have done quite well in your first year. All your supervisors say so. I don't see any reason to prolong this line of questioning. Everything indicates that you have a bright future here."

Hayden was shocked. He had a sense that Connelly was being more kind than normal as a counterpoint to Bolton, who had clumsily taken over Connelly's preeminent position on the panel. That's what the grin was about. He'd allowed Bolton to continue and then taken delight in pulling the rug out from under him.

Bolton was sitting back in his chair looking deflated. Apparently he'd been trying to rattle Nick and plant some seeds of doubt about an agent who hadn't come from the Patrol. They knew nothing after all.

Fasco followed up with a couple of innocuous questions about what types of investigations Hayden most enjoyed. Then Connelly resumed control and, without asking the others if they had further questions, congratulated Hayden on successfully completing probation and dismissed him from the room. Bolton, his face flushed, shot a baleful glance at Connelly.

As Hayden closed the door behind him, an enormous sense of relief swept over him. He felt he was gliding inches off the floor as he walked back to area control.

———

The day after his probation hearing, Hayden, curious about what he'd accomplished in his first year, leafed through the leather-bound logbook that recorded all of the unit's arrests and deportations. He counted over five hundred illegal immigrants arrested during the past year with his name next to theirs, which meant that he'd done the paperwork on them and, in many cases, personally arrested them. In all, the Chicago office had been responsible for removing or placing in deportation proceedings some ten thousand illegal aliens during that year. Considering the logistics of moving around that many people, it was a remarkably efficient operation. Yet politicians, activists, and pundits regularly pillaged INS, in no small part *because* of its efficiency. Agents were accused of insensitivity, brutality, and racism, even though cases of outright cruelty or abuse were extremely rare. Hayden had been struck by how meticulous agents were in making certain that the children of illegals were not left unattended when one or both of the parents were arrested. While agents from the FBI or any number of other federal agencies were routinely glorified and thought of as heroic, INS agents fought a lonely and unheralded battle, more often objects of derision than praise.

——

The small studio apartment where Hayden had been living for the past year was on the North Side of the city in a vibrant area of businesses—restaurants, bars, and small shops—intermixed with apartment buildings and three-flats. After work he sometimes played basketball at a nearby field house—pickup games with anyone who showed up. It was a good way to blow off steam and got him away from the habit of stopping at McGinty's to trade war stories with his colleagues, which always left him feeling empty.

There were many attractive single women in his neighborhood, and it wasn't difficult to meet them. Some were obviously turned off by his gritty line of work, while others found it intriguing. Either way, he was so consumed with the job that he hadn't the time or energy to be drawn into anything beyond brief liaisons.

His most meaningful personal encounters took place at the Veterans Hospital in Maywood, just west of the city. He'd noticed an article in the paper that mentioned a need for volunteers to visit bedridden veterans, particularly those without families, who would often fall into intense boredom and depression. Most were older men, many of them World War II or Korean War veterans, who enjoyed talking about their war experiences and were fascinated with Hayden's INS work. Hayden tried to get there once a week, usually on the weekends. Though the men were appreciative of his visits, he often thought *he* was getting more from the experience than the patients.

The shooting of Frank Kelso and its aftermath had deeply affected Hayden, as he had lost the most important and supportive relationship in his life. From the beginning, the circumstances surrounding that terrible event had been vague, and he'd formulated countless theories to fill in the blurry picture; but without solid evidence they would remain nothing more than speculation. Though Willis had provided only a general description of the incident, Buck Tatum's extreme reaction suggested that the situation might not have been as straightforward as Willis seemed to believe. Hayden had hoped more facts would emerge after talking to agents who had worked with Kelso, Landau, and Tatum, but none of them had direct personal knowledge, and they seemed to accept the results of the investigation conducted at the time. His unusual curiosity could raise suspicion, potentially costing him his job.

He'd passed the first professional hurdle by making it through probation. Now he was determined to sharpen his investigative skills and try to earn a position in one of the units that worked the more challenging criminal cases. He would have to be patient and wait for the right moment to make further inquiries about the shooting.

———

Hayden usually didn't remember his dreams and made little effort to do so. To him they were mere flights of the imagination, not to be taken seriously. But there was one dream he'd begun to have almost every week, and it disturbed him. It would always begin in a desert, the sun blazing through a cloudless sky—the peaks of dry, craggy mountains looming hazily in the distance. Several figures dressed in brown hooded robes, like those of Franciscan monks, shuffled slowly along a sandy path. The hoods hung loosely over their heads so that he couldn't make out their faces. It was a peaceful scene, the figures blending with the washed-out earth tones of the desert. They plodded along, a methodical purpose to their gait, as if they had traveled this path before and knew exactly where they were going. Nick, from a distance, would call out to get their attention, but they couldn't hear him. His voice had no strength behind it and always vanished into the air.

4

It was a windless day in the city of Guadalajara, the air thick and humid. A vast cloud of exhaust fumes filled the sky, diffusing the sunlight. On the Calle de Leon there were no trees or landscaping—nothing but concrete pavement and a long line of buildings with little or no space between them. A pack of bony dogs sniffed through garbage that lay next to a toppled metal container. The dogs scattered when a pickup truck pulled in front of the decaying six-story apartment building.

Miguel Chavez stepped out of the passenger side and looked up at a third-floor window where his son, Paco, was leaning over the windowsill.

"Papa!" the boy shouted happily, his voice echoing down the street.

Miguel, dressed in loose-fitting jeans, work boots, and a tan shirt with the sleeves rolled up, waved and walked toward the building, carrying his metal lunchbox. He had straight black hair combed cleanly back from his forehead. Broad-shouldered and thick at the waist, he moved with the unhurried ease of a man older than his thirty-six years. Miguel went inside and climbed the sagging stairs.

He had barely closed the apartment door behind him when Paco, ten years old and small for his age, began excitedly searching his father's pockets. "Where is it, Papa?" he cried in Spanish.

Carmen was watching from the kitchen. "Let your father breathe, Paco. He didn't promise. He only said he *might* have something." She looked at Miguel's face for some sign but could tell nothing from his placid expression.

Finding nothing, Paco stepped back and looked sadly at the floor.

"Here, son, take this to your mother," said Miguel, handing over his lunchbox.

Paco cradled it in his arms and marched slowly toward the kitchen.

"You might want to open it," Miguel murmured softly.

Paco's face lit up as he placed the box on the kitchen table, fumbled with the metal latch, and flung it open. He pulled out a bright blue Chicago Cubs cap, the red letter C on the front. Beaming with delight, he ran to his father and hugged him around his waist.

"The Cubs are my favorite team, Papa!"

"Yes, why do you think I got that one?" Miguel laughed and stroked the boy's hair. "Go show Luis your new cap. I saw him out on the landing." Paco smiled and raced out the front door.

Carmen, with a restrained smile, looked at the basket on the kitchen counter where their two-month-old daughter, Maria, slept peacefully, undisturbed by the commotion. "This one will sleep through anything," Carmen said.

Miguel kissed his wife's forehead and looked down at Maria, his expression now solemn.

"What's wrong?" Carmen asked.

"They won't need me for at least a week, probably more. Before long we'll have to find an apartment where the rent is lower, and it will probably make this place look like a palace."

Carmen looked away, afraid of what was coming.

"We're moving backwards," Miguel said pleadingly. "Something has to change. We have to consider the jobs in Chicago my cousin has written about. I've been praying . . . waiting for an answer."

Carmen, with worry in her large, brown eyes, looked out the kitchen window and then back at Miguel. "But they don't want us there."

"Then why do they let so many without papers live and work there? What they do is more important than what they say, and they don't seem to do much to stop anybody from getting jobs. They must want us."

She could feel her resistance beginning to crumble.

"I can go first," said Miguel. "You can stay with my parents until I send for you."

Carmen let out a deep sigh and rested her head gently against Miguel's chest. Perhaps he was right. Perhaps they *were* wanted north of the border. Thinking of it that way made it seem more reasonable.

———

Miguel crouched next to a shack on a rock-strewn hilltop in Juárez. He carried no clothing or other possessions except a wallet with the eighty dollars he had scraped together. It was hot—the late afternoon sun shining brightly. He peered down at the river, all that separated Mexico from the United States, yet here the Rio Grande was no more than a ribbon of brown water that cut through the valley. Women from the Mexican side went down to the river with buckets to capture the water and then returned to a cluster of small huts made of scrap metal, plywood, and tar paper. On the other side of the river, a steep, rocky hillside crested to a busy highway. Miguel watched as two men waded across the river, climbed the hill, and hopped into a waiting truck. To his surprise, there was no sign of the Border Patrol on the Texas side of the river. Mostly it was quiet, with an occasional gust of wind rappelling through the canyon.

When the sun disappeared and dusk set in, Miguel made his move—still fearing that sirens and spotlights would greet him. He descended the slope, sloshed across the knee-high river, and scrambled up the steep embankment, his feet crunching through dried branches and mesquite. He was sweating heavily and his heart was pounding when he reached the top. He walked briskly along the shoulder of the highway toward the tall buildings in the center of El Paso, less than a mile away, as cars and trucks roared past him. Where were the border agents? Don't think about them, he told himself. Just keep moving and follow the instructions. As it grew steadily darker, he relaxed a little, figuring he was less likely to be noticed.

He made his way to the bus depot in the downtown area and boarded a bus for Las Cruces, New Mexico, about fifty miles to the north. There were several others on the bus who looked around nervously and appeared to be in the same situation, but he didn't speak to them. As they waited for the bus to depart, he looked out the window and for the first time saw a green-and-white Border Patrol vehicle parked at the curb just twenty-five feet away, but the agents inside were looking down, apparently doing paperwork. He could make out the heads of two prisoners in the backseat of the vehicle.

The bus left without incident, and he got off an hour later in Las Cruces. Following the directions he'd been given, Miguel made his way to a large park, which had thick bushes and a small grove of trees at one corner. He lay down beneath the canopy of trees, but his mind was racing and he couldn't sleep. At the first light of dawn, he got up and walked straight to the restaurant parking lot where he'd been told a man named Carlos would be waiting.

———

They had been driving for nineteen hours when they arrived at the outskirts of Chicago. It was Saturday morning, so the traffic was relatively light as the pickup truck traveled at just below the speed limit, heading east toward the heart of the city. Carlos, a stoic, expressionless man of sixty, had insisted on driving the entire distance, turning away offers from Miguel and the other passenger, a seventeen-year-old Mexican boy who sat between them, his head propped sleepily against Miguel's shoulder. Carlos explained that he had driven this distance many times, and since they didn't have valid driver's licenses, it was safer this way.

They passed swiftly through the outlying neighborhoods— endless rows of apartments and businesses separated by faded green lawns and trees filled with colorful autumn leaves. Miguel peered at the distant skyscrapers, backlit by the emerging sun. The buildings had a surreal, bluish quality, lacking dimension, as though painted onto the horizon.

Carlos grunted tiredly and nodded toward the skyline. "Chicago," he said, with a faint smile.

"*Qué bonita*," said the boy, his eyes now shining with hope and fascination.

Suddenly there was a loud, wailing siren behind them. They all stiffened as two police cars, their blue lights rotating, sailed past them and quickly disappeared.

Carlos turned off the highway into the shadows of a seedy, neglected neighborhood. They passed an assortment of abandoned commercial buildings, dilapidated apartments, refuse-strewn alleys, and shabbily clad men—many of them standing in doorways, grasping bottles covered by paper bags. A pungent, rotting odor hung in the air—the smell of something burning.

Within minutes, they'd entered another neighborhood, this one not so impoverished and, judging by the people and the signs on the shops, populated mainly by Hispanics. They turned off busy Eighteenth Street onto a quiet, tree-lined street with small houses and two-flats on one side and a brick elementary school on the other. Carlos pulled in front of a narrow, brick two-flat covered with faded maroon paint. It was very close to the sidewalk, so there was no front yard.

"Here it is," Carlos said.

Miguel had armed himself with such limited expectations that this simple dwelling looked surprisingly attractive. "Are you sure?" he asked.

"I have been here before. The owner uses the first floor for storage. You are on the second floor. The key is under the mat."

"Do I owe you anything more?"

"No, your cousin has taken care of it. Good luck to you."

"Thank you," said Miguel, shaking both their hands. He stood on the street as they pulled away, his legs heavy from lack of movement. Carlos waved his large hand in a kind of salute and Miguel waved back. He watched as the pickup turned off the street and disappeared. Suddenly alone, he looked up at the building and then down the block, getting his bearings. The sky was gloriously blue, and a velvety breeze moved softly through the elm trees along the narrow parkway.

Miguel whispered a prayer of thanks as he shuffled slowly up the short walk to the front steps. The bottoms of his jeans, dried stiff from the muddy waters of the Rio Grande, rubbed together at his ankles as he walked.

———

Miguel stepped inside the dimly lit tavern. It was a gloomy little place—faded wood floors, a few small tables in the shadows, circular bar stools bolted to the floor—a place where people came to drink, not socialize. The aroma of stale beer and cigarettes hung in the air. A large overhead fan cut through cigarette smoke that drifted up from a scruffily dressed old woman sitting alone at the bar. The voice of Frank Sinatra singing "Summer Wind" filled the air, the tune's polished orchestration and upbeat rhythm contrasting sharply with the bleak mood of the tavern.

Chacon, a middle-aged man with a black goatee, sat at the end of the bar reading a newspaper as Miguel stepped up. Chacon looked at him with tired eyes and addressed him in Spanish. "What can I get for you?"

"I look for the man called Rico."

Chacon nodded toward a man sitting in the dark shadows opposite the bar. He was leaning back with his head against the wall and his eyes closed.

Miguel sat down in front of Salvador Rico and waited quietly, not wanting to startle him from his sleep. Something in the man's facial features made Miguel think he was not a Mexican, and a lip wound gave him a look of quiet menace. Miguel would tread lightly. For the moment, he needed this man.

The Sinatra tape ended and the silence stirred Rico, who opened his eyes and looked into the passive face of Miguel Chavez. "What do you want?" asked Rico gruffly in Spanish, pulling himself erect.

"The documents."

"Who sent you?"

"A man. I don't know his name."

Drowsy and hungover from a night of much tequila, Rico considered him for a moment through blurry eyes. "Come back tomorrow," he said finally. "This is not a good time."

"I can't wait that long," said Miguel evenly. "I need them to get work, for tomorrow morning."

"Eager to work, eh? You Mexicans. Well, it will cost you more on a Sunday," said Rico grumpily.

"How much?"

"Three hundred dollars for the green card and social security card."

"I don't have that much."

"How much *do* you have?"

Miguel smiled as if it wasn't a serious question.

"I will do you a favor," said Rico. "Two fifty."

They studied each other for several moments. Miguel knew he had no leverage, especially if he wanted them today. He'd heard that Monday was the big hiring day at the local factories, and he needed a job now. There was no way around it—it was just how things worked here, like paying off a cop in Mexico, even when you'd done nothing wrong. Fortunately, his cousin had left some money for him at the flat.

"All right," Miguel said.

"Give me the money."

"I will pay when you give me the documents." There was no edge to Miguel's voice; he spoke calmly, looking straight into Rico's eyes.

Rico glared silently at Miguel, getting the measure of him, and then he smiled. He was impressed. This Mexican was not docile and unsure like many others. "You'll get your documents," said Rico indignantly. He pulled a small notebook from the inside of his black nylon jacket, took a pen from his front shirt pocket, and began writing. "Do you have a social security number you want to use?"

"No."

"OK, we'll make one up. It takes years for them to figure it out, and by then you can get a good number." Rico tore a page from the notepad and handed it to Miguel. "Here, take this over to the photo shop around the corner. Knock on the back door and give the man this note. He will take your picture and give you the documents."

"I pay *him?*" asked Miguel.

"No, you pay me. That note will tell him I've been paid."

When Miguel looked at him suspiciously, Rico grinned and called out toward the bar, "Am I good for it?"

Chacon didn't look up from his newspaper. "He's good for it."

Miguel counted the bills and placed them in a neat stack on the table. He now had only thirty dollars left in his wallet and a few dollars in coins back at the apartment.

"You are sure he is there now?" Miguel asked.

"Of course. I pay him to be there," said Rico, stuffing the bills into his shirt pocket.

"Very well. You are Rico, no?"

"No more questions. Just go where I told you."

After Miguel left, Rico leaned back against the wall, swung his legs up on a chair, and looked lazily around the bar.

"Draw me a short one, would you?" he called out.

Chacon drew the beer from the tap into a small glass, marched over to Rico, and set it down in front of him. Rico looked at the beer as if it displeased him.

Returning to the bar, Chacon flipped over the tape and Sinatra came back, this time belting out "My Kind of Town." It was a bit too energetic for a quiet Sunday morning and mildly irritating to Rico, still struggling to come fully awake. He took a sip of beer and closed his eyes.

———

The foreman at the Poindexter Tube Company looked through the receptionist's window at three Hispanic men seated in plastic chairs. They appeared ready for work, dressed in jeans, work boots, and heavy-duty cotton shirts. One, considerably older than the other two, glanced up and just as quickly looked down. Staring was not his way.

They would speak little or no English, but the foreman knew they would have the necessary documents, probably counterfeits like most of the others. More important, they would be good workers, respectful of their bosses, and do their jobs quietly and efficiently. He knocked on the window to get their attention and gestured them forward.

As soon as he opened the heavy door to the shop area, they were greeted by a wall of musty heat, a sharp metallic odor, and overwhelming noise: churning machinery, buzzing forklifts, and workers yelling to be heard over the din. The sound rose up to the cavernous rafters of the plant and came back down in a cascade of colliding echoes. With windows mounted high on the walls, you could see only the sky and nothing of the surrounding community, making the shop seem like a world unto itself. Miguel peered up at the dirty haze and copper sunlight that streamed through the windows. It reminded him of Guadalajara.

The foreman led them to a huge, oblong machine that, at the moment, stood idle. He called over to a flaxen-haired young man who was using a hand-operated forklift to move a pallet of metal tubes. "Russell, show these guys what they're getting into, would you?"

Russell walked over and pushed a black button on the side of the old machine. A vibration shuddered through it, and dozens of tubes hanging from a track at one-foot intervals began moving into a large opening. Thirty seconds later the tubes reappeared through an opening at the opposite end. Dull and gray before, they were now glistening silver. Russell hit a red button and everything stopped. After removing the treated tubes he stepped over to a box of untreated tubes and demonstrated how to fasten them to the metal prongs hanging from the track. This would be their job: place the tubes on the prongs, run them through the coating machine, remove and stack the treated tubes on pallets for later shipping, and keep the machine supplied with paint solutions.

After Russell had demonstrated each part of the job, the foreman led them back into his tiny office. He made copies of their counterfeit documents and told them they would make $4.50 an hour. Ten minutes later, the three of them were back inside the plant, working the tube coating machine. They'd been hired.

The two younger men were good workers and deferred to Miguel, who instantly became their de facto foreman. Within two hours they'd become comfortable with the system and were already joking with one another as if they'd been processing tubes for weeks. Satisfied that the new job was going to work out and that the other two could handle things for a few minutes, Miguel excused himself.

As he walked to the washroom there were glances from other workers interested in the new face, and he nodded and smiled at them. In his head he calculated that he'd be earning over five times what he'd made in Guadalajara. He flashed on his family, now so far away but depending on him. They had no idea that their lives had just undergone a dramatic shift of fortune.

He was grateful to find that nobody was in the large, dingy washroom. Miguel stepped into the nearest stall and latched the door behind him. It was quiet except for the muted din of the plant machinery. He removed a handkerchief from his pants pocket and mopped the moisture from his face. Taking a deep breath, he braced himself against the walls with both hands and whispered a prayer of thanks. A wave of emotion shook through him. It was powerful and gained strength— like a deep, vibrating volcano. Tears began pouring down his cheeks. He held his handkerchief close to his mouth to muffle the sobs. What would they think if they were to find him here—crying like a child when he was supposed to be working? He blew his nose and dabbed the moisture from his eyes and cheeks. It took a minute to pull himself together.

Miguel couldn't stop smiling as he stepped back into the glorious, symphonic racket of the Poindexter Tube Company.

5

Marcos Ortega was curious about the shake in Sixto's voice and his reluctance to discuss the matter over the phone, but he wasn't worried. After all, Sixto was a bit high strung and tended to overreact to small problems. It was probably a minor issue with one of his vendors—the kind that came up from time to time.

They'd agreed to meet at the Fullerton Lanes, a bowling alley on the North Side. With pins clattering and bowlers shouting, it was a good place to talk and not be overheard. It was also far from Marcos's home, so they weren't likely to run into his friends or acquaintances.

The bowling alley was housed in an old brick building that covered several acres near the banks of the Chicago River. Inside were fifty lanes, a restaurant, bar, and poolroom. In the evening hours, it was crowded and there was often a party-like atmosphere. A cloud of cigarette smoke hung over the bowlers' heads, its odor mingling with that of popcorn, hotdogs, and pizza.

Marcos arrived early and ordered a large basket of French fries and two bottles of Corona. He took a table at the end of the dimly lit mezzanine in front of lane fifty, far from the other spectators. By the time Sixto arrived, Marcos had inhaled the fries and was relaxing like a well-fed cat with his legs stretched out, sipping his beer while watching a group of giggling young women roll gutter balls. He flashed a big smile when his friend stepped up to the table, but Sixto responded with only a sullen nod.

"I love this place," said Marcos breezily. "Best fries in town. Do you want a basket?"

"No. I don't like French fries," said Sixto. "Anyway, I'm not hungry."

"Well, I got you a beer," said Marcos, shoving the bottle across the table, a bit irritated with Sixto's grim mood. Sixto took a few sips of beer and stared distractedly at the lanes. They sat silently for a minute.

"So, what is it this time?" asked Marcos finally. "You sounded worried."

Sixto took a long swallow of beer and set it on the table. "It's Salvador Rico," he said.

"Ah, the Panamanian."

"Yes. I wanted to get as much information as I could before bothering you with it. I wanted to take care of it myself. But I'm afraid you will have to deal with Rico."

"What exactly is the problem?"

"As you know, I told him the rules and gave him an area. He set up shop in the back of a photo studio and was working like any of our other guys for the first few months. Then I found out he's been hanging around Sheridan and Broadway, working the streets like a drug dealer. It was getting people's attention."

"Did you talk to him?"

"Yes, of course. I told him we want a low-key operation. He said he understood, that he would do as I said. That was three weeks ago, but then one of my guys saw him over by Kedzie and Diversey doing business on the street again—way out of his area. I made his boundaries very clear, so there was no confusion about it."

Marcos grunted and shook his head.

"Now I find out he's hired vendors of his own," said Sixto. "He's got a guy assembling the cards for him in the back of that photo studio. He funnels business to his vendors from a bar called El Palacio on Sheridan—owned by a Cuban guy who lets Rico use his place for business and probably gets a cut."

Marcos listened calmly, though there was now a clear, hard look in his eyes.

Sixto continued. "He's charging two-fifty for a green card and social security card, sometimes more, depending on who he's dealing with. His guys are even hanging around the Devon area—going after the Indians and Pakistanis. He's overcharging and has no respect for boundaries."

Marcos glared coldly at the lanes, thinking about his conversation with Salvador Rico at the restaurant. It had gone against his instincts to take on a non-Mexican, even on a trial basis—his first serious blunder since starting the business.

Though the air-conditioned bowling alley was cool, Sixto's face was flushed and beads of sweat were popping out on his forehead. He grabbed a napkin from a canister on the table and wiped it across his face. "He's trouble, this guy," he said. "I went to talk to him again a couple of days ago. He acts like he doesn't know what I'm talking about. Finally, he doesn't deny it and says if Marcos has a problem with it, you should talk to him. He threw me out of the bar. I was lying there on the curb!"

Sixto took a moment to gulp what was left of the beer and looked nervously out at the bowlers, apparently hesitant to continue.

"There must be something else," said Marcos.

"Yes, and you're not going to like it." Sixto paused before continuing. "He's sending his boys down to work the mall on Twenty-Sixth Street."

Marcos's eyes flamed, and he slammed his huge fist on the table, sending both beer bottles flying to the carpeted floor, along with the empty basket. Sixto sprang from his chair and stepped back from the table.

"Why have you not told me of this earlier?" bellowed Marcos, leaning over the table. "This termite invades my territory, and you say nothing?"

Sixto scanned the surrounding area. The noise from the lanes had absorbed the outburst, and nobody seemed to have noticed. He retrieved the bottles and basket, and cautiously returned to his chair.

"I'm telling you now. I just found out yesterday about the guy at the mall," said Sixto unsteadily. "But this Rico is not going to listen to me."

Marcos ran his hand back through his hair, took a deep breath, and looked out at the bowling lanes for a few moments. Suddenly, a sheepish grin crossed his face.

"I am sorry, my friend," said Marcos. "You have done nothing wrong. It is I who made the mistake when I agreed to take him on." He reached across the table and patted Sixto on the shoulder. "Don't worry. I will take care of Rico. You wait and see."

———

When lunch hour arrived the next day, Marcos left the tortilla plant, and drove slowly down Twenty-Sixth Street and into the parking lot of the mall—a large, white building that housed small shops selling an endless variety of imported Mexican pots and trinkets, leather goods, and clothing. Shoppers could get a decent Mexican meal at one of the stands, where they cooked food on small burners. Prices were low, and thousands of people passed through every day. The music of a mariachi band blared out from loudspeakers mounted on the roof of the building.

Marcos bought a steak burrito wrapped in aluminum foil and returned to his car. Scanning the parking lot, he noticed a tall young man wearing bell-bottom jeans standing at the farthest corner of the lot in front of a coin laundry. He was wearing a T-shirt with the sleeves cut off and a Boston Red Sox baseball cap. The man gestured at a pickup truck to pull up close, and he leaned inside the open window. After a brief conversation, the truck pulled away. The man stuffed something into his pants pocket and counted the bills he'd just received.

Moments later the young man heard feet on the pavement and looked up at the massive figure of Marcos Ortega closing in on him. Before he could react, Marcos spun him around, grabbed him by the shoulder and seat of his pants, and flung him violently against a wooden fence that ran along the alley. The baseball cap went flying. The young man was on the ground, wedged against the bottom of the fence, looking terrified.

"Listen to me carefully, young fellow," said Marcos in Spanish. "You will not sell anything on the street again. Not here, not anywhere in this city. I am not a violent man, but nobody sells the documents around here without my permission. Do you understand me?"

"Yes, of course."

"Give me the money and the documents."

The young man, hands shaking, handed over a wad of cash, two small facial photos, and several counterfeit green cards and social security cards.

"So, you are working for Salvador Rico?" asked Marcos.

After a brief hesitation, the man spoke in a trembling voice: "Yes, he sells the cards to us and tells us where to go."

"Tell Salvador Rico that Marcos Ortega wishes to speak to him. He has twenty-four hours. Now get out of here and don't forget what I told you."

The young Mexican nodded meekly and began to pick himself up off the ground. Marcos let out a soft chuckle, turned away, and returned to his car. He drove slowly to the tortilla factory, certain that the matter would now be quickly resolved. Did Rico think he could just brush Sixto aside with no consequences? Even worse was sending vendors across town into *his* territory—a very personal provocation. So be it. Salvador Rico would be made to understand very clearly who was in charge of the counterfeit document trade in Chicago.

———

Wind swept through cottonwood trees along the river, the leaves rustling together like fine sandpaper. There was a quarter moon on the eastern horizon and a scattering of stars overhead. Below, the Chicago River moved like black ink, so narrow here that it seemed no more than a large, gurgling creek.

Marcos pulled off Fullerton Avenue onto a narrow road that wound through a grove of trees and descended into a clearing that served as the bowling alley's parking lot. The gravel lot offered privacy, as it was well below the street and was obscured by the trees. To his surprise, Fullerton Lanes was closed that Sunday night—the parking lot unlit and, so far as he could tell, completely empty. The darkened building, vaguely ominous, stood outlined against the sky like a huge ship at sea.

Had he known the lanes were closed, he would have suggested a different location. Still, he'd agreed to meet in the lot, not inside. He turned his brights on and drove in a tight circle to illuminate every part of the lot. Seeing nothing, he backed the car up to the bushes lining the banks of the river, turned the lights off, and shut off the engine.

A wave of foul air from the river passed through the open window. He rolled his window up halfway and waited uneasily, expecting to see another pair of headlights at any moment. His watch said it was ten minutes past the meeting time of eleven o'clock. He thought about what he would say.

A few minutes passed. Then he could make out the faint sound of boots on gravel, obscured at first by the wind and rustling leaves, but it grew louder, a rhythmic scraping. Marcos looked to his left and could see an indistinct black form walking swiftly toward him in the darkness. A shaft of light from across the river flashed through the trees and for an instant fell on sharp-pointed cowboy boots with silver tips. He jumped out of the car and walked a few steps toward the advancing figure.

"What's going on?" he shouted into the wind. "Where's your car?"

The only reply was a bolt of orange and an explosion from a gun's muzzle. The .38-caliber bullet pierced Marcos's skull, and he felt a flame of intense heat. Staggering back, he caromed against the rear of his car and rolled heavily over a small stand of cottonwood saplings along the riverbank, coming to rest, facedown, over the embankment. For a moment there was only the sound of the wind in the trees.

The shooter slowly stepped over to the body. There was just enough light from across the river to see that Marcos was no longer moving.

Two minutes later a car emerged from behind the bowling alley and stopped momentarily, its headlights aimed across Marcos's motionless body. Apparently satisfied, the driver pulled slowly out of the parking lot.

———

The manager of Fullerton Lanes discovered the empty vehicle and Ortega's dead body the next morning. Detectives from the Belmont district were pessimistic, having little to work with—no witnesses, no other tire marks near the car, and no empty shell casings. The wind had apparently muffled the gunshot, as there had been no reports of disturbance in the area. Footprints could not be lifted from the hard-packed gravel, and five hundred dollars in cash was left untouched in his wallet, which seemed to eliminate robbery as a motive.

The coroner reported that the slug had entered the left side of Marcos's forehead at a slight angle and was fatal within seconds. The police made the usual inquiries: talking to his family and close friends, his boss, and a few coworkers at the tortilla factory. His young wife, who had only recently arrived from Mexico with their children, knew very little of her husband's illegal business and chose to say nothing about it to the police, nor did his friends, none of whom wished to become entangled in a police investigation. Sixto Montoya assumed Rico was responsible, but he decided that the safest course of action was to get out of the document business and stay clear of both Rico and the police. Weeks passed with no new leads, and the police closed the case.

"Marcos respected us," declared Joe Willis to a gathering of agents at McGinty's. "He told me once he wouldn't mind going into politics. Maybe it was some politician who had him knocked off—saw him as competition, a rising star. Hell, we'll probably never know." Willis lifted his glass in a toast. "Anyway, here's to Marcos Ortega, one of the few tonks who tried to make our job easier. I'll miss the big son of a bitch." They were the most sentimental words anybody had heard from Willis in years.

In a city where hundreds of homicides occurred every year, the violent death of Marcos Ortega faded quickly from memory.

Part II

6

She was picked up at Marshall Field's for shoplifting and turned over to INS by the store security guards, who found the Colombian passport she had carelessly left in her purse. The visa in the passport showed that she had entered the country as a tourist for thirty days—but that was in 1987, and it was now the fall of 1990.

Young and very pretty, she had almond eyes, radiant black hair, and smooth, cinnamon-colored skin. She was dressed casually but expensively in tight-fitting designer jeans and a white, sleeveless blouse that highlighted her beautifully tanned shoulders.

"I like older men," she whispered to Joe Willis, her eyelids falling seductively.

"Find my bald head attractive, do you?" snapped Willis, who had seen agents fired for yielding to this sort of temptation. As he continued typing, the girl became visibly nervous and produced a business card of DEA agent Ike Torres.

"He is friend of mine," she said, with a touch of defiance.

"I'll bet he is," said Willis, whose eyes lit up as he examined the card. "How does he like it? With you on top or is he into something a little more kinky?"

"Is not like that," she said bitterly. "You call him and find out."

"He said he would protect you from INS, didn't he?"

Taken aback by Willis's fierce glare, she was momentarily speechless.

Willis persisted. "That's what he told you, didn't he?"

"He is important federal agent, no?"

"He's a lying piece of shit. As far as I'm concerned he's a criminal for harboring illegals." Willis flashed his crocodile smile as the woman eyed him nervously and shifted in her chair.

As the time of his age-forced retirement grew more imminent, Willis, realizing opportunities for revenge were dwindling, had developed a list of enemies. He'd let slip to Payton just a few days earlier that Ike Torres was number three on the list.

"A list of enemies? Who the hell do you think you are—Richard Nixon?" said Payton with a shake of his head.

The seeds of Willis's hatred for Ike Torres had been planted months earlier, when he encountered a Mexican who admitted he was illegal but claimed he was "working for the government" and should therefore not be arrested. Willis had ignored the comment and grabbed him by the arm, whereupon the Mexican punched Willis in the nose, drawing a small amount of blood. There'd been a brief scuffle before Willis was able to handcuff him. Determined to charge the Mexican with assaulting a federal officer, Willis transported him to the office and threw him into lockup. The Mexican promptly called Torres, who had told him that he would protect him from

INS, as long as he supplied useful drug information. Though
he had no authority for it, this procedure had become routine
for Torres.

Ike Torres, learning of the Mexican's predicament, had
spoken to the DEA chief in Chicago, who, in turn, called
INS district director Jerome Farber to ask that the "misun-
derstanding" be overlooked and the man be released so that
he could continue working on a case that had the "highest
priority." Farber, more concerned with avoiding interagency
strife than the fate of one illegal alien, had not bothered to
inquire with Moretti or Willis before ordering the release.
So Torres and Farber were added to the enemies list, though
Farber was farther down as Willis made allowances for the
predictable betrayals of politicians and high-level bureaucrats.

Now this young woman, who desperately wanted to remain
in the United States, presented a rare opportunity. Convinced
that Willis now controlled her destiny, she provided detailed
information on two Colombian brothers, the Padillas—both
illegal—who were possibly holding several kilos of cocaine in
their apartment. One of the brothers had boasted just yesterday about the drugs. But was it only a boast to impress her?
She said she hadn't yet told Torres about the Padilla brothers
as she was still collecting information. Willis doubted that she
ever planned to tell Torres, but it made no difference. It was
his case now. If it checked out, Willis assured her, he would
see to it that she was released and given a year to depart the
country on her own, which they both understood meant that
she'd be allowed to disappear. On his way out of lockup, Willis told the detention officers to make sure she was given no
access to a telephone or visitors, particularly any government
agents such as Ike Torres.

Willis wasted no time in gathering a team to meet the next day before dawn. He located a file on Francisco Padilla showing he had been deported two years earlier. In a brief meeting with the agents, Willis distributed mug shots of Padilla. The agents couldn't get a search warrant because the US Attorney would find the probable cause weak and insist on bringing the DEA and Ike Torres in on the case, so they would have to be creative. The plan was simple: get into the damned apartment by whatever means necessary and find the cocaine without the assistance or knowledge of Ike Torres or anybody from the DEA.

———

It was a diverse neighborhood on the far north side of the city, dense with apartment buildings, small houses, and three-flats with tiny yards or no yards at all. A bit of gentrification was in evidence, with an occasional rehabbed graystone next to a dilapidated high-rise, but it remained a relatively high-crime area. As agents took up their positions, the first glimmers of light emerged, softly brushing the street with color.

Hayden had eagerly accepted Willis's invitation to participate in what sounded like an interesting criminal case, but he hadn't counted on being partnered with Tom Kane. It had been three years since their altercation over the fleeing Jamaican, and though Nick had always been curious about why there had been no repercussions from the incident, he'd thought it wiser to let the issue fade. Since they were both in area control, a complete lack of contact had been impossible, but the branch was big enough—some forty agents—that he'd managed to quietly avoid Kane.

They sat in Kane's Fury, one of several INS vehicles scattered throughout the neighborhood, watching for any sign of the Padilla brothers entering or leaving the apartment building. It was quiet except for occasional bulletins from Willis, always happy to fill dead airspace. Hayden decided the lull was an opportunity to clear the air.

"I've been meaning to ask you something."

"What's that?" asked Kane.

"You never told anybody about that problem we had with the Jamaican when I was a trainee, did you?"

"If I'd said anything, the ex–Border Patrol guys might've seen an opening. As I recall, you were partnered with Joe Willis, who hates all trainees. Once those guys get a bad feeling about somebody, it's all over. Anyway, you'd just started and didn't have a chance to figure things out."

"I was pretty naive back then," said Hayden. "The way I look at it now, if they come here illegally, they're not entitled to be treated like everybody else. If they don't like it, they can go back where they came from. I have zero sympathy for them."

"Everybody changes on this job," said Kane. "You have to, otherwise you get steamrolled."

"Well, I owe you one for not saying anything to Willis and the others."

"That's ancient history. Forget about it."

Despite their earlier confrontation, Nick had come to respect Kane, who had a solid work ethic and didn't play political games.

"You still want out of area control?" asked Hayden.

"Yeah, but they never want to move you if you're producing. I've done OK on short assignments to the fraud unit, so maybe I'll eventually get a shot at staying there."

Willis's voice came over the radio, this time with more urgency. A man wearing a black leather jacket and a Yankees cap had left the apartment building and was walking swiftly toward Kane's vehicle. It could be one of the Padillas, Willis said, but he couldn't be sure. If it was Francisco or his brother, Enrico, they were to take him down out of sight of the apartment building.

"Not just a doper, a Yankees fan," said Kane, who could see, through his rearview mirror, a figure walking toward them, about twenty-five yards away. "Here he comes, on your side."

In his side-view mirror, Hayden saw the man looking suspiciously over his shoulder. Perhaps he had spotted one of the other surveillance vehicles. More likely he was just paranoid, especially if they were holding several kilos of cocaine in that apartment. Nick feared the man would spot two guys in the vehicle, assume they were cops, and take off.

"I better grab him," said Hayden, stepping out of the car. In the faint light, he stood face-to-face with a startled man who had close-set eyes and a wide nose: Francisco Padilla. The Colombian spotted the gold shield on Hayden's belt and pivoted away, but Hayden grabbed him by the shoulder and thrust him savagely into the brick stairway of a two-flat apartment just off the sidewalk. Padilla gasped in pain as his knees slammed off the pointed edges of the bricks. Hayden pushed him into a prone position against the steps, pulled his hands behind his back, and quickly slid a pair of handcuffs around Padilla's wrists. Hayden thrust his right hand into the man's pants pocket, dug around, pulled out a ring of keys, and threw them to Kane, who had just arrived.

"What is wrong? Why you do this?" Francisco sputtered in heavily accented English, a gash on his nose leaking droplets of blood.

Kane pulled the man's shoulder back to view his face. "Yeah, this appears to be Francisco."

Hayden felt something metallic pressed between Padilla's belt and abdomen, and a clip attached to the belt. "Hey, what do we have here?" he chirped. It was a black leather holster holding a nickel-plated .38-caliber revolver. He handed it back to Kane, who was now standing at Padilla's feet. Kane looked up and down the street while Hayden continued his search, pushing his hand into the inside pocket of the leather jacket. He pulled out a small glass vial of white powder and passed it to Kane.

"You have any papers, Francisco?" asked Hayden.

"What papers?" asked Padilla.

"Immigration papers, you idiot. Do you have permission to be here or not?" demanded Hayden, as Kane pulled Padilla to a standing position next to the steps.

Padilla stared defiantly at Hayden.

"I'll take that as a no," said Hayden. "That means you're going back to Colombia. But first, let's make sure you have your passport and all your belongings. We wouldn't want to send you back there without your personal stuff. We know how important that is to you."

"I no need anything. I no have passport."

"Let's get him into the car for this," said Kane. They each grabbed one of Padilla's arms and shoved him into the back-seat of the Fury, Hayden climbing in beside him.

"Five-fourteen to Kane and Hayden," said Willis over the radio.

"We've got him, Joe. It's Francisco," said Kane.

"Good. Any trouble?" asked Willis.

"No. He had a gun and a small vial of powder. Give us a minute to talk to him."

Hayden knew as soon as they'd arrested Padilla how they would do it. He leaned forward over the seat. "Tell him Francisco wants to get his belongings at the apartment."

"I no live around here," sputtered Padilla.

"I guarantee the apartment key is on that ring," said Hayden. "And he's going to give us permission to go into that apartment."

"I no give permission!" cried Padilla.

Kane, a bit startled that Hayden would hatch such a scheme, paused for a moment before an impish grin came over his face and he lifted the mic. "He wants to get his stuff before being shipped, Joe."

"I think we can accommodate him on that," said Willis sarcastically.

Two agents were stationed in the alley beneath the second-floor apartment. Inside the dim hallway, six agents with guns drawn were poised just outside Padilla's apartment door as Willis inserted the key. Francisco Padilla stood at the end of the row of agents, cuffed behind his back. To keep him from calling out a warning, Kane wrapped his hands around Francisco's mouth from behind. Willis turned the key, and the bolt slid away from the doorjamb. He kicked the door open and, seeing nobody inside, waved the others to follow. The tension of anticipation released, the agents stampeded through the apartment like a herd of elephants.

Willis and another agent charged into the first bedroom off the hallway to find Enrico Padilla next to the bed pulling on his pants. He looked up, a mixture of fear and defiance in his eyes.

"Let me see your papers if you have any," said Willis, showing his badge.

"You no have right," Enrico blurted, standing unclothed from the waist up.

"Call the ACLU," barked Willis, already pulling Enrico's arms behind his back to cuff him. He looked a lot like his brother, short but muscular, with a barrel chest and a wide nose with flaring nostrils.

It took only minutes to check the obvious places where several kilos of cocaine might be stashed: closets, dressers, mattresses, appliances, kitchen cupboards. Al Winfield even unscrewed the grilles on the heating vents, but to no avail. All they found was a loaded .357 revolver and the men's Colombian passports under Enrico's mattress. It was a spare, clean apartment and, given the absence of personal clutter that tends to accumulate over time, appeared not to have been occupied very long.

The Padilla brothers were sitting on the couch in the living room, handcuffed behind their backs, when Hayden marched in from the hallway.

"What do you do for work . . . to make a living?" asked Hayden. Francisco glowered, while Enrico hung his head and looked at the floor.

Hayden thought there were too many reasons to believe the girl—the guns, the vial of cocaine, Francisco's jumpy and belligerent reaction. He decided to give Francisco's bedroom a second look. The room had old hardwood floors that had recently been refinished with a fresh coat of polyurethane. He pulled up an imitation Oriental rug that was lying alongside the bed, and he was about to move on when he noticed an unusual configuration in the oak boards. At first glance the smooth finishing obscured the variation, but now he could see that a number of boards had been shortened to end at the same place, the edges forming an almost perfect square.

"Anybody got a flathead screwdriver?" he called out.

In the living room, Francisco exploded. "You have no right for search! I want lawyer," he bellowed angrily, rising to his feet. Kane shoved him back onto the couch.

Winfield pulled a screwdriver from his belt tool holder and walked past the Padillas to deliver it to Hayden, whereupon Francisco became even more animated. "Is illegal search!" he cried.

"You guys must be getting close," Kane shouted toward the bedroom. "Francisco's a human Geiger counter."

Hayden worked the screwdriver along the edges of the suspicious square until it came loose. The hollowed-out cavity beneath the square was only a few inches deep, but it widened beneath the floor, and they could see a number of packages wrapped in brown tape.

"We hit the jackpot!" said Willis excitedly. "Better get some photos. We need fingerprints, so nobody touch the bags without rubber gloves."

Winfield came in with a 35 mm camera and took several photos of the opening and packages. Slipping on rubber gloves, Hayden removed the packages—seven kilos altogether—and stacked them on the floor. He used a pocketknife to create a tiny slit in the wrapping of one, revealing a sparkling white powder. He looked up at the hovering Willis.

"Looks like good coke," he said.

"Good work, Hayden," said Willis. "Damn fine work. I'll take the dope in. You and Kane can take Francisco in, if you don't mind. I'll have other guys take Enrico."

Hayden couldn't believe Joe Willis would ever say "if you don't mind" without a touch of sarcasm. That alone was worth more than whatever accolades might come from his supervisors.

In the car, a scowling Francisco Padilla sat awkwardly in the backseat with his hands cuffed behind him.

"Nice job, Nick," said Kane, pulling the car away from the curb.

"We got lucky," said Hayden, unable to restrain a smile. It wasn't false modesty. He knew it hadn't taken any great skill. But everything was different now. The key had been his willingness to do something he wouldn't have considered a year earlier—sidestepping laws that seemed to him designed to thwart legitimate efforts to get criminals off the streets. In so doing he was reaping tangible benefits: a major seizure of drugs and the admiration of his colleagues, even Willis. He'd finally penetrated an invisible wall that had separated them.

They sped down Lake Shore Drive beneath a clear indigo sky, everything glowing in the morning sunshine. On Lake Michigan, rolling waves broke smoothly near the shoreline. Beyond the waves the lake spread out, flat and shimmering, appearing as vast as an ocean. Buoyed by an unfamiliar sense of belonging, Hayden felt something close to euphoria.

———

The cocaine had a street value of over a million dollars. The story was on the front pages of the Chicago papers and among the lead stories on television. District Director Farber was delighted to answer questions from the media that were, for a change, not about some perceived gaffe or violation of policy, and Jack Connelly received a congratulatory call from a top INS official at headquarters. It was good for morale; even agents not involved in the bust seemed to carry themselves with a bit more swagger. Joe Willis took great pleasure in letting Ike Torres know that his unauthorized "informant" had supplied the tip that led to the seizure. Though he feigned indifference, Torres was furious.

Fingerprint analysis would seal the fate of the Padilla brothers. The slick tape on the kilo-sized packages proved to be an excellent surface from which to lift fingerprints. The brothers couldn't plausibly claim that they'd known nothing about the seven kilos found in their apartment because their prints were all over them.

Still, their attorneys declared the search illegal, and this led to a suppression hearing at which Hayden and Kane were called upon to testify. They looked like young bankers in their dark suits, and testified almost identically: Francisco had provided a key to the apartment and given them permission to search it, which led to the discovery of the cocaine. According to them, it was all very straightforward.

Then the defense attorneys pounced. Why hadn't the agents obtained written consent to search? There was no legal requirement for it, said Hayden correctly, and there had been a witness to the verbal consent.

"If Mr. Padilla was giving his voluntary consent, why was it necessary for one of the agents to cover his mouth in the hallway?" inquired Francisco's lawyer.

"You never know if a person will panic and decide to warn someone inside the apartment. It was just a precaution. He never gave any indication he was withdrawing permission to conduct the search."

"Are you familiar with the crime of perjury, Agent Hayden?"

"Yes, of course," he replied calmly. The defense attorney asked several more questions about the search, getting nowhere, and the judge instructed him to move on.

Francisco Padilla did not make a good witness. His testimony was emotional and defensive, in stark contrast to the agents' professional presentation. The judge, a tired, cynical man of sixty-five who had grown bored with the drug cases that flooded his docket, looked down at the Colombians with unconcealed disdain and ruled there was insufficient evidence to find the search illegal.

Having no reasonable expectation of success at trial, the attorneys quickly negotiated a plea agreement resulting in a sentence of ten years in prison, followed by deportation to Colombia. The word from Willis's female informant was that certain Cali cartel members would be waiting for the brothers, who owed them several hundred thousand dollars.

Charlie McCloud's response was muted. Watching events from afar, he was as pleased as anybody about the Padilla bust. It sent a message to the DEA and the FBI who, by routinely stealing informants and eliciting information with no thought of returning the favor, had not endeared themselves to INS agents. But McCloud was skeptical about how Hayden and Kane had obtained entry into Padilla's apartment. Colombian dope dealers, McCloud knew, weren't in the habit of leading a team of agents into their stash house voluntarily. The Colombians' vehement denials of having done so raised suspicions that were confirmed when McCloud was having a drink at McGinty's. The Padilla bust came up in conversation with agents Al Winfield and Tim Reynolds, both of whom had participated in the seizure.

"That was a nice bust you guys pulled off," said McCloud.

"Yeah, about time we got some good publicity," said Winfield.

"Sounds like Padilla made it easy to do the search," McCloud offered mildly between sips of beer. A furtive glance passed between Winfield and Reynolds before Winfield said, "Yeah. The Colombians were stupid." He then looked away and changed the subject a little too quickly. That was enough to confirm it for McCloud.

Having observed the gladiator syndrome in other agents, and even in himself earlier in his career, he could see that it had arrived in force for Nick Hayden. McCloud was now troubled by what he perceived as Hayden's metamorphosis from a smart, thoughtful agent to one diminished in stature, though the conventional wisdom in the office was that Hayden was one of the rising stars.

During Hayden's first year, he and McCloud had frequently gone out to lunch to discuss whatever minor problems Nick was having in area control, and how to prepare for exams he would have to pass as part of his training regimen. Their conversations had often veered into other areas of mutual interest, such as politics or literature. They had always had a similar code of ethics, but that appeared to have changed, and the relationship had become a bit strained. McCloud suspected that Hayden had come to think of his former training officer as being from the "old school," disconnected from the realities and challenges of modern-day law enforcement.

Hayden was well aware of his own evolution—his life was now almost completely consumed and defined by work. Confident in his abilities as an investigator and driven by a clear sense of purpose, he often worked late into the night, reviewing leads and planning operations. Outside interests had faded. It had been over a year since he'd been to the Veterans Hospital in Maywood. His romantic relationships were still limited to brief liaisons that never progressed to a more meaningful level. The city itself was his most steadfast companion, offering endless diversions.

Though he'd assumed he would eventually finish law school, the thought of being an attorney had lost its appeal.

Compared to this job, the work of lawyers appeared stuffy and tedious. The action was on the street, not in the courtroom; attorneys were there mainly to sort out the mundane details. Though the Kelso shooting still came to mind periodically, he knew that if he made further inquiries, aside from raising suspicion that could cost him his job, he might not get the answers he wanted.

———

Hayden hadn't noticed McCloud's door partly open as he strode down the hallway.

"Hey, Nick, you got a minute?"

Hayden stopped just past the door. "I'm kind of busy, Charlie."

"It'll only take a minute," said McCloud.

Hayden walked into the room and stood rigidly behind a chair in front of the paper-strewn desk. "It's been a hectic time, Charlie. You know . . . the Padilla bust and all. I've got a lot to do."

"Sure, we all have a lot to do," said McCloud, leaning back in his chair. "Interesting piece of work, the Padilla thing."

"Yeah, it worked out well."

"You might not be so lucky next time."

Nick was momentarily taken aback. "What's that supposed to mean?"

"Have a seat, Nick." McCloud motioned toward the chair. "We need to talk."

"I'm not a trainee anymore, Charlie."

"Shut the door, would you? I've got something to say," said McCloud bluntly.

Hayden considered walking away but instead turned and closed the door. This conversation was inevitable; he might as well get it over with.

"What's bothering you, Charlie? Afraid we bent the rules a little to do something good?"

"Sounds like you did a little more than just bend them."

"Who said that?"

"Nobody said it. I've been around long enough to put two and two together."

"Come on, Charlie, I—"

"Look, guys like Stark and the front office—they might encourage you to take these kinds of risks, but if you get caught, they'll throw you to the wolves."

"I'm not doing it for them. It's what *I* want." He reluctantly sat down. "Things might be a little different than when you were on the street."

"You've been doing this stuff for four years, and you're going to tell *me* what it's like on the street?" said McCloud with a sardonic grin.

"It's a game, Charlie, and it's gotten worse. There are wets on every street corner now, and they're not afraid of us. A lot of them are involved in stuff like these Colombians, and we're supposed to just sit back and let them do whatever they want? You try to win the game—however you can."

"So perjury is part of the game?"

"Come on. It's not like they're innocent."

"And the end justifies the means? You're supposed to be above that sort of thing."

"You're giving me textbook stuff, Charlie. It doesn't hold up in the real world."

"That's been said by every gladiator cop who was too lazy and full of himself to do things professionally," said McCloud.

"I hear you were working with Kane. He doesn't know where to draw the line."

"I can handle Kane. He has no influence on me. Besides, what we did with the Colombians was my idea."

McCloud held up his hands in a gesture of mild exasperation. "OK, but remember—when things are crystal clear in this business, you're in trouble. I told you this gladiator syndrome is full of land mines. You start thinking you're indestructible."

They stared coolly at one another for several moments, but each knew the other wouldn't yield.

"I'm only telling you for your own good," McCloud said with a tone of weary resignation. "But you're right—you're not a trainee. So go ahead. You'll find out the hard way. Do whatever you want."

"That's good advice, Charlie. I *will* do what I want." Hayden went out, closed the door behind him, and stood in the hallway for a few moments. Then, with a disgusted wave toward McCloud's door, he turned away.

———

Sam Payton was retiring and moving back to San Antonio. They'd already had a retirement dinner with his wife and family in attendance, but at the end of his last day his colleagues gathered at McGinty's for a more casual send-off. When Hayden and Kane arrived, they found a circle of agents at a table in the corner. Payton, a heavyset, steady man, had an affable way about him that had made him one of the more popular agents in the office. He was now regaling his colleagues with stories about the old days in the Patrol and investigations, recalling the colorful characters he'd worked with.

When the laughing subsided for a moment, somebody asked why Willis wasn't there. "I saw him in the office putting in a request to stay past age fifty-seven," said Payton. "That's only two weeks away. They never grant those requests, but he says he's got nothing to lose. He's coming over later."

They all seemed to contemplate Willis for a few moments before Al Winfield posed a question: "Sam, what was the worst thing that happened during your time here?"

"What kind of thing is that to ask on his last day?" said Kane, shaking his head.

"No, that's OK," said Payton. "Let me think it over a second." He took a sip of beer, as the others waited quietly.

"I'd have to say the shooting of Frank Kelso," Payton began. "Kelso was a nice fella—everybody liked him. And it did something to Buck Tatum. He wouldn't talk to anybody about it—even me, and I was pretty close to him. When he retired, Tatum wouldn't keep in touch with anybody. He left the area, and his wife didn't want to go with him—divorced him. It was strange, his reaction. Cut himself off and went into hiding. And the trainee, Landau—he got fired and committed suicide a year later, right around the time Tatum retired and disappeared."

Payton's eyes narrowed, deep in recollection.

"Connelly asked me to pick up a copy of the police report and photos the day after the shooting," Payton continued. "I don't know how Kelso made the guy as a wet. He was from Argentina, but he looked like a typical, long-haired American guy. The report said he had blue eyes. Anyway, I always thought there was something that never came out—the way Tatum clammed up. And it never seemed right that Landau took all the blame. It was like a piece of the puzzle was missing—maybe more than just *one* piece. It's a gut feeling. But I guess we'll never know . . . just part of this business."

After a brief pause, somebody asked Payton to tell his favorite Joe Willis story before Joe arrived, and the gathering again turned lighthearted and jovial. But Hayden had backed away from the table. He quietly slipped out the door and into the night without saying a word to Kane, who watched him curiously.

Hayden felt dazed as he walked slowly to the parking garage. He got into his car and drove through the Loop into light evening traffic on Lake Shore Drive, the lake looming dark and silent to one side, the city lights on the other.

Though he had more than enough to deal with already, the uneasy feeling sent a clear message. He'd kept it all buried but now realized it was simmering just beneath the surface. With Payton's suspicions about the shooting arousing such a visceral reaction, he knew he had no choice but to resume his search for the truth—even if it meant losing a job he'd grown to love.

7

The tiny Peruvian walked stiffly through the cold, swirling wind. When he reached the corner, he glanced sideways down Sheridan Road and noticed the door to El Palacio slightly ajar, even though it was only ten o'clock in the morning. He'd bought his share of drinks there over the last couple of years. Perhaps that would count for something with Chacon.

Hernan Garza was covered in layers of clothing so that, like a cat with long fur, he appeared larger than he really was—five feet two and a hundred and twenty pounds. Sweaters and shirts were covered by an overcoat that fell to the tips of his black gym shoes. The coat was threadbare and badly frayed. With a blue knit cap covering his ears, he looked like a merchant seaman. He clapped his hands against the cold, stuffed them into his pockets, and headed toward the bar.

Garza slipped inside, hoping to drift unnoticed into a darkened corner, but the door's creak pierced the quiet. Chacon and Salvador Rico were standing at the bar, staring at him. Garza could tell from Chacon's sour expression that he wouldn't be welcome unless he were a paying customer.

He pulled the scarf away from his face and addressed Rico in Spanish.

"Mr. Rico, would you have a minute, sir? I would like to discuss something important with you." Though he had never spoken with Salvador Rico, he'd heard plenty—a leader of sorts, and ruthless. There was talk of the killing of a rival in the document trade.

"Important? Important to who?" asked Rico sharply.

"Please, just a minute of your time, sir," Garza pleaded.

Rico had seen Garza at the bar—heard that he was a heavy user of alcohol and cocaine who eked out a meager existence as a small-time dealer. Had Rico been busy he would have dismissed him, but he found Garza to be an amusing, almost cartoonlike character.

"Come," said Rico, pointing to his favorite table in the corner.

They sat down, Rico with his back against the wall. Garza pulled his cap off to reveal a matted shock of graying hair. He elaborately unraveled the scarf from around his neck and used it to wipe the melting icicles from his mustache. Rico sat watching him, captivated by his every move.

Though he was only forty-one years old, Garza could have been mistaken for sixty. His florid cheeks were weather-beaten and pockmarked, his teeth riddled with brown stains. Garza laid the hat and scarf on the table and looked up earnestly, like a man eager to confide in his lawyer. "I have been hoping to meet you, Mr. Rico. My name is Hernan Garza," he declared in surprisingly crisp Spanish as he held out his hand. Rico looked at it for a moment, then reached across the table and reluctantly gave it a quick shake.

"Yes, I have seen you. So what did you wish to discuss?"

"I know you sometimes hire people, those who are familiar with the street . . . those who can help you. I am very
discreet. I see and hear many things. Perhaps I could be of
service to you," said Garza, his glassy eyes taking on a hope-
ful glitter. Though it was an idea improvised to purchase a
few moments of warmth, he suddenly realized it might have
merit. He knew Rico had plenty of money.

Rico studied him. Garza was not lacking in intelligence,
though drugs and alcohol had obviously taken their toll. While
Rico had no interest in a business relationship, he sensed
that Garza, ubiquitous on local streets, possessed a wealth of
information. Perhaps he could glean something useful.

"You were working with Mario Duran, no? Before he got
busted?" inquired Rico. Duran, also from Peru, had been a
familiar presence at El Palacio until he'd been arrested a week
earlier by the DEA for possession of two kilos of cocaine. The
mention of Duran sparked an immediate reaction in Garza.

"I did work with Mario, yes, but don't believe everything
you hear, Mr. Rico. There are men who lie for their own
purposes." Garza's eyes were suddenly brimming with emotion. "You heard it was *me* who informed on Duran, didn't
you? It's that filthy Colombian, Bautista, I tell you! He puts
the word out that it was me, but Mario knows better—he
knows I would never do such a thing."

"I did hear something about it," Rico lied.

"Bautista works both sides. He sells drugs and is an informant for the DEA and the state police. They protect him.
Bautista made at least two thousand dollars for ratting out
Duran. Plus he gets rid of a competitor." Garza's hands were
desperately gripping the edge of the table.

"How do you know this?"

Garza turned and looked nervously around the bar, still empty except for Chacon. He then spoke in a whisper. "Bautista was the only one who knew about the two kilos besides me, but then he tells people it was *me* who ratted. He set me up!"

"How do you know the federal agents pay that much for information?"

"It came out in court last year. The FBI paid six thousand to an informant after they got six kilos of cocaine. Do I look like I've got thousands of dollars in my pocket?" Garza leaned closer and smiled, revealing several gaps where teeth were missing. His reeking breath arrived in a sudden wave, prompting Rico to back away from the table.

"I don't want dirty money from ratting," Garza continued frantically. "Bautista is holed up in his apartment with a lot of 'coca' right now. But even on Bautista I won't squeal!"

Rico listened intently, yet betrayed no more than casual interest. "Do you want a drink?" he asked.

"Yes, perhaps a shot of whiskey." Garza smiled appreciatively and began to salivate in anticipation.

"Bring over a shot of whiskey for my friend," Rico called out to Chacon. He looked back at Garza. "So, Bautista was working with the feds, eh?"

"Yes, of course. I had to defend myself . . . tell people it was Bautista and not me. Now nobody wants to deal with *him* either. That is why he is holed up. People are afraid to deal with him."

"I see. Now I understand your side of the story."

Garza's face broke into a smile at this apparent breakthrough. "If I wanted to make easy money, I would go to the cops about Bautista. But I have too much integrity to do that, even though he lies about me."

"Yes, I can see that—a man of integrity."

Chacon arrived with the whiskey and set it in front of Garza, who grabbed the glass with a trembling hand and immediately tossed the amber liquid to the back of his throat. His eyes twinkled, and he let out a pleasurable sigh. He took a moment to admire the empty glass and set it down on the table.

"Listen, Hernan," said Rico, "I don't believe what they say about you. And I will let you know if I need you." Rico dug into a back pocket of his slacks, pulled out a wad of bills, and peeled off a fifty. He reached across the table and stuffed it into Garza's hand. "Here, take this," he said. "But don't tell anybody we talked. If you do, I will not be pleased."

"Yes, I understand," said Garza gleefully, stashing the bill into the inside pocket of his wool coat. "I say nothing."

"And don't come in here again," said Rico, a firm edge to his voice. "If you need to talk to me, get word to one of my people."

"Of course. I know how to do things properly."

"I think you'd better leave now." Rico had gotten what he wanted and was no longer interested in Garza.

"Yes, Mr. Rico. Thank you for your time." Garza stood up, pulled his knit cap over his ears, and wrapped the scarf around his neck. He nodded toward Rico and marched toward the door. Though he desperately wanted another shot of whiskey, he wouldn't spend any of his fifty dollars here—to hell with Chacon! Garza went out the door into the freezing air, convinced that his visit had been a complete success. He had not only escaped the cold but also gotten a free whiskey and made fifty dollars!

It was quiet again in the bar. Rico sat in the corner and mulled over how to best utilize the windfall of information he'd just received. He chuckled softly at the image of Hernan Garza. It was his good fortune that the little Peruvian had stumbled into El Palacio.

———

Hernan Garza sat in the corner of a donut shop on Lincoln Avenue and slurped a hot cup of coffee. It was another frigid, gray February morning. He looked out the window at cars plowing through a fresh layer of snow and contemplated his dilemma. With Duran in jail, his brief career as a dealer of small bags of cocaine was over. He was almost broke, having spent most of the fifty dollars Rico had given him a week ago. The thought of robbing a liquor store passed through his mind. He'd noticed an inviting target on Pulaski Road, though he knew he had to consider getting a regular job. The thought depressed him.

He looked down at a *Chicago Tribune* somebody had left on the table and was about to page through to the classifieds, when the headline near the bottom of the front page caught his attention: COCAINE BUST NETS TWELVE KILOS. The name jumped out: Raul Bautista! His nemesis, Bautista, had been arrested by the FBI for possession of twelve kilos of high-quality, uncut cocaine.

Garza's head felt like it was on fire. He knew he was now in grave danger. His instincts told him that it had to be Salvador Rico who was responsible for Bautista's arrest. Rico was the only one he'd told about the Colombian holding the cocaine and that the FBI would pay thousands for the information. To protect himself, Rico had probably already spread the word that Garza was the rat. Bautista and his friends, having every reason to believe this story, would seek violent revenge. Suddenly, every passing vehicle and person was a threat. How incredibly foolish he had been—all for fifty dollars and a bit of warmth on a frigid morning.

He tried to calm himself and think it through clearly. He didn't have enough money to relocate to another city, yet it was too dangerous now to stay in Chicago. His mind worked feverishly for several minutes before it came to him—a route to safety that would cost him nothing.

Garza had been sleeping nights in the utility room of a three-flat in the Humboldt Park area on the West Side. With the furnace rumbling and pipes dripping overhead, he'd made a home of sorts, paying the building custodian a small amount each month to allow him to use the space. There was an industrial sink in one corner and a toilet in the adjoining supply room. Reasonably certain that the Colombians didn't know of his hideout, he decided to risk one last visit.

After checking the street and alley for signs of the Colombians, Garza darted down the cement stairs and through the basement door. He took time only to take the loose brick from the wall and remove the passport from the space he'd carved out. He left the .22-caliber revolver and the half-full bottle of Wild Turkey and replaced the brick. He then fled, pulling the collar of his wool coat up to hide his face and protect it from the freezing wind.

He jumped out of the train when it reached Jackson Boulevard and felt great relief when he passed through a revolving glass door and into the warmth of the Federal Building. Garza strode quickly along the marble floor to a stainless steel elevator that whisked him up to the third floor reception area of the INS office. He told the deportation officer he had no papers and had been unable to find work. Life was too hard here, he confided sadly, and he hadn't sufficient funds to go back to Peru on his own.

The INS office was always looking to pad their apprehensions of OTMs—"Other Than Mexicans"—if only to deflect charges that they discriminated by targeting Mexicans. Whether illegals were arrested or came in voluntarily, they all counted on the department's monthly tally sheet. Garza waived a deportation hearing, and they had sufficient funds on hand for airfare to Lima, so he would be allowed to return voluntarily at government expense.

Garza felt safe in jail. Ironically, he would do time in the same jail (the Metropolitan Correctional Center) as Raul Bautista. But Garza would be placed in the minimum-security area, several floors below Bautista and other high-flight-risk prisoners. Deportation officers would need time to get clearance from the Peruvian Consulate and to make travel arrangements, so it would be several days before his departure via jet from Chicago to Lima. That was fine with Garza. He liked the warmth of the jail. He liked the three regular meals a day and watching television on a big screen. He liked talking to other prisoners, trading stories and ideas on the best places to cross the border.

Still, as the days passed behind bars, Garza's thoughts drifted to Salvador Rico. And when the self-recriminations subsided, a loose plan for revenge began to emerge.

8

Six Months Later

Francisco Campos shuffled through the marble-floored pavilion of the Federal Building, pushed his way into a crowded elevator, and hit the button for the fourth floor. A short, chunky man with a thick mustache, Campos had the manner of a struggling, small-time businessman. A look of anguish seemed permanently etched on his face, as though he had just caught a whiff of old cheese. Nobody recognized him as an alderman, the elected representative for Chicago's Twenty-Fifth Ward.

Despite Campos's frequent public criticisms of the Chicago INS office, District Director Farber respected the feisty alderman. After years of being stabbed like a human piñata, Farber had developed the hide of an alligator and didn't take the attacks personally. Besides, he knew he couldn't refuse to meet with a member of the city council. It would only provide grist for another INS-bashing news conference.

Farber had his secretary usher the alderman into his office. Campos declined the offer of coffee and donuts and sank into the burgundy leather chair in front of Farber's desk. He folded his hands together on his lap—his face creased with worry. Farber, a portly but elegant man who favored expensive three-piece suits, smiled cautiously and settled into his chair. He passed a soft hand lightly over his wavy hair and sighed, girding himself for the next crisis.

"Well, now. How can I help you, Alderman?"

"There is a problem, Mr. Director," said Campos ominously.

"Yes, of course. There are always problems."

"Certain unsavory individuals have taken control of the counterfeit document business," Campos murmured dryly.

"You mean those who controlled it in the past were *not* unsavory?" asked Farber with a playful grin.

Having little sense of humor, Campos ignored the comment. "The vendors are now working openly on the streets," he said. "They used to work behind the scenes. Now they are becoming a nuisance, flagging people down, getting in the way of ordinary shoppers, especially on Cermak and Twenty-Sixth Street. Alderman Baez is equally concerned."

"What about the police?" asked Farber. "Can't they get rid of them?"

"They say it is an INS problem. There is the mayoral decree that prevents them from cooperating with INS enforcement efforts. Most of the vendors are undocumented, and city workers aren't supposed to assist in arresting them. Besides, they don't have the manpower to continually pick up people for misdemeanors like vagrancy."

"You supported that mayoral decree, Alderman. In fact, you were one of those who initiated it."

"Yes, but I don't agree with their interpretation of it in this case."

"I see."

"Perhaps a modest allocation of manpower would return things to normal, Mr. Director."

Farber considered Campos and the situation for a moment before speaking.

"Need I remind you, Alderman, of the conversation we had three years ago? You complained that having agents working counterfeit document cases was a waste of time. I agreed and ordered that ordinary document cases not be worked—only cases on major distributors. You seem to have changed your mind."

"It's different now. Before, they were operating reasonably. Now they are doing business openly. The businessmen are complaining about them."

"Ah, of course . . . the businessmen." Farber smiled knowingly.

"Yes. We must do something about it."

"Get them to 'operate reasonably.' That's how you put it?" said Farber.

"Yes, not so visibly."

"Who *are* these people who have taken over?"

"They are organized, but I don't know who is behind it. The leaders are not Mexicans, from what I hear. Perhaps a couple of your better agents can look into it."

"If I do as you wish, what do I get in return?"

"Well, if you do nothing, I would have to get the media involved. And I can assure you it would be very embarrassing," said Campos evenly. There was a silence as he let Farber think it over. The alderman knew he was holding the cards. He looked toward the wall at a collection of photographs of Farber and various dignitaries; then his eyes slowly drifted back to Farber. "In the end, you will have to do something.

If you wait, it will appear you are only reacting to pressure. If you do it now, bad publicity can be avoided, and you appear to be in control."

Farber considered the irony of Campos as political counselor and sudden advocate of INS enforcement. He sifted through likely scenarios—television crews filming vendors on the street, front-page news stories charging INS with incompetence. He knew how little it took to get them started. They would have no sympathy for excuses about manpower. That never worked. The accusatory interviews would put him on the defensive, and the news would find its way to region and headquarters. If things were as flagrant as Campos suggested, there was a possibility of national media exposure. It wouldn't matter to officials at headquarters that they had intentionally ignored the problem of counterfeit documents. *He* would be blamed. Where the hell was Jack Connelly? It was his job to stay on top of things like this. But Connelly was burned out and ready to retire, so disengaged that Francisco Campos was more diligent in rooting out violators than his own director of investigations. Farber knew that he was trapped and had no real choice.

"I'll see what I can do, Alderman. I may need a month or two."

"Yes, of course, but the sooner the better. I can't guarantee the press won't pick up on it before you are able to act." Campos always knew the right buttons to push.

"No, I suppose not," said Farber. "Please contact me before you bring in the media."

"Certainly. And it is to our mutual benefit that the substance of this meeting should never be discussed, don't you agree?"

Farber smiled. "We have only been discussing how to improve community relations."

"You are always a very reasonable man, Mr. Director." Given Campos's past public criticisms, it seemed a ludicrous statement, yet he appeared to be completely serious.

"I would appreciate it if you would pass those sentiments along to your friends in the media, Alderman."

For the first time there was a hint of a smile in Campos's eyes. "You know, Mr. Director, I can only go so far."

"Of course," said Farber. "I understand very well."

———

Hayden and Kane, having no idea why they'd been called in, took seats facing the two supervisors. Lou Moretti, looking depressed, peered through reading glasses at a roster of agents, trying to figure out how to make up for the loss in production. "Well, boys, the big time is calling," he said, smiling beneath flat, joyless eyes. He looked like the weary manager of a minor-league team about to lose his best players to the majors.

Richard Stark, standing behind Moretti's desk and casually leaning against a filing cabinet, chuckled at Moretti's implied compliment. Or *was* it a compliment? He was never quite sure if Moretti was being sincere or sarcastic.

Stark was a tall, lanky man in his early forties with small gray eyes that shifted restlessly beneath bushy eyebrows. As a field agent, Stark had managed to garner outstanding performance evaluations, not through hard work but by fawning over his supervisors, dressing well, and carefully avoiding the controversies that seemed to dog his more productive colleagues. His ambition was so transparent, however, that he had no real friends, only temporary allies.

Everything was going according to plan for Stark. He'd been promoted to first-line supervisor and a year later to his current position as chief of fraud investigations. Now he desperately wanted to succeed Jack Connelly as Chicago's director of investigations. Looking around the office, Stark found only one serious competitor—Ed Gleason, a solid field agent in his day, a competent supervisor for twelve years and, at least on paper, the most qualified to take over for Connelly. With Connelly retiring in three months, Stark knew he didn't have much time to position himself ahead of Gleason. He saw the counterfeit document task force ordered by Farber as a vehicle to push him over the top, but because fraud had become a low priority, he found himself supervising slow-moving dinosaurs who were mainly killing time before retirement. The obvious solution was to poach a couple of young, ambitious agents from another section. With Farber's directive applying the needed pressure, Jack Connelly agreed to Stark's request for Moretti's best agents: Tom Kane and Nick Hayden.

"We thought you two might be interested in working criminal cases in our shop," said Stark. "I want somebody to work counterfeit documents again. Vendors are now dealing out in the open. I've been trying to convince the front office for some time that we can no longer ignore it."

Moretti rolled his eyes, recalling that the day before he had seen Alderman Campos on the fourth floor. Now it all made sense.

Stark continued. "No dress code. You can wear jeans and gym shoes. It would be a two-month detail; then we'll see where we are. As you know, a number of guys detailed to fraud from area control have ended up with permanent assignments."

Hayden and Kane looked at Moretti, who said nothing, feigning indifference. Stark, following their eyes, rushed to fill the void: "Of course, Lou fully supports this."

"Yeah, we'd be interested," said Kane. "At least, I would be." All eyes shifted to Hayden.

Nick was surprised he wasn't more excited about the offer. From the beginning, the fraud investigations unit had been the most attractive. Yet there was something in Stark's demeanor that made him hesitate.

"So we'd be partners, Tom and I?" he asked.

"Right," said Stark. "Normally I'd want you working with a journeyman, but everybody is tied up with other cases at the moment. You've both already spent time on details in fraud and gone through the usual training. Two months is plenty of time to clear the vendors off the street and take a crack at the guys behind it. I think you can handle it. Naturally, I'll be there for guidance along the way."

Moretti grimaced. Guidance? The only thing Stark would be able to instruct them in would be how to skillfully caress the posteriors of superiors at the district and regional offices. And the only thing the old-timers in fraud were "tied up with" was happy hour at McGinty's. The bullshit had grown too intense. Moretti pretended he was wearing thick earmuffs, swiveled in his chair, and peered out the window, trying to spot an attractive female on the street below.

"When would we report?" asked Hayden, who knew he couldn't pass up the opportunity.

"Next week. But you guys can start moving your stuff down any time now. There are a couple of desks in back," said Stark. "I've also arranged for two seized vehicles to be at your disposal, a Camaro and a Firebird. Good for surveillance."

Hayden again glanced at Moretti, knowing it was bad form to eagerly accept a detail out of the unit without his tacit approval. But he could immediately tell his concern was misplaced.

Moretti was now staring out the window, his gaze fastened on a young woman in a leather miniskirt and high heels making her way poetically down the street. Moretti wished Stark would get the hell out of his office so he could lock the door, get out his binoculars, and peer down Jackson Boulevard in peace.

———

Kane and Hayden had both reached a point where their jobs and identities had merged into one—it had become very personal. Those who violated the immigration laws or committed crimes that fell within their statutory authority were a threat, not just to the rule of law but to their very identities. Though they'd never spoken of it, they observed the same messianic fire burning in the other and thought it could be the basis of an effective working relationship.

A few days after the meeting in Moretti's office, they sat in Kane's Camaro, just off Twenty-Sixth Street. It was the center of commercial activity in the largely Hispanic Little Village area, featuring a long line of small but thriving businesses: restaurants, clothing stores, and other retail shops. The buildings were old, two-story brick structures, each with unique architectural details, unlike the generic strip malls that had sprung up more recently. Thousands of pedestrians flocked to the area every day, and police cars rolled by slowly every half hour or so. The popular Mexican import mall was just a few blocks away.

The two agents watched as a car pulled into a parking spot on Twenty-Sixth and a man in an orange shirt and a straw cowboy hat walked up and stuck his head inside the passenger window. He and the driver appeared to be negotiating a deal. Looking farther up the street, Kane and Hayden could see at least two other vendors, one at an intersection about half a block away, and the other working from the doorway of an apartment building. The men engaged almost any pedestrian indiscriminately. To passing vehicles they flashed a sign with their thumb and forefinger in the rectangular shape of a card.

"It's an open market," observed Hayden.

"Yeah, like shooting fish in a barrel," Kane agreed. "We could go after these guys and flip them against their boss or supplier. Most of them have to be wet."

"Right," said Hayden, lifting the binoculars to his eyes, "but if they don't cooperate and word gets back to the boss that we're onto him, he gets nervous and closes down until our detail is over. If they're just low-level vendors like these guys, they know they won't get much jail time, so there's not enough pressure to get them to flip on the boss."

The man in the cowboy hat walked to the curb, stuffing bills into his pocket, and the car proceeded down the street.

"I wonder how many orders he takes before delivering them to the pad where they make the cards," said Hayden.

"We've got less than two months," Kane responded. "And we don't have teams of surveillance units or manpower for wiretaps."

"No, but if we can get somebody to go undercover, we have a shot at making a really good case, not just taking foot soldiers off the street. They're getting sloppy because they don't think anybody's working these cases. We have to take a shot at whoever's behind all this. These clowns couldn't organize a one-man parade. *Look* at him!" Hayden was pointing at the cowboy-hatted vendor, who had spotted several girls in a car and swiveled his hips seductively as if dancing with them.

Kane couldn't help grinning at the street performer. "I guess we have a little time," he conceded. "These guys aren't going anywhere. They're having too much fun."

9

Hayden left the office, walked swiftly through the fading sunlight on Jackson Boulevard, and turned down a narrow street that was shadowed by tall office buildings. The stores at street level were closed, but the purple neon sign of McGinty's cast an inviting glow. Glancing through the tavern's window, he recognized the bearlike shape of Charlie McCloud hunched over the bar, apparently lost in some inner conversation. It had been several weeks since their tense encounter in Charlie's office, and the casual setting of the bar seemed like a good place not only to clear the air but also to ask an important favor of McCloud.

McGinty's had a long mahogany bar, dark wood tables and chairs, and soft lighting. The atmosphere was heavy and masculine—a comfortable refuge for federal agents, many of whose offices were located nearby. It was Wednesday, so the bar was relatively quiet. Tony Bennett crooned softly in the background, enveloping the place in a sort of timeless, sleepy warmth. Hayden recognized a couple of IRS agents at the far end of the bar and a familiar collection of secretaries from the DEA and the US Attorney's office huddled in a corner. Nick leaned against the bar just inches from McCloud and swung a shoe onto the brass foot rail, giving off a metallic ring, but McCloud was so preoccupied he didn't react.

"A wise training officer once told me drinking alone can be dangerous," whispered Hayden into Charlie's ear.

McCloud was momentarily startled—then smiled in recognition and gestured toward the empty stool next to him. "I was picturing myself retired. It used to seem like heaven. But now that it's closer . . ." His voice trailed off, and he quaffed deeply from his mug of beer. Hayden noticed an empty shot glass in front of McCloud.

"I would think you'd be relieved to get out."

"Everybody thinks that when they're young." McCloud paused and, knowing Hayden wouldn't understand, decided to change the subject. "So, you and Kane making any progress?"

"It's only been a few days. We're getting our bearings. We could take down some vendors on the street right away and work it from the bottom up, but we have a little time."

"You'll need a good informant," said McCloud, who signaled with his hand to the bartender to bring a beer for Hayden.

"You know of any we could use?" asked Hayden.

"Well, I'd be happy to give you one of my old ones. They're good, but they've gone to seed a bit—they've got families and jobs. They'd be going in cold. You're better off looking for one who's arrived in the last couple of years. They would know who the current players are—maybe even had contact with them."

"We're looking through leads for somebody like that."

"Good—you're better off developing your own informants, unlike the FBI or DEA. They say they'll borrow—then they steal them."

"So I've heard."

McCloud could tell Hayden was distracted and ill at ease. "What's on your mind, Nick?"

"I owe you an apology, Charlie. The conversation in your office—I know you were trying to help."

McCloud smiled. "It's OK. You're a gladiator, right? I was there at one time. Now I'm an over-the-hill pussy who's afraid of his own shadow. When you're a gladiator, nobody can tell you shit." McCloud sipped his beer before continuing. "Some never come out of it. Those guys implode and break into a million pieces."

Hayden was surprised that McCloud wasn't softening his earlier comments. Not wishing to reignite that debate, Nick steered the conversation to a recent incident involving a DEA agent who'd killed a drug dealer in self-defense in an alley off Howard Street. The agent, who was shot in the neck, was now doing better. It was the first use of deadly force by a federal agent in Chicago since the Kelso shooting, and a useful pretext for where Hayden wanted to go.

They sipped their beers for a moment. Nick had never asked Charlie about the Kelso shooting because of McCloud's curiosity about the name Hayden when he'd first reported for duty. But now he felt he had to risk it. "By the way, Charlie, what do you know about the shooting in '74 when Frank Kelso got killed?"

"I had no direct knowledge—just heard the story that went around the office."

"Payton said something didn't smell right about it, like something got buried."

"Something *always* gets buried. I wasn't in area control at the time so I wasn't as familiar with the details as Payton and some others."

"It's frustrating that nobody seems to know the details of how it all went down." Hayden paused briefly. "You know, I wouldn't mind seeing a copy of the report on the shooting."

"How you gonna do that?"

"Since you're a training officer, maybe you could justify getting it for training purposes."

"Ah," said McCloud with a wry smile. "You want *me* to get it for you."

"Only if you can do it without any trouble. It's not worth sticking your neck out."

"Why so much interest?" inquired McCloud.

"Partly because of what Payton said. An agent died—I'm just interested in what happened." There was a hint of defensiveness in the shrug of his shoulders and his voice, suggesting that McCloud ought to understand without further explanation. McCloud watched him through the mirror behind the bar, but Hayden just sipped his beer and offered nothing more.

"Well, it was obviously tough on everyone involved," said McCloud. "Kelso dies. The wet dies. Trainee lost his job over it. And Buck Tatum . . . poor guy was never the same again." He paused a moment before continuing. "I don't blame you for not taking what Willis says at face value."

"It's vague," said Hayden. "And apparently Tatum wouldn't talk about it."

"Clamming up isn't unusual after the trauma of a shooting. I guess nobody wanted to push him. The trainee, Landau, was smart but not one of the guys. It was pretty tough down there in area control. If you hadn't been in the Patrol, there wasn't much room for error. He'd been a social worker or something—that didn't help with that crew."

"Maybe they pinned the shooting on him to dump him."

"I don't know about that, but whatever Landau had to say at the time wouldn't have been given much weight. A lot of it had to come down to what Tatum said, because I don't think there were any other witnesses." McCloud took a swallow of beer and wiped the foam from his mustache.

"I assume Tatum had to talk to the investigators about it," said Hayden.

"Yeah, they would have gotten a statement." McCloud paused. He suddenly remembered something. "You heard what happened to Landau after he was fired, didn't you?"

"Yeah, Payton mentioned it."

"I don't know if it had anything to do with the shooting."

"Couldn't have helped."

"So, Kelso and the wet die, Tatum is an emotional wreck, and Landau ends up losing his job and killing himself. Not a pretty picture. I was so absorbed in my own cases, I don't even know who did the shooting investigation." McCloud paused briefly. "That was around the time my wife left me, so my head was spinning."

"That's understandable," said Hayden. He could feel McCloud's eyes studying him.

"OK, I'll see what I can do about getting the report," said McCloud finally. "I'll have to find the right person up at the regional office. They live to deny requests like this."

Hayden took a final swallow of beer and laid money on the bar for McCloud's next round.

"I'll let you know when I get the file," said McCloud.

"Thanks, Charlie," said Nick as he stepped away.

McCloud watched as Nick went out the door and disappeared into the shadows. He had to admit that something about the Kelso shooting didn't add up. Just as intriguing, he had a feeling that Hayden was hiding something.

———

Charlie McCloud's old friend Hank Balsam had done a five-year stint in the Chicago INS office of investigations and then, in a life-altering pivot, accepted a higher-grade staff position at the regional office in Minneapolis. Soon after arriving, however, he realized that he'd entered a world of surreal, Kafkaesque logic that made sense only to the most jaded, hard-core bureaucrats. Much of his time was now spent reviewing vacancy announcements and planning his escape with the desperate vigor of a soldier tunneling from a prison camp.

Balsam whispered into the telephone: "If you stay up here too long, you become one of them, Charlie—the hollow eyes, the zombielike devotion to screwing people in the field offices. I feel like I've been abducted by freakin' Martians. It's frightening."

"I warned you, Hank."

"Don't remind me. And listen, I'm still using you as a reference on my applications, OK?"

"Of course, Hank. Anything I can do to help," said McCloud sympathetically.

Balsam didn't think twice about McCloud's request for the file on the Kelso shooting. Not wanting to take the time to copy the whole file, and not willing to let a secretary in on the conspiracy, Balsam personally packaged and mailed the original.

McCloud's curious mind was finally zeroing in on the case. Any shooting would be traumatic, but why had Buck Tatum's response been so extreme? He'd completely cut off contact with anybody from INS, been divorced by his wife of twenty years, and, if still alive, was squirreled away somewhere in self-exile, though nobody knew where. Landau was dead . . . now Hayden's peculiar interest.

McCloud received the file on Monday, shoved it into his top desk drawer, and waited until early evening so there would be no calls or distractions while reviewing it. After picking up a cup of coffee from the shop across the street, he returned to the deserted office. He then shut off the fluorescent lights in his room, turned on the green-shaded desk lamp, which was easier on his eyes, and removed the file from his desk drawer with the sense of anticipation he used to feel when searching out evidence on a good criminal case.

CONFIDENTIAL had been stamped diagonally in large black letters across its cover, and a metal-rimmed label identified it as KELSO SHOOTING FILE, CHI 50/001.1974. McCloud started with the supporting documents and exhibits on the left side of the file. It was an old habit—reviewing the physical evidence first and then comparing his analysis of it with that of the case agent, whose report would be on the right side.

The first item was a copy of a report dated March 9, 1974, from the Chicago police officer who responded to the shooting, scribbled out in longhand and barely readable. McCloud moved his finger down the blocks of information.

OFFENDER: ANTONIO CANO. Date of birth: 4/20/49.
Nationality: Argentina. Residence address: unknown.
VICTIM: FRANK KELSO. Date of birth: 7/11/34. INS
agent, c/o INS office, 219 S. Dearborn St., Chicago, Illinois.
WITNESSES: MICHAEL LANDAU and WILLIAM
TATUM, INS agents, c/o INS office, 219 S. Dearborn
St., Chicago, Illinois.

There was a brief description of the shootings, followed by a statement that the homicide division had taken photos and handled the preliminary evidence collection, but that federal authorities would conduct a thorough follow-up investigation.

Next in the file was a yellow property envelope containing a stack of black-and-white photos—good quality, six-by-eight-inch images. The first in the stack were of Cano, a young man with high cheekbones and long, blond hair. His body was wedged into a sitting position against a brick wall, his hair matted with streaks of drying blood. There were several photos from different angles, then the close-up photos of Cano's face, showing a single perforation just above the nose, gunpowder burns on the forehead, and a line of dried blood running along his nose and through his mustache. It appeared to be a direct frontal shot through Cano's forehead. His pale eyes were half open and glistened from the flash of the camera.

The photos of Frank Kelso sent a wave of nausea through McCloud. Kelso had been the sort of happy-go-lucky guy who'd clearly found his niche in life. He was often smiling, rarely complained, and drove his partners to frustration with a work ethic that was unmatched by anybody in area control. He had a remarkable knack for ferreting out illegals in a crowd—often able to identify their nationalities based on factors so subtle that even *he* couldn't always articulate them. In this case, it would have been difficult to distinguish Cano from any young American with long hair.

One photo showed Kelso lying flat on his back on the pavement with arms spread straight out, his legs close together, as in a crucifixion pose. His sport coat was unbuttoned, and the shirt beneath it was completely saturated with blood. There was a sharp tear in the shirt's fabric at the bottom center of his chest, which was swollen—the flesh pressed against the shirt. His black hair, streaked with gray, had fallen in front to his eyebrows and his eyes were shut. The slightest upturn at the corners of his lips added an odd, lighthearted quality to the image, as though Kelso was only playing at being dead.

McCloud carefully examined a photo of Kelso taken from several feet away that showed the full length of his body. Along Kelso's left hip, where the open sport coat had fallen away, McCloud could see Kelso's empty black holster fastened to his belt. He must have been left-handed, thought McCloud. He didn't remember that about Kelso. Then, looking closely at the shape of the holster, he realized it was backwards—the side facing forward bowed out to enclose the trigger guard. This meant that Kelso was right-handed but had been wearing his gun in a "cross-draw" fashion on his left hip—prohibited because it would take longer to reach in an emergency. Even more important, an assailant could more easily grab the pistol, because the handle would stick out invitingly. McCloud had known a couple of older agents who insisted on wearing their guns that way because they felt it was easier to pull the gun out across their bodies. He wondered how such a crucial piece of information could *not* have been widely known throughout the office in the wake of Kelso's death, and it made him curious about who had conducted the investigation.

The coroner's report indicated Cano had traces of heroin in his bloodstream and a series of needle marks on his left arm. The .357-caliber, hollow-point bullet had exploded in Cano's brain, causing extensive and irreversible damage—his death quick and relatively painless.

Kelso had not been so fortunate. He would have been partially conscious for several horrible minutes. As McCloud had expected, and the coroner's report confirmed, the heart had been pierced by the .38-caliber bullet, and the main coronary artery had been severed, causing massive internal and external bleeding. Kelso had literally felt his life fading away as he lay on the pavement.

McCloud leaned back in his chair and pictured the scene on Clark Street. Two bodies lay dead or dying on the cold cement, blood covering the sidewalk, a crowd quickly gathering. Landau and Tatum had no doubt called for an ambulance and were ministering to the fallen Kelso. A police squad car or two would have arrived to establish order and sort things out. And then, after the street had been cleared, those first quiet moments for Tatum and Landau to consider what had happened—measuring their degree of guilt or responsibility. The images would be seared permanently into their minds— life forever divided into two eras: *before* and *after* the shooting.

McCloud left the photos scattered on his desk and moved to the next item—an FBI rap sheet that summarized Cano's known criminal history in the United States:

March 1969: Armed Robbery; New York City Police Dept.; no disposition

December 1969: Solicitation of Prostitution; Chicago Police Dept.; dismissed

January 1972: Armed Robbery; Chicago Police Dept.; TOT INS

March 1972: INS warrant for deportation issued; Chicago INS office; no disposition

McCloud had seen countless rap sheets like this one and knew how to read between the lines. INS in New York hadn't been contacted following Cano's first arrest, and he skated free on the robbery charge. He came to Chicago, where he got caught in a prostitution sting and was released, the police again not delving into his immigration status. The charge was

later dismissed. Then he was arrested for another armed robbery. This time somebody checked his alien status, and he was
turned over to INS. The cops would get credit for a felony
collar without the paperwork and would hand him over to
INS for what they thought would be immediate deportation.

But McCloud knew it didn't work that way. Prompt
removal for non-Mexicans was a relatively unusual event. All
they had to do was request a deportation hearing, and soft-
hearted judges could be counted on to lower the bond to as
little as five hundred dollars, or release the alien on his own
recognizance, even if he had an arrest record. Once released,
the delays could be endless. A deportation hearing could be
scheduled a year or more after the initial arrest, and attorneys
could get delays of many months or years after that.

Cano had been released, probably after posting a nominal
bond, and hadn't shown up for his deportation hearing. A warrant would have been issued, and the file would have been sent
to investigations to locate and arrest him. There were several large
file cabinets in area control containing hundreds of these cases,
which were supposed to be worked by agents when they had
time between daily field operations. McCloud scratched Cano's
eight-digit file number on a notepad. He'd check on it later.

Beneath the rap sheet, McCloud found another property
envelope, this one filled with the investigator's notes scribbled
on the backs of business cards and scraps of paper. The handwriting had a distinctive quality—small, precise lettering with
sharpness at the corners that suggested rigidity. It was vaguely
familiar. He tried to match the writing with a name, but all
he could summon was the unpleasant essence of somebody
from the past.

McCloud looked at the pink sheet on the right side of
the file. INVESTIGATOR'S REPORT had been stamped across it

in large black letters. He flipped past it to the administrative page. There, in the middle of the page, was the author's typed name: WILLARD SMITH.

"Oh no, not that son of a bitch," he said aloud.

Willard Smith had come to the Chicago office from Texas in 1967—about the same time as McCloud. They were soon followed by Joe Willis, Buck Tatum, and Sam Payton, among other Border Patrol agents—the agency's belated response to the presence of vast and growing communities of illegals in America's big cities. Some, like Smith, who had left the Patrol for higher grade plainclothes positions, had spent their lives in the rural Southwest and now became immigrants themselves, as disoriented in a sprawling metropolis as the illegals they pursued.

Images of Willard Smith flooded McCloud's mind. Six feet tall, the rugged Smith exuded an air of confidence, though he found the noise, size, and diversity of Chicago intimidating. Smith, never timid about expressing his opinions, frequently lashed out at Chicago and other large cities as fostering the "moral decay" of America.

McCloud was initially partnered with Smith—an awkward pairing to say the least. The two of them patrolled the South Side of Chicago, picking up illegal Mexicans at bus stops or looking for ship-jumpers who had fled foreign vessels docked at Calumet Harbor, south of the city. Smith would drive slowly to their destination, defying the rush of the city while chain smoking Camels, his eyes shielded by mirrored sunglasses. Wearing polyester slacks that were too short, a bolo tie, and cowboy boots, Smith was uncomfortable around McCloud, who was considered an intellectual by other agents.

"Why'd a smart boy like you wanna go down to the border in the first place?" Smith had asked one morning as they cruised down Damen Avenue.

"That's where the work was."

"Didn't care for it down there, did ya?"

"It was fine. I got along OK," McCloud had replied, refusing to take the bait.

Smith and most of his former Border Patrol colleagues had been adamantly opposed to hiring investigators "off the street"—those who hadn't first passed through the Border Patrol gauntlet. When the agency began doing so a couple of years after Smith arrived in Chicago, the policy shift represented a challenge to the Border Patrol's preeminent position within the enforcement hierarchy. Smith and other former Border Patrol agents felt slighted by the perceived disrespect to the Patrol and threatened by the new recruits, most of whom had college degrees and more contemporary views of society. Several trainees had been dismissed on specious grounds at the conclusion of their one-year probationary period. Meanwhile, former Border Patrol agents who came north had been welcomed with open arms.

Tolerance and flexibility had no place in Smith's emotional universe, McCloud had observed. He was instinctively opposed to change or anything that did not reinforce his prejudices and narrow worldview. As the country moved through the turbulent 1960s, the status quo had to be fiercely defended, and Smith had been determined to do his small part.

In 1972 Willard Smith had moved on to the regional office in Minneapolis for a higher grade, survived two tedious years there, retired, and returned to Texas at the end of 1974. A month later, he had dropped dead from a heart attack. Shortly before retiring, however, he had been tapped to conduct the Kelso shooting investigation. It had evidently not occurred to regional officials that Smith's previous assignment at the Chicago office created a rather obvious conflict of interest.

McCloud flipped to the synopsis page and began reading Smith's summary:

On March 9, 1974, Criminal Investigators Kelso, Tatum, and Landau attempted to arrest Antonio Cano, an illegal alien from Argentina. Cano violently resisted, disarmed Investigator Kelso, and shot Investigator Kelso in the chest with Kelso's service-issued, .38-caliber Smith & Wesson revolver. Investigator Tatum, in justified self-defense, shot Cano in the head. Investigator Kelso and Cano both died at the scene.

It was the second paragraph that had spelled the end of Michael Landau's career with INS:

Investigator Tatum used an appropriate level of force, and the use of his revolver to subdue the offender was fully justified. The shooting of Investigator Kelso might have been prevented if Investigator Landau had taken more positive and forceful action.

McCloud cringed. Smith had stated an opinion as though it were fact. Any opinion, if necessary at all, was reserved for a clearly labeled investigator's comments section. It had no legitimate place on the synopsis page, which was supposed to be purely factual.

McCloud gulped what was left of the coffee and flung the paper cup into the wastebasket. He folded the synopsis page back and started in on the details section of the report.

Smith, with the help of a Chicago homicide detective, had put together a series of diagrams showing the positions of the individuals involved in the shooting in relation to physical landmarks such as the street and nearby businesses. He had attached and summarized the coroner's report to establish Cano's and Kelso's causes of death.

Finally, there was Smith's description of the shooting itself:

Investigator Kelso encountered Cano near Cleo's Vintage Books in the 5300 block of North Clark Street at approximately 5:45 PM. As he attempted to place the subject under arrest, Cano resisted and was able to remove Investigator Kelso's .38-caliber Smith & Wesson revolver from his waistband holster. A struggle followed during which Investigator Landau attempted to restrain Cano but, without the use of deadly force, was not able to prevent the shooting of Investigator Kelso. Cano fired one deadly shot into Investigator Kelso's heart. Investigator William "Buck" Tatum then used his .357-caliber Smith & Wesson revolver to fire one deadly shot to Cano's head. Both Investigator Kelso and Cano died at the scene before medical personnel arrived.

McCloud was shocked and disgusted. Smith had compressed an enormously complex event into a one-paragraph summary without details provided by Landau and Tatum. As a result, there was no way to visualize, except in a general way, what had actually happened that night. Nor was it possible to examine discrepancies between their accounts or to reconcile those discrepancies with the physical evidence. There was no indication that Smith had attempted to locate other witnesses to the shooting, nor was there mention of the position of Kelso's holster on his left hip. McCloud's eyes fell to the next short paragraph:

The interviews of Investigators Tatum and Landau concerning this incident were tape-recorded by this investigator. No other persons were present during the interviews. The cassette tapes are attached in a property envelope in this file.

McCloud flipped the page over to the last item in the file, a mustard-colored property envelope. Willard's distinctive handwriting was at the bottom: TAPES OF INTERVIEWS WITH TATUM AND LANDAU.

McCloud lifted the envelope from the bottom but could see it was empty and completely flat, without the creases usually formed over time by the edges of a tape or tape case.

Unless the tapes could be located, it wouldn't be easy to piece together what actually happened that night. A search of Smith's notes revealed nothing concerning his interviews with Tatum or Landau. That, too, was odd, even if the interviews had been recorded.

McCloud realized his shirt was damp with sweat. He felt trapped in his small office, bombarded with visions of the unsavory Willard Smith and gripped by a sense that something had gone terribly wrong in the wake of the shooting. He suddenly felt the need to get out of there and breathe fresh air.

It was past ten o'clock when he stepped away from the building, the night air cool and bracing against his face. He noticed the huge American flag on the plaza across the street hadn't been taken down and was whipping in the wind. A clasp on the flag's rope clanged loudly against the metal pole— a discordant note on an otherwise quiet evening.

———

The next day McCloud called Balsam to inform him that the tapes were missing from the shooting file. "There's an envelope for them, but it's empty. I need you to look for the tapes up there, Hank."

Balsam quickly checked the regional evidence locker and found nothing. He then conducted a thorough search of the filing cabinet where the shooting file had been stored to make sure nothing related to Smith's investigation had been misfiled, but again found nothing.

McCloud could think of only one other place where the tapes might turn up. "Hank, I need Landau's personnel file. They may have needed the tapes for the probation hearing and left them in his file."

"I'll check the file and if the tapes are there, I'll send them to you."

"No, I need to see the personnel file." There was a moment of silence before McCloud continued. "Look, I'm very suspicious about how Smith handled this investigation. I don't even know exactly what I'm looking for, but I want to see every piece of paper connected to this thing."

"We both know a personnel file is even more sensitive. What's my cover for sending it to you?"

"Chicago's training officer requested it. I'll take full responsibility if there are any questions."

There was only a brief hesitation before Balsam spoke: "What the hell—maybe I'll have a better chance of getting out of here if I piss them off. OK, I'll send it."

A large, yellow envelope appeared on Charlie McCloud's desk three days later. He immediately tore it open and found the pale green personnel file of Michael Landau. He laid the file flat on his desk and went through both sides, not pausing to read anything, just looking for a property envelope that might contain the tapes. But there were no tapes to be found and no indication they had ever been there. Though disappointed, McCloud began a more thorough examination of the file's contents.

On the very top was a clipping from the obituary section of a Portland newspaper that reported the death of Michael Landau. There was no photo. It was the kind of lean article one would expect to see for a skid row bum.

Beneath the news clipping, McCloud found a form that documented Landau's dismissal on May 25, 1974. PROBATIONARY NONRETENTION had been typed into one of the blocks.

The review panel recommendation form was next. McCloud's eyes fell to the signature blocks at the bottom of the form for the three review panel members. To his amazement he found the signature of the suddenly ubiquitous Willard Smith. Even after Smith's damning report on the shooting, somebody had allowed him to be on the panel that would decide Landau's fate. Next to Smith's signature was an X in the square indicating recommendation for nonretention.

The next signature was that of Thomas Reilly, the head of investigations at the Chicago office at the time of Landau's hearing. Reilly would certainly not have resisted Willard Smith's recommendation, especially if he'd believed that Landau couldn't be relied upon in difficult situations. The third and final signature was that of the head of investigations for the Detroit office. All had recommended nonretention.

On the second page of the review panel recommendation form, one sentence was scrawled in the hand of Thomas Reilly:

Although Agent Landau received acceptable performance ratings his first year, his actions in the shooting death of Agent Frank Kelso, as outlined in the report by Willard Smith, cast doubt on his ability to use deadly force.

That had made it clear. The entire hearing would have been perfunctory at best.

McCloud flipped through the remaining documents in the file. There was a copy of Smith's report, along with evaluations by journeyman agents who had worked with Landau. He had done extremely well on written examinations and had finished second in his class at the academy.

Then, a final document, buried at the very bottom: Landau's original application for employment, the standard government form SF-171, which included personal biographic information. McCloud scanned the blocks. Landau was born in 1940 in Hinsdale, Illinois; graduated with honors from the University of Illinois; received bachelor's and master's degrees in social work; was hired by the Veterans Administration in 1965. This guy was even more of a misfit than I'd imagined, thought McCloud. It reminded him of Hayden, or the way Hayden had once been. He moved down the page to the section for dependents and relatives. Michael Landau's spouse, Joyce Landau, then her maiden name: Hayden.

In the space for the couple's children, there was one entry: Nicolas, age eleven years.

———

Hayden spent two hours alone in McCloud's office combing through every piece of paper in the shooting file. Even the smallest details held a lurid fascination for him. But when he was finished, he felt empty. He'd hoped he could fit the pieces together into something coherent and conclusive, but that hadn't happened. He now had more information, but the crucial question—whether his father had acted appropriately under the circumstances—remained unanswered.

Hayden knew that if his father had not used deadly force when it was necessary to save the life of another agent—if he'd been unable to respond appropriately—his dismissal was justified. But that case hadn't been made by Willard Smith, and the tapes that might have provided some clarity were missing. There was a glaring absence of detail about what had happened in the moments before the shooting.

Though he was trying to keep an open mind about his father's conduct, he couldn't help feeling resentful toward Smith for what appeared to be a lack of thoroughness and for improperly stating opinions instead of simply presenting facts. The report suggested that Smith was either inept or biased against his father. As a result, Nick was left with a picture that was far from complete, and it appeared Buck Tatum was the only potential source of additional information—if he was still alive.

When McCloud returned to his office, Nick, careful to conceal his emotions, offered his observations about the position of Kelso's holster and what appeared to be unorthodox liberties taken by the report's author. "We still don't know what really happened, Charlie."

"Yeah, there's definitely something missing here, and the principals aren't around to clear things up—except maybe Tatum. Even if Smith were alive, you couldn't trust anything he'd say. I worked with him here in Chicago. He was a horrible investigator—driven by animosities and prejudices. He thought the Border Patrol was the only worthwhile part of INS. Anything he said in that report is suspect." McCloud paused. "By the way, I found Cano's file. The judge set bond at five hundred dollars, so he had no trouble making it, and he never showed up at his deportation hearing—ordered deported in absentia. Only thing that seemed strange was that there's no indication the file was sent to investigations to locate him. Maybe the court screwed up and it was sent to the file room by mistake."

Silence lingered for several moments until Hayden became aware that McCloud was looking at him differently. He wasn't sure if it was sympathy or suspicion, but it was now McCloud who was hiding something.

"You know, don't you?" Hayden asked softly.

McCloud nodded. "Yeah, I know."

———

Though Hayden had concealed his relationship with former INS agent Michael Landau, McCloud wasn't angry, only curious about what else might have been covered up. He assured Nick that he hadn't yet told anybody in the office but would need more details before deciding what to do. They agreed to meet after work in a side room at McGinty's that was usually deserted and fairly quiet, except for the muffled sound of traffic on Dearborn.

Nick busied himself with paperwork for the rest of the afternoon and arrived early. He wanted to be as clear-headed as possible, so he ordered a Coke instead of a beer and waited anxiously at one of the tables. McCloud soon came in and set his mug of beer down across from Hayden. "I've got plenty of time, Nick, so don't feel rushed," he said, draping his coat over the back of a chair and taking a seat.

"I hope you didn't have to rearrange your schedule," said Hayden.

"No. It's not like I have a thriving social life. Besides, this is important." McCloud paused and fixed Nick with a sober stare. "Listen, I don't want to be blindsided, so I need you to be straight and not hold anything back, OK?"

"Sure. You can trust me to tell you everything."

"I thought I could. Just relax and tell it at your own pace."

"OK, I appreciate it, Charlie."

"After we talked I pulled your personnel file and saw that on your application you identified Michael 'Hayden' as your father, and you didn't mention that he ever worked for the federal government."

"I was pretty sure that if they'd known I was the son of a federal agent, they would have checked into his background and I wouldn't have been hired."

"That's a reasonable assumption."

"So I had to say that I had no relatives who had been employed by the federal government, except my mother. I knew they would interview her as part of the background investigation, and she agreed not to mention that my father had worked for INS if they didn't bring it up and, fortunately, they didn't. She thought I was crazy for wanting to do this work, and I couldn't tell her the truth—that I had to find out what really happened—because I didn't want her to know how it haunted me. But I couldn't see any way to get the job without concealing his connection to INS."

"They could charge you with making a false statement on the application, though I doubt it would come to that," said McCloud evenly. "Your dismissal would probably be sufficient."

"Yeah, they'd have to fire me." Hayden searched McCloud's passive face a moment before continuing. "Anyway, I knew there was a risk that you or somebody else would find out once I started digging into it . . . and I know you're in an awkward position. If you feel you need to tell somebody, I'll understand."

"I'll let you know if I need to do that . . . after I hear more."

Nick looked out the window for a moment to collect his thoughts. "Well, I guess it all started with my mother. She's the one who wanted my father to take the job with INS. He was working as a social worker at the Veterans Administration Hospital in Maywood, and she was a secretary at the DEA down here in the Loop. She heard about the job openings at INS, and I think she liked the idea of my father being in law enforcement. She seemed to be impressed with the DEA agents she worked with and thought his job as a social worker sounded dull, though I don't know that he ever complained about it. He had a master's degree in social work, so it was what he was trained for, and I have a feeling he was pretty good at it. But the INS job paid more because of overtime, and my mother was always concerned about money. So he took the job at least partially to please her. I have to say I've wondered how my parents ended up together in the first place. My dad was more of a thinker and did a lot of reading. Maybe it was physical attraction they took for love, because they didn't seem to have much in common.

"Anyway, things were going along well enough between them as far as I could tell until that night in March. I think I was twelve at the time. I had gone to bed already, but I heard a car pull up and looked out the window from the second floor. It was snowing a little, and somebody was dropping off my dad. I knew he was working a late shift that day, and I didn't think much about it. So he comes in the back way, and I had my door open upstairs and I hear him talking to my mother in the kitchen. And he says, 'Joyce, something terrible has happened.' They sat down, and he talked kind of low so I couldn't hear everything, but I remember him saying an agent and another guy had been shot and killed. The name Buck Tatum was mentioned as one of the agents involved. For some reason that name stuck in my mind. Anyway, after he told her what happened, it got real quiet and Dad said, 'Well, I did the best I could do. I wish I could have done more,' and I was waiting to hear something comforting from my mother, but I don't think she said anything. There was just an awkward silence.

"The next day I asked him about it, and he seemed surprised that I'd heard them talking. And he told me that an arrest got out of control, that an agent had been killed, and Buck Tatum had shot and killed a guy from Argentina. He said something like, 'It was a terrible thing, but it sometimes happens in this line of work. You just have to deal with it as best you can.' That was about all he said.

"But starting from that point, everything was different between my parents. They seemed to stop talking to each other, and my mother became very quiet and withdrawn. It was like she was ashamed of him. My dad wasn't the same either, although at first he seemed to be OK, and then gradually he became more distant, probably because he was worried about losing his job, which he did about two months later."

"So you were an only child?" asked McCloud.

"Yes. Much later I asked my mother why they didn't have more kids, and she said my father wanted more, but she wasn't ready, which is not surprising because I always had the feeling that she didn't really enjoy being a mother.

"So my father was suddenly out of work, and I remember that he talked about it as if he was better off doing something else. Nobody ever said that he was fired from the job, but even though I was young I could tell what happened. Pretty quickly he got a job unloading trucks, which was hard work but the pay was OK, and my mother was still working for the DEA. But within a couple of months he told me he was moving out; that he and my mother had to live apart for a while. He asked me if I wanted to live with him, and I was a little surprised that my mother would be OK with that. But she wanted to be alone, so I moved in with Dad, which was fine because my father was just a warmer and more supportive person by nature. We were living in Forest Park at the time, and he got a small apartment only a couple miles away so I could stay in the same school.

"But my dad was having a tough time. He got home from work exhausted, and he tried to hide it, but he seemed depressed . . . kind of emotionally fragile. I think his confidence had been shattered—first the shooting and losing his job, then my mother wanting the separation. It got worse when my mother asked for a divorce. After that, he just seemed completely dispirited. But I still wanted to live there with him instead of with my mother. Then one weekend there was a series of phone calls between them. I couldn't hear what was said, though my father raised his voice a couple of times, which was unusual. The next day, out of nowhere, he told me that he wanted to scout things out in Portland, Oregon. For some reason he thought it was a good place to get a fresh start, and he said that if I wanted to join him later out there, I could. I didn't know what to think because I'd never been there, but the idea of moving didn't seem too bad. Anyway, a few days later he dropped me off at my mother's place and said he would be in touch within a couple of weeks.

"But I never talked to him again. About a week later my mother and I were sitting in the living room and the phone rang and I answered it. It was a police officer calling from

Portland. Somehow I knew why he was calling. I asked him if my dad was OK, and he didn't answer—just asked to talk to my mother. I went to my bedroom, feeling sick to my stomach. And then I heard my mother crying. She eventually came into my bedroom and told me that Dad had died. Later I found out he'd hanged himself in his room at the YMCA.

"My dad may not have been the strongest person around, but he was a good man, and I missed him a lot. My mother got over it quicker than I did, and that angered me . . . that it didn't seem to affect her as much. She quit her job at the DEA and started a career in real estate and did quite well. She had her occasional boyfriends, and they were nice to me in a distant sort of way. When I started high school she decided that we should both change our last names to her maiden name. I didn't want to, but she insisted, telling me that it was the perfect time to make a switch. I had the feeling that she was still somehow ashamed about her connection to Dad; like she wanted to leave him completely behind. We had a decent relationship, Mom and I. We weren't at each other's throats, but it was more like living with an aunt who had no choice but to care for an abandoned nephew. It was OK with me, though, because I was independent and pretty self-sufficient as I went through high school and college. I was lucky because I was interested in my studies, especially history and literature, and I got involved in sports, mainly baseball. Most of my friends were guys I met playing sports.

"But as the years passed, I became more and more curious about where all the problems seemed to start for my father. I kept wondering—what exactly happened that night? My mother had not gone after details as far as I knew, and simply assumed when they fired him that he'd not done enough to prevent Kelso's death. At one point she said he was too gentle and civilized a person for law enforcement work. To her the fact that he'd been fired suggested he'd failed, but a 'suggestion' wasn't going to satisfy me, and I had to have as many details as possible. The name change to Hayden made it possible to get hired, and I thought being on the inside was the only way to find the truth. My plan was to stay at INS long enough to find out what really happened and then go on with my life. But when I found how much I liked the work, I came up with reasons not to look further into it. And I began to realize that I had a powerful need to prove that I could do the job well, regardless of whether my father had. That became more important for a while than learning more about the shooting . . . until Payton said a piece of the puzzle seemed to be missing. Then I *had* to know the truth, no matter what might happen to me and my career. That's when I reached out to you to get the file, though I knew you might figure it out."

Hayden paused. He felt relieved to have told somebody but was suddenly very tired. He peered out the window as a cab sped by, its red taillights sailing smoothly through the night. "That's pretty much it, Charlie," he said wearily.

"I'm sorry about your father, Nick. I didn't have much contact with him, but he seemed like a good guy. I wish I'd known him better."

"You two would probably have gotten along well together."

"Yeah, I think so."

McCloud pulled a folded piece of paper from his shirt pocket and passed it across the table. "This was all I could find," he said. "I couldn't get a street address."

Hayden opened it to find a handwritten note that read, "Buck Tatum, PO Box 133, Hollins, Florida."

10

The voice was so loud that she held the phone away from her ear.

"It's about time this country stands up and doesn't take this shit anymore," the man growled. "These damn wetbacks come across the border; next thing you know they're taking good jobs from American citizens. Like this guy I just told you about."

Rita Bustos, a petite, middle-aged woman with a billow of black hair and rimless reading glasses, sat in a corner of area control, her desk covered with stacks of leads she'd written up. She'd taken thousands of such calls from discontented workers over the previous ten years.

"What is his job at the plant, sir?" she asked politely.

"They just made him a damn foreman, for chrissakes," the man said. "Been here less than four years and already he's in management. Hell, I've been workin' there eight years. Guess I'm not the right color. I ain't black, brown, or yellow, so I ain't worth shit!" She carefully took down the information, and then remembered Hayden's request that she ask all callers what they knew about phony documents.

"Does he have counterfeit documents—a green card or social security card?"

"Course he does. They all do. What a laugh!" he said, letting out a bitter cackle. "I've heard about guys selling 'em in bars around here."

"Do you know who sells them, sir?"

"No, I don't know any *names*," he said. "But a couple of years ago I heard some Mexicans flappin' their jaws about this bar called the El Paladio or El Palacio or somethin' like that. I guess that's where they go for the documents. It's over on Sheridan . . . a tonk bar."

"But you don't know who sells the cards at this bar?"

"How would I know that? I don't go to tonk bars," he barked. "Hey, I'm calling about this one guy, is all, and you're askin' me about all this other stuff! It's *this* guy I want picked up!"

"Yes, sir, I understand. I just need to get all the information you have. It helps us do our job."

"Well, I'm an American citizen. I want this damn wetback picked up and I want him picked up now!"

"Can you give me your name and number so an agent can call you if there are any other questions, sir?"

"You got enough information. Remember, he's driving a tan Fairlane."

"Yes, I have that."

"And listen, if he's not picked up damn quick, I'll call my senator and tell him you all ain't doin' your jobs down there. You hear me?"

Rita said nothing.

"You got it?" he demanded.

"We have it. Thank you, sir."

Rita placed the report on a far corner of her desk. Just before leaving that day, she walked down to fraud and left it on Nick Hayden's desk.

———

Hayden and Kane sat in the shadow of the "L" tracks, the trains thundering overhead. Between trains it was quiet, a morning breeze gently stirring a line of trees on the parkway. Kane had parked between a pair of abandoned cars about fifty yards south of the entrance to the Poindexter plant. They were watching the tan Fairlane that had been mentioned in the tip Hayden had received from Rita the day before. It was thought to belong to an illegal Mexican named Miguel Chavez, who worked at the plant as a low-level shop supervisor. The rusted-out Fairlane was parked with a few other vehicles in a makeshift lot beneath the tracks. At seven o'clock, they could hear the distant ring of the shift bell from inside the plant.

Hayden, in the passenger seat, suddenly felt the presence of a figure to his right: a middle-aged man with muttonchop sideburns, wearing a knee-length overcoat and a pair of ragged construction boots. The man swayed unsteadily as he squinted to focus on the car with two men inside.

"Hey, are you guys a couple of homos or what?" the man bellowed, looking around for somebody with whom to share his discovery. He staggered in short steps to the front of the vehicle to get a better look.

Hayden grimaced. "Great, our guy is coming out in a few seconds and this wino shows up. I'll get rid of him." He got out of the car and advanced toward the drunk, who looked up with frightened eyes, and then tried false bravado.

"Who 'n hell do ya think—" he sputtered, but Hayden had grabbed his coat at the back of the neck and was walking him to the sidewalk. The man instantly became docile. "Hey, I didn't mean nothin' by it."

Hayden launched the drunk headfirst into a clump of bushes adjacent to the parking area. The man fell awkwardly into them, a pint bottle of liquor falling out of his coat pocket. Hayden kicked the bottle, and it skidded down the sidewalk.

"Get the hell out of here," ordered Hayden. "If you come back, I'll take your bottle and throw you in jail."

The man slowly extracted himself and began to walk away shakily. Hayden gave him a swift kick in the butt, and the man staggered down the sidewalk, muttering and casting angry glances over his shoulder. Silence returned to the street as Hayden got back in the car.

"Never a dull moment," said Kane, grinning.

A few minutes later a small cluster of men, some Anglo and some Hispanic, emerged from the alley next to the plant. They dispersed quickly, some climbing the stairs to the "L" platform, others retrieving cars parked on the street or beneath the tracks. Then a dark-skinned man appeared in the alley, an unhurried dignity in his gait. He made his way to the Fairlane, got in, and slowly pulled away.

"Let him drive off," said Hayden. "We can keep a loose tail on him until he stops somewhere."

Irritated with his partner's recent habit of issuing orders, Kane defiantly pulled the Camaro right up behind the Fairlane at a stop sign. They could see the driver looking curiously in the rearview mirror.

"So much for a loose tail," said Hayden. "Now he's watching us. What's the idea?"

"Just because he looks at us doesn't mean anything," said Kane coolly.

They followed the car as it moved smoothly through the traffic along Montrose Avenue and then south on Ashland. Kane dropped back and another car cut in, separating them from the Fairlane. As they came to a stop at a red light, he rhythmically tapped his fingers on the steering wheel while both of them leered at two young women in short skirts waiting at a bus stop. The light changed, and they passed through the intersection.

"This is kind of a long shot, isn't it?" said Kane. "All we know is this guy *might* be wet, *might* have phony documents, and *might* have gotten them from somebody at a bar on Sheridan."

"That's why we're out here—to find out if it's good information . . . if he cooperates. Anyway, what else have we got?"

A couple of miles farther down Ashland Avenue, the Fairlane veered sharply into a grocery store parking lot.

"He's trying to find out if we're tailing him," said Hayden. "Stay back unless he gets out of the vehicle. We don't want him to take off in the car."

Kane smiled. He would have been delighted if the car had sped off so he could pull out the flashing light, get the siren going, and begin weaving wildly through traffic.

As they entered the lot in front of the store, they watched the man pull into a parking space, hop out, and walk briskly toward a pay phone near the corner of the building. He picked up the receiver and for a moment, as they came closer, seemed to be making a call. The man glanced over his shoulder, spotted the vehicle bearing down on him, and a look of alarm crossed his face. He dropped the receiver, ran to the nearby corner of the building, and began to fight desperately through a cluster of bushes that hugged the side of the building—trying to reach the alley behind the store.

Nick leaped from the car in pursuit. Kane flipped on the siren and sped out of the lot to intercept the man in the alley.

Chasing people had been fun for the first year or so, but now it aroused hostility in Hayden. How dare they defy his authority? He pushed through the bushes—purple berries smearing his leather jacket. This son of a bitch was going to pay, he thought, pushing through the sharp branches with his elbows. Finally he burst free of the bushes and into the alley. To his left he saw the momentary flash of a green jacket as it disappeared through a space between the garages that lined the alley. Where the hell was Kane?

Hayden darted between the squat, shingled garages and down a narrow cement walkway. Hearing footsteps, he circled the garage until he again faced the alley and a tall, cross-hatched metal fence—the man climbing it frantically.

"Stop right there," Hayden called out in Spanish. "Federal agent."

The man had reached the top rung of the fence when Hayden grabbed his belt from behind and pulled hard, so that the man lost his grip and tumbled to the cement, sprawled out helplessly at Hayden's feet. For a moment they stared at each other, both wheezing from the run. As the man slowly raised himself, Hayden, feeling a surge of anger, thrust his elbow into the man's chin, a jarring blow that knocked him on his back.

Hayden, suddenly dizzy and weak, dropped to the ground, his hands and knees on the cement. Even after thousands of arrests, many of them rough, he'd never struck a person except in legitimate self-defense, and he felt a twist of shame.

He was woozy and not sure how long he'd been on his knees when he realized he was being helped to his feet by the dark-skinned man he'd struck. There was a cut and a bit of blood on the man's chin.

"I sorry, sir," said the man calmly. "Is foolish to run. You are *la migra?*"

Hayden needed a moment to steady himself before answering. "Yeah, Immigration," he said weakly and nodded at the man's chin. "Sorry about that."

"Is not bad."

"You speak good English. You're Chavez?"

"Yes, Miguel Chavez," he said, holding out his hand to Hayden.

After a moment's hesitation, he shook Miguel's hand. "Good to meet you," he said. It was an odd thing to say to a person he had just assaulted and arrested, but Hayden knew the man could have escaped—could easily have scrambled away instead of helping him.

At that moment Tom Kane appeared breathlessly around the corner of the garage to find Chavez and Hayden facing each other.

"What the hell's going on here?" said Kane, his face flushed. Not waiting for an answer, he grabbed Miguel's arm and pushed him against the side of the garage.

"It's OK," said Hayden. "He's all right."

"You pat him down yet?"

Chavez, sensing Hayden's disorientation and Kane's impatience, placed his hands up against the garage.

"Is he our guy?" asked Kane, as he checked Miguel's pockets.

"Yeah . . . Miguel Chavez."

Kane handed Miguel's wallet to Hayden and was about to handcuff him behind his back.

"We don't need to cuff him, Tom," said Hayden, wiping sweat from his forehead with his handkerchief.

"He already tried to escape," Kane said. "Now you're both covered with fucking berry stains, you're all scratched up, he's got a bloody face, and you don't want to cuff him?"

"That's right," said Hayden firmly. "We won't need the cuffs."

Miguel stepped between the two agents with his hands outstretched. "Is OK," he said to Hayden.

"No, Miguel," said Hayden, and then to Kane, "We don't need them."

Kane's expression eased, and he looked at Chavez cautiously. "Well, if we aren't going to cuff him, you'll have to sit with him in back."

"OK," said Hayden, patting Kane on the back. "What happened to you, anyway?"

"Damn garbage truck was blocking the alley."

Hayden peered absently out the window as they drove to the office. He was replaying the incident in his mind, the elbow driving forward, Chavez falling back on the cement, then helping him up. How had it come to this? For most of his life, Nick had thought of violence, except to protect yourself or another person, as cowardly. His father had taught him that.

"Nick, you OK?" Kane was looking at him through the rearview mirror.

Hayden shifted in his seat and cleared his throat. "I'm fine."

"You gonna check his documents?"

Hayden wiped his sweaty brow with a handkerchief. He opened Miguel's wallet and pulled the contents from beneath a buttoned leather flap. There were frayed business cards and a driver's license issued nearly two years earlier with an address on Francis Street. Then the photos—a girl, perhaps three years old, in a pink dress; a boy with a baseball glove; a woman with a humble smile and black hair swept behind her ears; then the family together, the children laughing as if the photographer had made a funny face. Nick had rifled through countless wallets like this but had never paused to look at personal photos.

Finally he came to the counterfeit permanent resident card—the quality of the printing quite good, but not good enough to fool an agent. It looked identical to any number of counterfeits he had come across in recent months. The social security card was also an obvious phony.

Kane had been looking curiously at Hayden, who was moving at half speed, and adjusted the mirror to view Chavez, who was sitting impassively. Blood was now trickling down his swollen jaw.

"How'd he cut his chin?" asked Kane.

Before Hayden could speak, Chavez said, "I cut on fence."

"It looks like more than a cut," said Kane. "Your whole chin is starting to swell up."

Chavez shrugged and looked out the window. Hayden offered his handkerchief. "Here, Miguel, your chin is bleeding."

Nick then turned to Kane: "The cards look the same as the ones we've been finding. They're all coming from the same printer."

———

Hayden leaned over the sink, splashed cold water on his face, and patted himself dry, but the nausea grew more intense.

He staggered into an open stall and threw up violently into the bowl. Perspiration rose in a hot wave from his forehead as he gripped the sides of the stall. He was pulling himself together at the sink when Tom Kane entered the washroom.

"Jesus, it smells like puke in here," said Kane.

Hayden was wiping his hands with a paper towel and said nothing.

"What the hell went on back there between you and the tonk?" demanded Kane.

"He just tried to get away," said Hayden.

"Did he come at you?"

Hayden looked wearily at Kane through the mirror.

Kane persisted: "Come on—I need to know what to expect from this guy, especially if he's going to work for us."

"He didn't do anything. He's fine." Nick knew Kane wouldn't understand. Or, worse, he *would* understand and suspect that Hayden was going soft.

"Well, whatever happened, I'm gonna keep an eye on this guy," said Kane.

————

Miguel Chavez sat in a chair beneath the flat, fluorescent light and wondered whether it had all been worth it. He thought back to the trip north, finding work, arranging for his family to join him, the enormous effort of it. Now it was over. Still, he had earned more money in the past two years than he would have earned in ten years in Mexico. He had even gotten used to the precarious nature of his life. His wife and children would be terribly disappointed, of course, as they were now comfortable here. He knew of others who had lived here for years without papers and never had an encounter with INS. Eventually they were able to legalize their status. The quickest and most certain avenue was to fake a marriage to a US citizen, but he could not do that. It was one thing to cross the border without papers, quite another to enter a dishonest scheme like that.

He felt a subtle pounding in his chin and ran his fingers over the cut. If he were in Mexico and had run from the police, he would likely have been severely beaten. This was nothing.

Miguel hesitated briefly before answering the agents' questions about the documents, but there was no reason to protect Salvador Rico. He told them how he had met and bought documents from Rico at El Palacio, the rumors about the demise of Marcos Ortega, and how Rico had taken control of the counterfeit document trade. Though Rico told people he'd been born in Puerto Rico, there was talk that he was really from Panama. Hayden and Kane listened intently until Miguel had told them everything he knew or had heard about Rico.

"You may be able to help us and yourself at the same time, Miguel," said Hayden.

"How?"

"If you're willing to do undercover work for us, we can let you stay here and keep your job at Poindexter," said Hayden. "You won't have to go back to Mexico. It could end up being permanent."

"What you want me to do?"

"You would have to meet with Rico and wear a wire," said Hayden, who reached to the far side of his desk and picked up a wire with a tiny microphone attached to its end. He held it up for Miguel to see. "You'd be buying a lot of documents this time."

Miguel nodded. "And my family?"

"They could stay. But you'd have to be willing to testify later, if the case against Rico goes to trial. You need to understand that," said Hayden, who noticed Kane frowning. The idea of testifying in open court wasn't normally thrown at a potential informant right away. Many were scared away, so it wasn't mentioned until later, if at all.

"We stay and get the papers if I do this?" Miguel asked.

"We could carry you as an informant as long as we want," said Hayden, "but you'd have to be productive. You know, help us make criminal cases. There's a possibility of getting permanent papers if you're here long enough."

Miguel stared at the floor, mulling it over for several moments, and then looked at Hayden. "Is dangerous, no?" he asked.

"We'll be there along the way," said Kane. "There's nothing to worry about."

"There *is* danger, of course," said Hayden. "We have to assume Rico and his buddies will be armed and dangerous. But we'll provide protection. If you come through, we'll take care of you. You can trust us to do that. In a worst-case scenario, we may have to move you to a different part of the country, but we'll protect you."

Miguel wasn't so sure about the other agent, but there was something about this man that he trusted, despite their altercation. "Yes, I do this. I think the Lord wish it for my family . . . and for him also."

"For who?" asked Kane.

"This man . . . Salvador Rico."

11

Kane felt like the captain of a small submarine. On his knees in the back of the van, he gripped the handles of the periscope and scanned the street in front of El Palacio. A series of lenses inside the periscope column delivered an image from a mirror on the van's roof that could be adjusted by pushing the handles left or right. The mirror was concealed by a metal cap that looked like an air vent. Parked in front of a small grocery store, the van was an inconspicuous part of the scenery along Sheridan Road.

Wearing jeans and a sweat-soaked T-shirt, Kane muttered profanities at Floyd Baker, the cerebral little technician responsible for outfitting the only legitimate surveillance van in the Chicago INS fleet. Thanks to Baker there was no cooling system in the rear of the van, aside from a small fan, and almost no ventilation. This was fine during the cooler months, but now, the second week of an unusually hot and humid September, it was like a furnace. To provide cover for the van, Baker, with unintentional irony, had attached removable magnetic signs that read, FLOYD'S HEATING & AIR CONDITIONING SERVICE.

A week of surveillance had revealed a pattern of sorts. Rico would arrive at El Palacio in midmorning, parking his black Volvo directly in front. At about eleven o'clock, a colorful assortment of young men would begin parading through the bar. Unlike regular customers who would come for drinks or Chacon's greasy tamales, they would remain for only five or ten minutes, just long enough to conduct business with Rico and his subordinates. Wearing gym shoes and T-shirts, some carried backpacks or thin briefcases. Though they weren't from the neighborhood, the area surrounding the bar was such a revolving farrago of pedestrians and vehicles that their comings and goings went largely unnoticed by the casual observer.

Through license plate checks and photos, Hayden and Kane had identified two men as lieutenants in the Rico organization. Rosario Nieto was a large, muscle-bound Bolivian, whose arms and neck were covered with tattoos. INS records showed that he'd been deported twice. The other, Felix Pinal, was a thin, studious-looking man who had no known prior deportations but was presumed to be illegal. Both of them spent a good deal of time at El Palacio and could often be seen conversing with street vendors in front of the bar. Salvador Rico usually remained inside, hidden from view.

On alternate days one of the agents, in the suffocating heat of the van, would snap photographs through a camera with a powerful telephoto lens. The other agent would conduct surveillance from a separate vehicle, parked close enough to pick up a loose tail on Rico's business associates.

On this day Nick had followed one of Rico's briefcase-wielding associates to Twenty-Sixth Street and sat in his Firebird watching the young man and others ply their trade. Cars pulled up, and items were exchanged and passed to couriers, who would deliver the orders to pads where the cards were manufactured. The customers would return in a couple of hours to pick up their orders. The whole operation churned along briskly, unimpeded by authorities and ignored by almost everybody, aside from business owners, who sometimes angrily chased vendors from one sidewalk location to another.

As he watched, a question began to prey on Nick's mind: Who *was* Salvador Rico? They had done criminal checks using the name and date of birth on Rico's driver's license and come up empty. But it made no sense. A confident man in his midthirties, firmly in command of a large criminal enterprise, doesn't appear out of nowhere. Hayden's gut told him that Rico had a history, probably a bad history, and wouldn't hesitate to blow to smithereens anybody who would threaten his little empire—precisely what they were asking Miguel Chavez to do.

———

As Nick climbed the staircase to Miguel's flat, the scent of old wood gave way to the savory aroma of fried sausage and onions. A makeshift coat rack was fastened near the door—a length of plywood with several nails sticking out. A crumpled Cubs baseball cap hung on one of the nails. He rapped on the door and could hear the shuffle of feet and the muffled ebb and flow of conversation.

When the door opened, Miguel and his family were standing in a row, like soldiers awaiting inspection.

"Mr. Hayden," said Miguel, who was wearing a stiff white shirt with ironed creases at the shoulders. "Is great honor to welcome you. Please come in." Miguel quickly introduced his family. Paco stood rigidly beside his father, while the tiny Maria leaned against her mother's leg and smiled radiantly. Miguel's wife, Carmen, appeared shy and uncertain.

Hayden was touched by their innocence and sincerity. "Thanks for inviting me, Miguel," he said, reaching out to shake his hand.

Nick glanced around the flat. The hardwood floors badly needed refinishing, and the old plaster walls had a few cracks and blemishes, but the overall atmosphere was clean and warm. There were handsome moldings and baseboards, which he'd noticed were common even in modest houses built in the early 1900s. The flat was furnished with old furniture they had probably found discarded or at flea markets.

"Would you like beer or soda, Mr. Hayden?" asked Miguel.

"What are you having?"

"Ginger ale. I no drink anymore."

"Ginger ale is fine."

Miguel gave him a can of soda and went into the kitchen to help Carmen, while Hayden sank into a lumpy armchair in the living room. On the wall behind the sofa was a framed image of Jesus that looked as though it had been cut out of a magazine. A white plaster-of-Paris sculpture of the Virgin Mary hung next to it. A Bible with frayed edges rested on a small end table next to the chair.

Nick became aware of Paco sitting on the sofa, watching him curiously. Hayden spoke in Spanish. "Is that your cap out in the hallway, Paco?"

Paco smiled, showing teeth that looked exceptionally white next to his tan cheeks. He replied in English with only a slight accent. "Yes, my father got it for me. Are you a Cubs fan, Mr. Hayden?"

"Yeah, big Cubs fan. Your buddies down here on the South Side must give you grief about that—not being a White Sox fan."

"What is 'grief'?"

"You know, they must razz you about being a Cubs fan."

"'Razz'? I don't know that word either."

Hayden silently cursed his ineptitude. "It's just that . . . the Cubs aren't too popular down here."

Paco smiled. "I like both teams the same."

"That's a good attitude, Paco."

"Do you want to see my baseball cards?" Paco had already grabbed a stack of cards from a shoebox on the sofa.

"Sure, let's take a look."

Paco shuffled through the stack, stopping in the middle. "This is my favorite, Ozzie Guillén," he said, standing and handing the card to Hayden. "He's a great shortstop."

"No question about it," said Hayden, pleased with so quickly finding common ground. "You've got a nice collection here."

Paco sifted through the deck as Hayden looked at the back of the card showing the player's career statistics. Nick had collected hundreds of baseball cards as a boy and understood their magical quality—as though possessing a player's card established a personal connection with him.

From the dining room, Miguel announced that dinner was ready.

"We can go through the rest after dinner, Paco," said Hayden.

The Chavez family stood, politely waiting for Hayden to take his seat. A small ceiling light cast a soft glow over the table, which was covered with a freshly ironed white tablecloth.

When they were all seated, Miguel said a short prayer in English and then very rapidly in Spanish, thanking God for food and blessings, and for introducing his family to Mr. Hayden. The family all crossed themselves and then quietly waited for Nick to fill his plate from the large, steaming bowls. Rich food aromas filled the room.

"This is quite a feast, Carmen," said Hayden.

Carmen was wearing a light green dress. Her hair was swept back, which accented the largeness of her brown eyes. She smiled, but her blank expression told Nick she didn't understand. He repeated the words in Spanish, and she nodded agreeably.

"Thank you," she said softly in English.

"Her English is improving," said Miguel. "Is hard because she is home all day. Paco already studies English before he comes here. Maria learns also." Maria, wearing a flowered dress, was sitting next to her mother in a high chair, staring at Hayden.

"Please go ahead, Mr. Hayden," said Miguel, who began serving the others.

"You have a nice family, Miguel," said Hayden. "You're a lucky man."

"Yes, is true. Perhaps you someday have family. You would be good father."

"I don't know about that, but thank you," said Hayden. It was one of the kindest things anybody had ever told him, but he wasn't at all sure it was true. He'd already concluded that it was unlikely he would ever get married.

After dinner, Paco helped Carmen clear the table, while Miguel and Nick sat down in the living room with cups of coffee.

"Have you known many guys like Rico?" asked Hayden.

"Yes. I am not so different when I am younger."

"That's hard to believe."

"I never go so far as him, so far bad, but before I find the Lord, my life is different. I was very foolish," he said with a sheepish grin. "I not say I am smart and wise . . . just not so foolish like before."

Nick looked at Miguel inquisitively, waiting for more.

"I love the tequila," said Miguel finally. "And women. I live for the body, what the body wants. It was, how you say . . . shallow, very shallow life—has no meaning. I no keep any job. I live like child. One morning I wake up in alley in city of Morelos, many miles from home. I no remember how I come there. And I find wound in my stomach and was bleeding. It is long cut, right here, from knife." He motioned with his finger across his abdomen. "I get up and walk down street. I am very thirsty—my mouth feels like desert. I need water, but everything is closed. Then I come to small chapel and door is open. I go inside. I think maybe priest give me water. But there is nobody there, no priest. I am alone. I sit in back of chapel, and I look up and I feel very small. He is there up on cross and something happen. My heart come open, and He speak many things to me. He say nothing of stupid things I do, just I should trust and follow His way, and He protect me. And I feel like I am hit by . . . how you say . . . the lightning! Life is never same since that time. Men who are blind think those who follow God are weak, but is not true. I am stronger. Maybe because I am stronger, the Lord give me Carmen, the children. He let me come here—to this country. And He bring you to our family. Many good things come to me. So I am very blessed." He smiled warmly at Hayden, who was lost in the scene Miguel had described. Nick had always respected those who could sift some higher meaning and order from what often seemed the arbitrary chaos of life.

"Yes," said Hayden finally. "I can see that, Miguel."

A sharp knock rattled the front door. Miguel looked up with an expression of mild concern. "I take care of this," he said calmly. Carmen stepped out of the kitchen and looked nervously at Miguel. When he opened the door, Tom Kane was leaning against the wall next to the stairway.

"Mr. Kane. Please, come in," said Miguel, opening the door wide.

"No," said Kane coolly, staring past Miguel at Hayden, who had risen from his chair. "Something came up, Nick. We have to take care of it."

"Carmen, please get Mr. Kane a beer," said Miguel.

"No," said Kane. "I can't stay. We have to go right away. It's important." Hayden was now at the door beside Miguel.

"What's up?" inquired Hayden.

"I'll tell you about it outside," said Kane.

"Mr. Kane, please, you must meet my family while you are here," said Miguel.

"Maybe some other time," said Kane, already starting down the stairway. Hayden stood at the doorway, annoyed with Kane's brusque manner.

"Paco, please get Mr. Hayden's jacket," said Miguel.

Hayden thanked Carmen for the meal and apologized for the hasty departure. He promised Paco he would return to see more of his baseball cards and bring his glove so they could play catch. Miguel insisted on going down the stairs and outside onto the porch with Hayden. Nick again thanked him for his hospitality, while Tom Kane stood next to his car and watched, scowling.

Hayden strode toward Kane, making sure Miguel had closed the door before speaking. "How'd you find me?"

"I was checking things out on Twenty-Sixth, to see if Rico's guys were out on a Friday night. Saw your car when I was driving down Eighteenth Street."

"So what's the emergency?"

Kane glanced around the neighborhood, apparently concerned their conversation would be overheard. "We can't talk here. I'll meet you at the usual place on Cermak."

The lot was nearly empty as they parked next to each other along an old railroad embankment a good distance away from the front of a large grocery store. It was darker now, and an overhead streetlight at the center of the parking lot cast a pale light that barely reached them. Hayden had spent the drive over telling himself not to jump to conclusions, but his adrenaline was pumping when he stepped out of the car and advanced toward Kane, who was casually leaning against his Camaro.

"What's this all about?" demanded Hayden.

"The question is, what was *that* all about? We can't be socializing with informants," said Kane. "You know as well as I do that you can't get too close to them or—"

"So that was a lie about there being something urgent—is that what you're telling me?"

"Would you feel better if I told Miguel you were putting him and his family in danger?"

"We need these people to trust us if we ask them to risk their lives."

"That's bullshit," Kane retorted. "All we need is for them to be frightened enough to do whatever we want them to do. We're supposed to *handle* 'em, not *coddle* 'em."

"I'll deal with him as I see fit," said Hayden sharply, his chest bumping against Kane's.

Kane shoved Hayden as though he were weightless, sending him reeling awkwardly back on his heels. "He's not *your* informant, you know," said Kane, his face red with anger. "We both arrested the son of a bitch."

Hayden gathered himself and drove into Kane with his shoulder, pushing him hard against the hood of the Camaro. Kane, though off balance, quickly righted himself and pushed Nick aside with a thrust of his powerful arms. Suddenly a bright spotlight engulfed them, and there was the squeal and skid of a fast-moving car as it came to a stop. Two uniformed cops jumped out of a squad car, one grabbing Hayden, the other Kane.

"OK, up against the car," said the cop who had grabbed Hayden, pushing him toward the Camaro.

"Hey, guys, we're cops," shouted Kane, as he grabbed the roof of the car. "Check my inside pocket." The officer reached around Kane's back and inside the leather jacket, slipping out the shiny black credentials case, the gold badge embossed on its cover. He flipped it open and pointed his flashlight down to view the ID and photo. Hayden's cop did the same, and the two, both rangy men in their thirties, relaxed and stepped back.

"So, you guys been partners too long or what?" said Kane's cop, now amused by the situation.

"Just a little spat," Hayden said between deep breaths. "You know how it is."

"Oh, yeah . . . we know," said the other cop with a knowing grin. "It's not unusual in our precinct, but we try to keep it out of public view."

The cops were looking at Kane, the spotlight from the squad car on his face. He squinted against the light but said nothing, still catching his breath. They seemed to be waiting to hear something conciliatory so they could be on their way.

"We'll be fine, guys," said Kane finally, pulling his jacket back into position. He forced a weak smile. "Sorry we caused you any concern."

Kane's cop flipped the credentials back to him. "Don't make us come back, all right?"

"Don't worry," said Hayden. "We know you've got better things to do."

The spotlight went off, and the police car peeled out of the lot, leaving Hayden and Kane facing each other.

"It's good for you those guys came along," said Kane, pushing his wildly tousled hair back into place. "You were about to go down."

Hayden knew Kane could make short work of him in a real fight. Besides, it was no time for a rift that would permanently undermine the partnership, both of them being keenly aware that there were only about three weeks remaining in their detail. They leaned against the Camaro, silently looking down at their shoes when Kane remembered the six-pack of beer in the trunk.

Sipping the warm beer, Kane eventually conceded that "maybe" it hadn't been wise to barge in on the Chavez family, regardless of his misgivings. It could have been discussed later. Hayden acknowledged that he'd been wrong to suggest he had sole control of Miguel and that he should have informed Kane of his plans. By the time they'd each had a couple of beers, they were trading office gossip, and the heaviness had lifted. As they prepared to leave, Hayden gave

Kane a brotherly pat on the shoulder to suggest that there were no hard feelings.

They got in their cars and pulled out of the parking lot but headed in opposite directions on Cermak Road.

12

Chacon had cleared away the empty bottles of Corona and was wiping off the counter when he noticed a man standing at the bar watching him.

"What can I get for you?" asked Chacon in Spanish.

"I'd like to see Mr. Rico, if you don't mind," replied Miguel.

"It's not like before," said Chacon impatiently. "There are people on the street that can help you. Not here anymore."

"No, this is something else. I must talk with Mr. Rico, please," said Miguel firmly. "I am Luna."

Though he was under orders from Rico to get rid of such people, there was a forthright, serious quality about the man that made Chacon consider him for a moment.

"Wait here," said Chacon, who disappeared through a beaded curtain into a room at the end of the bar. Miguel looked around. The place seemed to have undergone a facelift since he'd been there two years before. The dusty wood floors had been replaced by black and white tiles arranged in checkerboard fashion. There were sleek-looking tables and chairs, fresh curtains, and an elevated square of parquet flooring in a corner with a stand-up microphone on it. Clearly there was more money coming into the bar these days.

Chacon returned. "Through that curtain," he said curtly.

Rico was sitting behind a large mahogany desk, about twenty-five feet from the door. There was an oblong banker's lamp on the desk and a single light bulb overhead that cast weak, grainy light throughout the room. Two small windows against the wall behind Rico's desk had been covered with black paint, blocking the light from outside. Miguel noticed that Rico's face was heavier, his hair expensively styled. He wore a tan blazer of thin leather over a black shirt, open at the top to reveal a heavy gold chain.

"I understand you have business," said Rico gruffly in Spanish.

Miguel stood inside the door, respectfully waiting for an invitation into the inner sanctum, his eyes adjusting to the frail light. There was a sofa against the wall to the left and two wooden chairs in front of Rico's desk.

"Yes, Mr. Rico. That is correct," said Miguel.

"Well, come closer," said Rico. He motioned toward the chairs in front of his desk. "Have a seat here." He was alert and studying Miguel intently.

"We met a couple of years ago," said Miguel, sitting down. "It was out there." He gestured toward the bar.

"I remember you now," said Rico softly. He paused and leaned back into his chair. There was an aura about this man that encouraged Rico to defer to him, to seek his favor. Self-conscious under Miguel's calm stare, he needlessly picked up an ashtray and set it on a stack of papers. "Well, then . . . you are Luna?"

"Yes, Miguel Luna. I bought the documents. You were kind enough to help me with this."

It was a reasonable statement, but directness of speech was not a desirable attribute in Rico's business. "I don't know what you are talking about," said Rico. "What sort of business do you wish to discuss?"

"I am a Mexican. I know many people on the South Side. Many are afraid to buy the documents from those on the street."

"Is that so? Why are they afraid?"

"Some are still afraid to do these things in the open. If you give me the opportunity, I can sell many of the documents quietly and professionally."

Rico considered Miguel thoughtfully. Was he wearing a wire, or was he just plainspoken by nature? Rico pointed toward the wood-paneled wall to his left and rose from his chair. "Put your hands up against that wall," he said evenly.

Miguel looked at the wall and then back at Rico with the hint of a smile. "You don't have to worry about me, Mr. Rico."

"Maybe not, but you're not walking out of here until I search you."

Miguel paused for only a moment. "Yes, of course," he said, standing. "It is always wise to take precautions."

Miguel spread his legs and placed his hands high against the wall. Rico gently patted him down. Miguel was wearing work pants and a thin nylon jacket over a long-sleeved work shirt, the type of loose-fitting clothing that could easily conceal a recorder or transmitter. Finding nothing suspicious, Rico stepped back, staring at Miguel's midsection.

"OK, now take off your jacket and shirt."

Miguel removed them and faced Rico. He was wearing a ribbed undershirt with narrow straps over the shoulders. There was a tattoo of a heart with an arrow through it on his upper right arm. Rico lifted the undershirt, exposing a ten-inch diagonal scar across Miguel's stomach just below the ribs. Rico looked up with a smile.

"What do we have here, my friend?"

"That is from an accident," said Miguel. Rico looked at him for further explanation, but Miguel offered none and pulled the shirt back over his stomach.

"OK . . . unbuckle your pants," said Rico.

Miguel wasn't expecting a crotch search. He looked at Rico for several moments in defiant contemplation.

"Do you think I like doing this?" barked Rico. "Pull 'em down!"

Slowly, Miguel released his belt buckle and dropped the pants down to his knees with one hand, revealing a pair of boxer shorts. "Turn around," ordered Rico. Miguel shuffled awkwardly in a circle, holding his pants at his knees, until he had come fully around. Rico, finally satisfied, turned away. Miguel pulled his pants up, refastened his belt, and put his shirt and jacket on.

"We must be careful," said Rico triumphantly, stepping behind his desk. "Men are tempted if their circumstances are desperate."

Miguel knew the word "we" represented an important shift, and that he probably had Rico where he wanted him. Rico appeared relieved as he settled back into his chair. "These federal cops don't seem to care about what we do. But that could change, and we must be ready."

"Yes, I understand," said Miguel, sliding his jacket back on and returning to the chair.

"Now we can talk freely," said Rico. "Do you want some coffee? A beer?"

"No, thank you."

"So, what do you have in mind?"

"Perhaps I could buy a couple hundred documents to start—green cards and social securities. I believe I could sell them quickly."

Rico could feel his reservations melting away. This fellow was a leader—no posturing or game playing. He almost felt complimented that Miguel would come to him. If this deal worked out all right, perhaps he would hire him to keep the wild Mexican vendors in line. He opened his top desk drawer and removed a copper box of cigarettes, opened the lid, and pushed them toward Miguel, who politely declined. Rico quickly lit a cigarette and exhaled a line of smoke.

"Do you have the money already?" asked Rico.

"How much?"

"Let's say nine thousand. I'm giving you four hundred documents altogether, when you include the social securities. Those two hundred sets are worth at least thirty or forty thousand on the street if you do it right. You'll quadruple your money. But you have to stay away from where my people are working on Cermak and Twenty-Sixth Street."

"As I said, I would not work openly on the street. But I was hoping the price would be a bit less," said Miguel.

Rico broke into an open smile that clearly showed his deformed lip. "Where did you get that idea?" he asked. "If this becomes a regular thing, I can drop the price some."

"By Wednesday of next week I will have the money. Is Thursday all right with you?"

"It doesn't matter to me what day." Rico scribbled a note on a calendar that lay open on his desk. "I've put you down for ten in the morning on Thursday, September 27."

"OK."

"Use this number if you need to contact me." Rico pulled a business card from a plastic holder and flipped it to the

front of the desk. "But don't say anything about the documents when you call. If you do anything stupid like that, the
deal is off."

"Of course," said Miguel, who looked briefly at the card
and shoved it into his jacket pocket.

"One other thing," said Rico. His small eyes had gone hard
and cold as he leaned forward and clasped his hands together
on the desktop. "If I ever find that you're working against me
in any way, I won't hesitate to do what is necessary to you,
your family, anybody close to you. Do you understand?"

Miguel had no doubt that Salvador Rico meant what he
said. He was looking at a man who had probably killed and
would kill again.

"Yes, of course," said Miguel. "I understand very well."

———

Hayden had chosen a remote section of Lincoln Park for the
debriefing—down a winding, tree-lined road to a deserted
parking lot. Shortly after leaving El Palacio, Miguel drove into
the lot, making sure he wasn't followed, and joined Hayden
and Kane in Nick's Firebird. It took him only a few minutes to
report what had transpired in the meeting with Rico. Though
both agents were pleased, Hayden's reaction was subdued.

The prosecutor with the US Attorney's Office had
requested that an undercover officer accompany Miguel to
meetings with Rico, but the agents had explained that trying
to involve a person Rico had never met would probably kill
the deal before it got started. Fortunately, they had been able
to convince him that one large purchase by Miguel would be
sufficient, as long as it was tape-recorded.

The agents had provided Miguel with a set of license plates that, if checked, would come back to a "Miguel Luna" at the address of a large apartment building with hundreds of residents. They had also made sure through surveillance that Miguel would find Rico alone in his office at El Palacio. Had his two subordinates been present, it would have been more difficult, if not impossible, for Miguel to establish a personal relationship. Nieto and Pinal would probably be at the next meeting, but the agents thought it was likely that Rico, now apparently comfortable with Miguel, would not allow another awkward search of a man he wanted to hire.

After meeting with the agents, Miguel took the long, slow way home—west to Ashland Avenue, and then south, where he would encounter sluggish traffic and lights at every other corner. It was a pleasant day to take a leisurely drive, and he was working the graveyard shift at the plant, so there was no hurry. He rolled down the window, and a gust of warm air blew in.

Although Miguel had tried to ignore it, a sense of unease was building. He had told Carmen very little, stating vaguely that he would help INS from time to time in their investigations and his identity would be protected. The agents would always be there to make sure he was safe, he'd assured her. Paco knew only that his father was friendly with the agents and that the family was allowed to stay—mainly because of Mr. Hayden.

Rico's threats came as no surprise to Miguel. In his younger days, before he'd found the Lord and started a family, they wouldn't have fazed him in the least. But now he was a man with responsibilities, and everything he did had repercussions for his wife and children. In that light, threats from the lips of a person so utterly devoid of conscience were disturbing. His

palms grew damp and thoughts of a hasty departure passed
through his mind. They could, after all, return to Mexico and
enjoy relative peace, if not prosperity. But he knew instantly
that this seemingly reasonable thought had sprung out of fear.
He could not allow fear to overrule whatever plan the Lord
had for his life.

Miguel glanced up at his rearview mirror and noticed a
silver-and-black sedan driven by a swarthy man with a black
beard. The man seemed to look away as soon as Miguel
noticed him. Perhaps Rico was having him followed. Coin-
cidentally, he was on the same stretch of Ashland Avenue
where Hayden and Kane had followed him just weeks earlier.
Then, abruptly, the suspicious man wheeled into the left lane,
roared past him, and turned into the parking lot of a Middle
Eastern restaurant, where several yellow cabs were parked
and a small group of men had gathered. Miguel slowed and
watched the man jump out of his car to greet the others. He
was wearing a white sarong that hung like a skirt to his ankles.

Though relieved, Miguel felt foolish. Paranoia, it seemed,
was a price he would have to pay to remain in this country.

He continued slowly down Ashland Avenue. People were
moving purposefully all around him—workers filling potholes
with fresh blacktop, masons tuck-pointing the wall of an apartment building, cab drivers ferrying passengers to their destinations. He enviously imagined their lives as uncomplicated,
free of worry—anonymous players in the grind and bustle of
a vibrant city. Meanwhile, *he* was risking everything—leading
his family into a potential crisis they knew nothing about, the
outcome of which could be disastrous.

Less than an hour earlier he had been cool and unruffled,
even while meeting with a man who wouldn't hesitate to kill.
Now his hand was trembling as he pulled it away from the

steering wheel. He had never seen his hand shake like that, even in his heavy drinking days.

Miguel had left the North Side and entered an area of public housing—scruffy bars, liquor stores, and abandoned buildings. He drove a bit faster and within minutes was back in the familiar Pilsen neighborhood. He turned onto Francis Street and pulled slowly into the shade of the elm trees in front of his home. Miguel shut off the engine, closed his eyes, and began to pray—asking forgiveness for his imperfect faith.

He believed that only by God's grace had he and his family found their way here, to this secluded little street that seemed protected—an island of tranquility. He was convinced that he had been led here as part of a divine plan. As Miguel sat quietly, a feeling of deep peace gradually swept over him.

13

Rico drove his Volvo slowly through rows of empty vehicles and pulled in a few spaces away from a black BMW. It was their usual meeting place—the parking lot of a dreary shopping center near Midway Airport. He shut off the engine and watched cars entering and exiting the lot from Cicero Avenue. He'd recently sensed that he was being followed, though he had seen nothing to give credence to his suspicions. So far, it was only a feeling.

Rico left his car and strolled to the BMW. He'd removed his heavy gold chain and expensive clothing and was now wearing gym shoes, baggy pants, and a black T-shirt—a more subdued, working-class look. When he slid into the front passenger seat, Byrd muttered a cool greeting and sat stiff and silent, like a spurned lover.

FBI agent Jerry Byrd wore his hair in a military-style crew cut and was dressed casually in a golf shirt and blue jeans. Although the agent was in his early forties and had been with the bureau for eleven years, to Rico he seemed naive—willing to accept at face value that Rico was no more than an ordinary, law-abiding citizen who held down a dull job as manager of El Palacio. Byrd hadn't even asked for proof of Rico's spurious claim to being born in Puerto Rico.

Months earlier Rico had dropped the Bautista drug case into Byrd's lap, and the seizure of twelve kilos of cocaine had no doubt enhanced the agent's career and professional reputation, though Byrd had done little more than execute a search warrant. Rico had benefited as well, collecting a ten-thousand-dollar reward, which he promptly invested in a large purchase of counterfeit documents. Now Rico was stringing Byrd along for protection and inside information. But today something seemed to be bothering the agent.

"You haven't been keeping in touch," said Byrd irritably. "I didn't *have* to give you that much money for Bautista, you know. Part of it was like a down payment. I've been waiting to hear more . . . about your new friends."

Rico was momentarily at a loss. New friends? Then he remembered he'd spoken cryptically in their last meeting of "getting close" to a group of Colombian drug dealers who frequented a bar on Montrose Avenue.

"I been working on this. These guys big," said Rico. "They no deal five or ten kilos like Bautista. They sell thirty, sometime fifty."

"Now we're getting somewhere," said Byrd, his mood brightening.

"They competitors to Cali organization."

"They have names?"

"I have only nicknames—one is El Flaco. Another El Gato. But no way I get last names yet. They very careful. I try to get license plates."

"Why are they willing to talk to you?"

A jet roared loudly overhead. Rico, looking at the sky, waited for the noise to pass as he thought it over. Perhaps it was time to take another risk—throw a line in the water to see if Byrd was as indiscreet as he was gullible.

"I help them get documents. You know, the fake documents," said Rico, pausing to observe Byrd's reaction. "I hope is not problem, OK?"

Byrd didn't look away or register an unusual reaction. "I'll cover for you this time," he said. "But from now on you can't break the law unless I say it's OK in advance."

"I no can be too clean. They don't trust. I only help them . . . to get close."

"Don't worry about it. In the meantime, see if you can get those plate numbers and more information about them."

Rico decided to probe further. "INS—they have cases on who sell the documents?" he asked, as though the thought had just occurred to him.

Byrd flashed on the image of his occasional drinking buddy Lou Moretti and smiled. "No, those bozos are too busy picking up Mexicans at factories. They may get to it in the next century."

"I no hear about these things," said Rico.

"You don't have to worry about falling into their net because the government doesn't *want* a net. They have a few hundred agents scattered around the country to round up millions of illegal aliens. There isn't time to look into counterfeit documents," said Byrd, who began to chuckle at what seemed the hopeless absurdity of the INS mission. Rico joined in, amused with the irony of Byrd confiding in him about the immigration mess, and relieved to hear that INS wasn't even working document cases.

Jerry Byrd was convinced that Rico's new case would boost his career even more dramatically than the Bautista case had. It was now clear how to proceed. He would ignore

Interpol's request for a better set of prints on Rico. What was to be gained by digging further? If it were found that Rico was wanted in another country or had lied about his place of birth, he'd not only lose a good informant but also the Bautista conviction might be reexamined. The fact that he hadn't thoroughly vetted Rico before registering him as an informant would tarnish his reputation and career prospects. And now that Rico was promising another high-profile case, there was plenty to lose in discovering anything incriminating from his past.

As it grew darker outside, Byrd and Rico exchanged final pleasantries, neither paying attention to the Camaro with tinted windows at the other end of the lot. At that distance, about a hundred feet away, they couldn't see the binoculars as Tom Kane lifted them to his eyes.

———

Rico lit a cigarette and stared dully across the desk at Felix Pinal, who wore a tan safari jacket with epaulets at the shoulders, black jeans, and cowboy boots. He could have been a photographer covering a foreign war.

A few months earlier, Pinal had come into El Palacio looking for a set of documents, and Rico had hired him on the spot. Pinal had attended university for a time in his native Venezuela and spoke with the smooth articulation of an educated man. He was not large—medium height and slender, clean-shaven, hardly an intimidating physical presence. But he was useful in handling administrative tasks, keeping track of the documents, and making deliveries to vendors—an obedient foot soldier.

On the other side of the room Rosario Nieto was sitting on the sofa against the wall, his muscular arms closed across his chest. He was one of the largest Bolivians Rico had ever seen—well over six feet tall, with broad shoulders tapering to a thin waist. He wore a blue denim jacket, jeans, and sharply pointed, alligator-skin cowboy boots. Nieto had a classic Indian face: the skin a deep bronze, and flat, high cheekbones.

Life's subtleties glided past Nieto's lethargic eyes, as though what appeared to the rest of the world in color was to him a dull monochrome. There was an absence of both joy and fear. He'd confided to Rico early on that he'd been involved in the cocaine trade in Bolivia, ended up on the wrong side of a heated drug war, and fled the country. Now he was Rico's enforcer.

The death of Marcos Ortega had paved the way for Rico's alliance with a team of flamboyant street vendors. Unlike Marcos, Rico had no benevolent ideas of keeping prices down. He kept his vendors happy by allowing them to charge whatever they could get. What was the point of controlling supply if you weren't going to take advantage of it?

Once he'd set up shop in a corner of El Palacio, the street traffic gave a huge boost to the bar, which had been on the brink of going broke. Rico's customers would stop for a beer or two, and word got around. It was no longer just a seedy watering hole for winos to idle away the hours. When the money started rolling in, Rico had paid for a thorough remodeling of the bar.

Rico was dressed in dark colors, his silk shirt opened at the top to reveal several sparkling gold chains around his neck. He told Pinal to get on with the weekly ritual of announcing income figures for the previous week but was distracted and hardly seemed to listen. He puffed hungrily on the cigarette until the ember was burning hot. When Pinal finished, Rico opened a side drawer, pulled out a silver stainless-steel semiautomatic handgun, and placed it on the middle of the desk.

"I want you to start carrying this, at least when you're around here," said Rico.

"I thought that's what he was for," said Pinal, nodding toward Nieto.

"He's not always here," said Rico seriously. "Besides, if somebody tries to take us down, they're not coming in with just one guy. We need all the protection we can get."

Pinal picked up the gun and with his thumb pressed the release button that dropped a loaded magazine from the bottom of the handle and into his left hand. He placed the magazine on the desk and pulled back on the slide, sending the one remaining shell flying into the air. He caught the shell with his right hand, looked into the empty chamber, and blew through the cylinder. "This is almost brand new," he said admiringly.

"Looks like you don't need Rosario to show you how to use it," said Rico.

"No, my father had a large gun collection."

Rico crushed his cigarette in the ashtray and turned toward Nieto. In the dimness of the room Nieto didn't notice the intensity in Rico's eyes. "So, how are we doing on Twenty-Sixth Street?" asked Rico.

"People are coming in from Wisconsin and Michigan just to buy documents from these guys," said Nieto. "There was a gang of farm workers yesterday who came up from southern Illinois. Word has gotten around. It keeps getting better."

Rico ignored what Nieto thought would please his boss. "I hear your boys are still acting up and drawing a lot of attention. I thought you were going to talk to them about that."

Nieto stiffened a bit. "I did. They do what they want when I go away. They're just wild Mexican kids."

"Those wild kids are supposed to be frightened of you! I hear one of our boys flashed himself to a carload of young girls last week." Rico paused and glowered at Nieto, who remained silent. "That is the kind of thing that could put us out of business."

Nieto said nothing. It was the best way to handle Rico's occasional eruptions.

"Anyway, I might have somebody who can help us down there," said Rico. "An older Mexican guy."

Rico waited a moment for some reaction, but Nieto and Pinal remained silent.

"He's coming back here next week, Thursday morning, to pick up two hundred sets of documents—green cards and social securities," said Rico. He nodded at Pinal. "Have them ready. And I want both of you here. He might be working with us, so I want you to meet him."

"What do we know about this guy?" asked Nieto.

"What do we know about any of them?" said Rico indignantly. "I did some business with him a couple of years ago."

"Did you go to him, or did he come to you?" asked Nieto.

"What's wrong? You afraid he's an informant for the government?"

"We have to be careful."

"Careful?" said Rico, exasperated. "I hired you, didn't I? Don't tell me about being careful. Anyway, they aren't working phony document cases. I have it on good authority. If it makes you feel any better, I checked him for a wire when he was here last week."

"Maybe we should check him again Thursday," said Nieto.

Rico grimaced. He knew Miguel wouldn't like it. On the other hand, what would it hurt? To hell with him if he didn't like it. "All right. We can pat him down again."

After a long silence, Pinal spoke up. "We've never discussed exactly what we'd do if somebody tries to rip us off or we find out he's an informant."

Nieto began laughing softly and looked toward Rico as if the question were preposterous. Rico's eyes narrowed and his mouth crinkled into a wry, contemptuous grin. "I didn't think it was *necessary* to talk about it."

14

It was another unseasonably hot day. Warm air that smelled vaguely of mold and sewage was being pumped through vents in the fraud unit. The building maintenance department had been contacted, but didn't seem in a hurry to address the issue. It made everybody irritable, especially Kane, who was fuming about the latest bizarre decision to come out of the Board of Immigration Appeals—as always, it seemed, destroying what remained of practical enforcement mechanisms in the immigration laws. Cursing loudly, Kane tore a copy of the decision into little pieces and tossed them into the wastebasket. Hayden tried to ignore the tirade. Three other agents in the unit, who knew that when Kane was angry he was like a gorilla on steroids, quietly slipped away. The phone ringing silenced Kane and zapped some of the tension from the room. Kane grabbed the receiver and listened, then nodded toward Hayden. "It's for you—Interpol."

Though they had agreed not to put a close tail on Rico, Hayden was pleased that Kane had recognized Jerry Byrd as an FBI agent he'd met in Moretti's office a few months earlier. Byrd was part of a drug unit the bureau had recently set up, so it was assumed he was using Rico as an informant. Contacting Byrd, they agreed, was out of the question. An FBI agent couldn't be trusted to do anything but protect his own turf and wouldn't be above spiriting Rico out of town, or even trying to take over the document case and claim it as his own.

But Hayden thought it possible that Byrd had checked with the Interpol office in France for outstanding warrants when registering Rico as a confidential informant. Perhaps Rico was using a different identity with Byrd. There was nothing to lose, so Nick had left a message for Interpol agent Ken Vogel, formerly with INS, requesting that he verify whether Byrd had done a record check in the past year on Salvador Rico or anybody else.

"I looked into it," said Vogel. "Byrd sent in a bad set of fingerprints on Salvador Rico several months ago, so we sent them back and asked for another set, but we've received nothing so far."

"My information is that Rico might be from Panama, even though he claims he was born in Puerto Rico," said Hayden. "I have no idea what his real name might be."

"We don't have that many fugitive warrants out of Panama right now. About how old is Rico?"

"Midthirties, I'd say."

"Hang on a second. Let me see what I can pull up on our database."

Vogel took a minute to search his computer before coming back on the line. "OK, I've got a couple of guys in that age bracket from Panama. Does your guy have any identifying marks or tattoos?"

"He's got a slightly deformed upper lip," said Hayden.

There was a brief pause as Vogel reviewed information on his screen. "Well, one of these guys, name of Liriano Solis, has what is referred to as a 'cut scar' on his lip, but it doesn't say if it's upper or lower."

"Do you have a photo of Solis?" asked Hayden.

"No photo, sorry. A lot of this stuff from Latin America is incomplete."

"What's Solis wanted for in Panama?"

"Murder and armed robbery. Looks like he and his pals knocked off a bank in Panama City about four years ago. Somebody must have gotten killed."

Hayden's heart was thumping.

"You still there?" asked Vogel.

"Do you have any details about the bank robbery?"

"No, we'd have to request reports and photos from Panama."

"I guess it's still a long shot, but I could use that stuff by next Tuesday. We've got a deal planned with Rico for next Thursday."

"I'll try to get our contacts in Panama to send it directly to you instead of coming through our office. That'll save a few days."

"I appreciate it, Ken. Listen, I have a concern about what Byrd would do if he found out."

"I'll keep it quiet," said Vogel. "Just let me know if you make an arrest."

Hayden hung up the phone and glanced around the squad room, which was still deserted in the wake of Kane's outburst. Kane had left too, probably to get coffee in the cafeteria. Hayden felt an impulse to get out of the office to consider the new information alone. He could fill Kane in later about his conversation with Vogel. Nick scratched out a message saying he had something personal to take care of, placed it on Kane's desk, and made a clean getaway.

Outside it was very humid, and a cloud of copper-colored exhaust fumes hung over the city. Hayden pulled out of the garage and onto the Dan Ryan Expressway, where he was immediately engulfed in a sea of fast-moving traffic: cars, trucks, and buses, all careening down the highway in the late afternoon rush hour. Feeling trapped, Hayden forced his way across two lanes of traffic, evoking honks and gestures of outrage from other drivers for not staying with the pack, and headed down the exit ramp. Relieved to escape the madness, he took a deep breath and drove slowly toward Eighteenth Street.

By the time he turned the corner onto Francis Street, the haze had thinned a bit, and there were traces of blue in the sky. A breeze passed in soft waves through the elm trees on the parkway. It was so serene and quiet that it was hard to believe he was still in the heart of a throbbing metropolis.

Paco was home, and the two of them played catch in the empty lot next to the house. Hayden threw balls high into the air, and Paco deftly snagged nearly all of them. Miguel soon pulled his car up slowly to the curb. As he walked toward them, his face opened into a broad smile.

"What a good surprise, Mr. Hayden," he said. "You stay for dinner?"

"Thanks, but I don't have time, Miguel. I need to talk to you."

"*Hijo*, go upstairs," said Miguel to Paco. "Tell your mother I come when I done talking to Mr. Hayden."

Paco, disappointed, walked slowly away.

"We'll play again soon, Paco," said Hayden. "I can see you're a good player."

Paco smiled shyly and went inside. Hayden and Miguel settled in on the porch, facing the empty schoolyard across the street.

"You should come more often, Mr. Hayden. You always welcome."

"I know, Miguel. I appreciate it."

"You are like hero to Paco. He knows because of you, we no hide. He is old enough that he understand."

"You deserve credit for that, not me. He ought to know that."

"Maybe some day he know, but not now. Even Carmen not understand all these things. Is better they not know."

"I guess you're right. They'd worry, especially Carmen."

They sat silently for several moments.

"Is reason you come now?" Miguel finally ventured.

Hayden looked at Miguel seriously. "You don't have to do it, you know."

"You mean with Rico?"

Nick nodded. "He won't hesitate to hurt somebody if he feels threatened. I'm not trying to scare you, but you have a right to know."

"No, I do this. I know he is person who would kill. He no have respect for life," said Miguel. "Is sad thing to see—a man lose his soul."

"It's not your job to reclaim his soul, Miguel."

"Maybe the Lord want this."

Hayden looked at Miguel as if he were naive to believe such a thing.

Miguel smiled. "You not religious man."

Hayden paused. "Not like you," he said finally.

"I not worried about this thing we do. I have doubt before, but no more. I have faith it happen as God wish."

Neither spoke for a few minutes. At the far end of the school-yard, a few children kicked a ball around, their cheerful voices echoing off the brick walls of the school. Nick felt no more comfortable than when he'd arrived, but could see no way to stop the momentum of the case and Miguel's role in it. He told Miguel he would be in touch.

———

Within minutes of leaving Francis Street, he merged back into the noisy chaos of the city. Hayden drove over to Twenty-Sixth Street to observe the vendors, scribbled notes about their locations, and did the same on Cermak Road. As dusk set in he headed north out of the Pilsen area and stopped at a Chinese restaurant on Division Street. It was a good place for eating alone, as it was never very crowded. Smooth, synthe-sized music was piped in over the speaker system. American songs he had never liked seemed more innocent and appeal-ing with the singsong intonation of the Chinese singers. The restaurant was staffed by pretty, smiling waitresses who could barely speak English and seemed not to have a care in the world as they glided past the tables with steaming plates of food.

From his table, Hayden watched the Chinese cooks through the open window into the kitchen. He figured that they, too, were probably illegal, having traveled thousands of miles through God knows what sort of horrible conditions, so that they could labor in a blazing hot kitchen for little money. Yet they appeared happy.

His thoughts gradually drifted to a grim reality. He was an INS agent, sitting in a restaurant staffed by illegals, in a city teeming with illegals of every conceivable nationality, looking for a way to extract Miguel, another illegal, from a looming crisis—a crisis he'd personally engineered. He now wished he'd gone along with Kane's suggestion to pick a few document vendors off the street and declare victory. But he knew his problems extended far beyond the Rico case. If he'd not allowed compulsive curiosity about his father to alter his career path—if he'd been reasonable and less emotional, he would likely be practicing law in the comfort of well-furnished offices and courtrooms. It seemed that almost everything in his professional and personal life was out of sync and out of control. He thought of Miguel's faith in a higher power, which until recently he'd dismissed as wishful thinking. Yet suddenly the idea of a random, godless world was a depressing notion to contemplate.

He finished the fiery kung pao chicken, left fifteen dollars to pay the ten-dollar check, and headed back to the office.

———

As Nick had hoped, the office was deserted when he arrived at eight o'clock that evening. There was much to do in preparation for next week's operation, and it was easier to concentrate without phones ringing and other interruptions. He spread out the photos of street vendors on his desk and sketched out a crude map identifying their locations.

It was now dark outside. As he looked out the window, he could see the lit-up offices in the other federal building across the street. Most of the building was unlit, but cubicles of light would snap on and off as the cleaning crew moved from one office to another. From this distance the workers were indistinct, though he could make out their powder-blue uniforms. They, too, were probably illegals, he concluded, just like the cooks at the Chinese restaurant. Wherever he went, even to government buildings, there seemed to be no escape. He tried to ignore them, recalling one of McCloud's dictums: "Looking at the big picture will drive you crazy. Just think about the case you're working on." He'd found that approach useful early in his career, but he now wondered why the hell he *shouldn't* think about the big picture.

Hayden sorted through the photographs, picking out the ones to be given to agents on the day of the operation. He pulled the desk lamp closer and was using a magnifying glass to make out the blurred face of one of the vendors, when he heard the murmur of voices and the scuffle of shoes in the hallway.

"*A la derecha* . . . in that door," said a deep male voice. The handcuffed prisoners shuffled in through the door at the far end of the room. There were six brown-skinned men, looking tired and disoriented, wearing heavily soiled work clothing. From across the room Hayden could smell the grease and sweat. He guessed they had been working on an assembly line in a manufacturing plant.

Phil Denton, a tall, businesslike agent wearing a wrinkled gray suit without a tie, entered the room behind the men. As always, he sported a toupee that looked like a flattened Brillo pad. A good-natured sort, Denton took a lot of heat for the toupee, but he didn't seem to care.

"You guys sit down there. *Siéntese alli*," he said, pointing at the metal radiator that ran along the wall. Slowly, awkwardly, the men sat down, the stainless steel cuffs clinking noisily.

Four women came next, also handcuffed together. Three of them were very young, probably teenagers, and looked at Hayden shyly. They too had been sweating, and their hair had become matted and stiff as it dried in the night air. One woman, much older than the others, looked woozily at the floor with half-closed eyes. The women sat on the radiator next to the men and were followed into the room by another agent, Henry De Rosa, a short, stocky man with dark features who rarely spoke and seemed to believe that his job was to act as Denton's chauffeur and valet. He stood silently at the doorway.

"I saw your light on up here, Nick," said Denton. "We picked 'em up out in Joliet about an hour ago. We could use something to eat before getting 'em to jail for the night."

"Want me to watch 'em for ya?" asked Hayden.

"Yeah, if you don't mind. We'll run across the street and bring something back," said Denton.

As Denton and De Rosa left the room, Hayden thought it fortunate the prisoners were cuffed and tired. They weren't going anywhere, so he could return to his work. But moments later a soft voice called out in Spanish.

"Excuse me, sir. Could she have some water?" It was the young man sitting closest to the older woman, who was now swaying slowly back and forth.

"They'll be back in a few minutes," said Hayden in Spanish. "They'll give you water." Nick was about to go back to his work when he looked at the older woman more closely. Her eyes were closed, her mouth slack and partly open. Her swaying stopped, and she leaned heavily against the young woman next to her. She appeared close to fainting.

Perhaps it was the quiet intimacy of the office at night. There was none of the usual office noise and activity that created an invisible barrier. Hayden studied the whole group, one by one. On the surface, they appeared no different from any of the thousands that had come before. Yet they *were* different now.

Hayden picked up the cup of lukewarm coffee from his desk and walked over to them.

"You're all from Mexico?" he asked, looking at the man who had called out.

"Yes, Mexico," said the young man with a smile that revealed several missing teeth. The outer edges of his two front teeth were lined with thin bands of gold. "When they took us, we had no break for four hours, and it was very hot in the factory. They let us go to the bathroom before we left, but we had nothing to eat or drink."

The older woman seemed unaware that Hayden was standing in front of her. He knelt down and held her left shoulder to steady her. Her eyes came partly open, and she said something in slurred words that he couldn't understand.

"Here, drink some of this," said Hayden, lifting the cup of coffee to the woman's mouth. She took a sip, then eagerly took hold of the cup with both hands and tilted it to drain the remaining coffee. It seemed to revive her a bit, and she looked up gratefully at Hayden.

Nick stepped into the hallway and went to the drinking fountain to fill the empty coffee cup with water. When he returned he gave the cup to the woman and she drank it eagerly, some spilling down her chin and onto the floor. She handed the cup back to Hayden and glanced at the water on the floor.

"I sorry," she said, and dropped to the floor on her knees. She wiped the wet tiles with the shirtsleeve of her unshackled hand and smiled weakly.

"That's OK," said Hayden. "Don't worry about it."

Hayden made several trips to the hallway drinking fountain and was filling the cup again when he heard the elevator bell and the low voices of Denton and De Rosa. When Denton turned the corner, he saw Hayden at the fountain and was instantly concerned about his untended prisoners.

"What's going on, Nick?" he asked. The two were carrying white bags, and the aroma of hamburgers and fries filled the hallway.

"They're all a little dehydrated," he said. Denton and De Rosa walked around him into the squad room but offered no comment.

When Hayden returned, the two agents were sitting at a desk, munching away silently. Hayden brought the cup of water to the last Mexican in line, a middle-aged man who sat looking at the agents, his face weathered and sad. The agents watched Hayden curiously as he handed the cup to the man, and an awkward silence enveloped the room. Hayden knew what Denton and De Rosa were thinking. He'd intervened in something that, according to accepted protocol, was none of his business. He thought of Denton as a good professional, not remarkable in any way, but a solid, reliable agent. He was neither overly aggressive nor too soft. If Denton had been aware of the woman's condition, he too would have provided assistance. Yet he no doubt found Nick's concern and involvement excessive. It took so little to arouse suspicion.

"They won't give them anything to eat at the jail until morning, but water will help a little," said Hayden. There was a silent pause as Denton and De Rosa looked at Hayden and kept eating. "One of the women here almost passed out after you guys left."

Denton grunted disgustedly at what he took as implied criticism. "The women always want special attention," he said. "They play games."

Hayden let the remark pass. He'd said exactly the same thing himself when dealing with women detainees. He

returned to his desk with an empty cup and tried to go back
to work but couldn't keep his eyes off the Mexicans, who
now seemed as interested in Hayden as he was in them. They
could feel the unspoken tension between Hayden and the
other agents. Finally, Denton and De Rosa finished eating
and rose from their chairs.

"OK, let's go," said Denton. The Mexicans stood up, their
handcuffs clinking together, and began trudging toward the
door. It reminded Hayden of his recurring dream of face-
less people in the desert. But unlike the dream, he could
see these people clearly, their eyes, their expressions—each a
distinct, individual presence. He felt a subtle shift, as though
a ray of penetrating sunlight had awakened something deep
inside him.

As they staggered out, the older woman looked back at
Hayden, smiled feebly, and gave a short wave of her hand.
Hayden nodded and lifted a hand in response. As the Mexicans disappeared out the door, Denton and De Rosa both
glanced curiously back at Hayden. He listened to them make
their way down the hallway and into the elevator.

Alone again, Hayden peered out the window at the cubicles
of light and the blue-clad figures methodically going about
their work.

15

A large envelope covered with bright yellow Panamanian stamps was on Hayden's desk when he arrived on Tuesday morning. He removed the contents: a report on the bank robbery, a two-page rap sheet, and mug shots of Liriano Solis.

Hayden had seen Rico only once during surveillance from at least thirty yards away, but Kane had taken photos of him. Nick spread them out on the desk, along with a copy of Rico's driver's license, which had a blurry photo.

There was no question: the rounded features, thick eyebrows, and small, flat eyes. Especially telling was the curvature of the upper lip. He wasn't surprised. It made perfect sense that Rico would have a criminal past, though confirming it certainly raised the stakes.

He flipped back to the rap sheet and found that Solis had been arrested for numerous petty thefts, armed robbery, and burglary. The final entry was the most serious—the warrant for murder that Vogel had mentioned in connection with the bank robbery. Hayden knew, however, that if anybody had been killed during a robbery, all those participating would be charged with murder, regardless of who pulled the trigger.

Hayden turned to the next page. There before him was a set of still photos transferred from a video camera mounted above the entrance of the Chase Manhattan Bank in Panama City. The six black-and-white images showed two men. One was running away from the bank and carrying a gunnysack in his right hand, his shoulders bent over as if he were trying to avoid shots fired from inside—a black hood covering his head. The man next to him was aiming a shotgun toward the entrance of the bank. This man's hood had been removed, perhaps to better view his adversaries. In the fourth shot of the series, a barely visible puff of smoke could be seen rising from the shotgun, its muzzle tilted up at a forty-five-degree angle from the recoil. Though the photos were blurry and taken from a distance of at least forty feet, he could see that the man carrying the shotgun was the same person known in Chicago as Salvador Rico.

The three-page report of the bank robbery stated that the getaway vehicle was cornered by a police roadblock just minutes after leaving the bank. The driver and another of the bandits had been shot down in a hail of bullets and the money recovered. But Solis had rolled out of the backseat of the vehicle and disappeared into the dense tangle of buildings in the heart of Panama City.

The manhunt yielded nothing in the days after the robbery, though it was rumored that the fugitive had fled south into Venezuela. Police intelligence officers were convinced he was still holed up somewhere in his Panama City neighborhood, though frantic searches of suspected hangouts produced nothing. Two days after the robbery, fingerprints on the shotgun identified Liriano Solis as the shooter.

Hayden looked over at Kane, who was contentedly munching a donut and reading the morning newspaper. "You need to take a look at this stuff," said Hayden, tossing the Interpol report onto Kane's desk. "I'm going downstairs for coffee."

The cafeteria on the second floor of the Federal Building was almost deserted when Hayden took a seat at one of the long tables, far from the cash registers and occasional customers. Since the coffee was always bitter and the collection of day-old pastries unappetizing, there was little activity between meals. Bright fluorescent lights and cheap plastic chairs did nothing to enhance the atmosphere. Still, it was quiet and there were floor-to-ceiling windows for an expansive view of the plaza, which was dominated by an enormous orange metal sculpture by Alexander Calder.

Rain fell against the windows as Nick sipped his coffee and tried to absorb the news confirming that Rico was a killer and would be desperate if cornered. Though Panama had no official death penalty, Rico would be keenly aware that prison guards could be counted on to avenge the dead security guard, probably through torture and grisly death.

It had suddenly become eerily dark outside. Deep volleys of thunder began to rumble overhead, seeming to shake the building, and rain thudded loudly against the cafeteria windows. The lights flickered off for a moment but almost instantly came back on.

Out of nowhere, Tom Kane pulled up a chair across from Hayden.

"That report from Panama is priceless," chirped Kane. "The bureau is using a killer as an informant." Kane cackled with delight and rubbed his hands together as though he'd won a pot of money in a poker game. "We've got Byrd by the short and curlies!"

"Byrd isn't the issue at the moment," said Nick seriously.

"Come on—this stuff on Rico is great."

"Great?"

"Absolutely. The press will love it, and so will Stark. The magnitude of the case just skyrocketed."

Hayden looked at Kane impassively and for a moment felt envious of his partner's blissful approach. "We could arrest Rico right now on a murder warrant," said Nick. "We know where to find him. He could split any time before Thursday."

"You mean before the operation?" said Kane, clearly startled by the suggestion.

Nick continued. "What if he gets suspicious, decides the whole deal with Miguel doesn't feel right? What if word leaks out about the operation? Byrd finds out, tips off Rico—then what do we have? We lose a killer and end up with nothing but a document case."

Kane was incredulous. "You wanna take him down on the warrant and that's it? It isn't just Rico we're after; it's the whole organization! Two more days isn't going to make any difference."

"We could still arrest some vendors," Hayden suggested, with little conviction. "Try to flip them on Rico's lieutenants. If they're holding large numbers of documents, we could get the US Attorney to file for possession. That's all they really wanted when this thing started."

"So we're supposed to throw away all the work we've done just to arrest Rico two days before we were going to arrest him anyway? Look, we need a criminal prosecution to make our detail a success," Kane said with finality. "I'm not going back to area control without something to show for it. Hell, I might never get out of there again. Stark wants something good, especially since we've briefed him. He's told the front office about it. It's out of our hands now."

Hayden stared out the window at the black sky and cascading rain. Kane was right. Stark was salivating at the prospect of a big case going down on his watch. There was no way he would approve of arresting Rico prior to the scheduled operation on Thursday.

Kane waved a hand across an invisible plane in front of Hayden's face. "Base to Hayden. You in there, little fella?" he said in a high, mocking tone.

"Knock it off, Tom. I need time to figure this thing out."

"No, you don't need more time. You're overanalyzing. I know what you're thinking—that Miguel is going in wired and he'll be in danger, and yeah, he will. But I've got a news bulletin for you. That's what informants do."

Kane waited for a response, but Hayden looked away and said nothing.

"By the way," continued Kane in a lowered voice, "I passed through area control earlier and heard Denton and some other guys talking. I guess you guys ran into each the other night, huh?"

"What about it?"

Kane leaned forward over the table and whispered. "I'm no shrink, but there's something happening with you, and it ain't good." He paused, hoping Hayden would confide in him, but Hayden, clearly annoyed, stared across the table. It was nothing he could speak candidly about with Kane.

"I know it's pretty bizarre, giving them water," said Hayden sarcastically. "It's downright neurotic."

"It's not just the thing with Denton," said Kane evenly. "It's ever since we collared Miguel. If you start caring too much about these people, you can't do the job. It's that simple. You're paralyzed."

Nick recalled a McCloud lecture about agents caught in the paralysis syndrome—frozen by an exaggerated sense of what might go wrong. That phase wasn't supposed to happen for years, if ever. And though Kane had a valid point, it *wasn't* that simple.

"McCloud used to tell us to never forget these are people we're dealing with," Nick said. "It doesn't mean you can't do what's necessary to get the job done."

"OK," said Kane, raising his palms defensively, "but we're getting down to crunch time, and I'm not gonna let a good case go down because of some irrational concern about an informant, so you better get your shit together."

Hayden said nothing, knowing his partner had the upper hand.

"It's too late to pull back," declared Kane, as he rose from his chair. "Anyway, we have a lot to do to get ready for Thursday."

As Kane stalked away, Hayden saw that the rain had stopped and it was suddenly much brighter outside. A column of sunlight slipped through a gap in the skyscrapers, illuminating the wet granite plaza. A few people emerged from buildings, glancing warily at the sky.

———

When informed that Salvador Rico was wanted for murder and armed robbery in Panama, Richard Stark, as expected, insisted that the operation go forward as planned. "We're not even sure it's the same guy," he said. "You can't rely on blurry photos. We'll need prints for a firm ID, and we'll have those on Thursday." Hayden, seeing it was inevitable, kept his silence, and the two agents resumed their preparations.

On Wednesday morning they were summoned to Connelly's office to brief him and Stark on the upcoming operation. They split up the briefing—Hayden going over the undercover deal with Rico, Kane outlining the anticipated arrests and searches of document-manufacturing pads in other parts of the city. Everything appeared to be a go for Thursday.

Jack Connelly, ninety days from retirement and wary of anything that might disrupt the serenity of his departure, was visibly nervous. "You fellas let Richard know if you need anything," he said, waving a hand toward Stark. "I've told him and the other chiefs that this case gets priority for manpower and equipment." The smell of vodka wafted across the desk. It was more excitement than Connelly could handle in the last weeks of his career, and he'd needed a jolt, even though Stark was for all practical purposes in charge. As the meeting continued, Connelly sat like a spectator watching a tennis match, his head bobbing back and forth between Stark and the agents.

Hayden and Kane were relieved when Stark announced that he would remain in the office during the operation. Supervisors in the field were problematic, often feeling the need to show they were in charge, which led to ill-informed decisions.

"Call me as soon as it goes down," said Stark with a thrust of his chest. "I'll handle the PR stuff."

"And I'll keep Director Farber informed," offered Connelly, glancing at Stark for approval. "He's very interested in this case, as you know."

"Yes, that's good, Jack," said Stark with a patronizing grin. Hayden was silently amused. All that was missing was a pat on the head and a cookie.

For the rest of the afternoon, Hayden and Kane flung themselves into final preparations. They briefed agents as a group and then each of the three teams separately so that everybody knew exactly what was expected of them. Gradually things died down and the office became deserted and quiet. It was the first chance to consider nightmare scenarios that could scuttle everything and place Miguel in even more danger. By now a lot of people knew about the operation, and the circle of knowledge was likely expanding with each passing minute.

"I can just hear them at McGinty's after a few drinks," said Hayden.

"We told them to shut up about it," said Kane. "What else can we do? Anyway, a beer sounds good right now."

"You go ahead. I want to go over a few things again."

"OK. I'll talk to you on the radio in the morning." Kane rapped his knuckles on Hayden's desk and smiled as he swaggered out with a backpack slung over his shoulder.

Alone in the office, Hayden continued looking over photos and thinking through the operation. Ten minutes had passed when he heard a slight movement behind him and turned around. It was Joe Willis, who had been forced to retire two weeks before. Though it was highly unusual for Willis to enter a room without loudly announcing his presence, there he was, sitting in Kane's chair, staring morosely at the floor. There were circles under his eyes, and his normally fiery cheeks had gone pale. Wearing one of his familiar black sport coats, he looked more like an undertaker than an agent.

"Joe, how long have you been there?"

Willis coughed weakly and looked up. "Not long. I was having a beer with Moretti. He mentioned your case."

Hayden paused, looking him over. "How are you, Joe? How's retirement?"

Willis ignored the question but came suddenly alive. "Hey, listen, I know it's not by the book, but how about I go along with you tomorrow? I'll stay out of the way. It'll be like old times, like the Padilla bust."

"It'd be OK with me, but with Stark in charge, there's no way. If he found out, he'd have my badge." That was true enough, but he could also see that Willis was different now—fragile and unsure. Who knew what he might do in the excitement of an ongoing operation?

To Hayden's surprise, Willis didn't fight it. "Hmm. I see your point. I guess I shouldn't have asked," he said softly. It was painful to watch him caving in so easily. Willis lifted his eyes pleadingly for a moment, giving Hayden a chance to change his mind.

"Sorry, Joe. I'll give you a call to let you know how it went."

"No, that's OK. You'll be busy." Willis was standing to leave. "Anyhow, I hope it goes all right," he muttered sadly, and then slipped out the door like a ghost.

By the time Hayden left the office, a light rain was falling. On the way to the garage he noticed McGinty's was unusually packed for a weekday, but he resisted the temptation to stop.

Back at his apartment, he ordered a pizza and watched a baseball game on television in an effort to slow the pace of his thoughts before going to bed. But he didn't sleep well—waking at four o'clock in a cold sweat. It was the recurring dream of marching figures in the desert. Once again, he'd been unable to make contact with them.

Part III

16

A bank of cool Canadian air had driven away the heat of the extended summer. This was good, Nick told himself. Miguel could wear a jacket without raising suspicion. It would go fine—unless Rico decided to again shake him down for a wire.

Nick and Miguel met in the parking lot of a boarded-up auto repair shop on the North Side. A tall, wooden fence surrounded the lot, so they couldn't be seen by the traffic on Belmont Avenue. Miguel parked next to Hayden's vehicle and remained in his car.

Nick grabbed the mic from under the dash. "Five-fourteen to five-eleven, I'm getting ready to wire him. How things look over there?"

Kane's voice came over the radio: "The Bolivian was looking around, so we all had to move a block away, but Meadows can still see the bar from his position, and we've got units that can see both ends of the alley behind it."

Hayden didn't like it. From that far away it could take the agents two or three minutes to get inside the bar.

"Ten-four," said Hayden. "It's nine thirty. I'll let you know when our guy is headed for the bar."

Miguel slid into the passenger seat of the Firebird and shut the door.

"How you feeling, Miguel?"

"Good, Nicolas."

Hayden had decided not to tell Miguel about the outstanding murder warrant in Panama, Kane having argued that they still didn't have a firm identification on Rico and that such a disclosure could make Miguel more nervous. Hayden finally backed off after convincing himself that Miguel would not have let the revelation deter him. As for being jittery, there wasn't the slightest hint of nerves on Miguel's part. He appeared to be as cool as the autumn air.

It took five minutes to make sure the Nagra recorder and a transmitter were properly fastened to Miguel's body. The Nagra was placed in a spandex holder at the small of his back and its two wires were snaked up his stomach to his chest. The transmitter was fitted inside padding just below Miguel's waist, its wire and tiny microphone taped just below his collarbone. This unit sent a signal to the receiver on the backseat of Hayden's car so that he could monitor the conversation. Draped in wires, Miguel looked like a suicide bomber, thought Hayden, and even a cursory pat-down would be disastrous. Baker had told him smaller devices were available, but their quality and range were very limited. Besides, a thorough pat-down would locate a wire, however small.

To make sure the equipment was working properly, Nick had Miguel briefly walk around the parking lot and speak. As Miguel got back into the car, Hayden checked his watch. It was nine forty-five. It would take about ten minutes to drive to El Palacio. He reached inside his leather briefcase and removed an envelope filled with cash.

"Here's nine thousand dollars in hundred-dollar bills," said Nick. "They're marked." Miguel slipped the envelope into the inside pocket of his nylon jacket.

Though they'd been over it before, Hayden again gave instructions on how the deal should go down. "Remember, ask to see the documents before showing him the money. If he asks to see the money first, just pat the inside of your jacket. As soon as they give you the documents and we hear you counting out the money, we'll be on our way in. I'll be listening to everything. If they start to search you, try to stall them. We'll come in right away. And don't forget, we'll make it look like we're arresting you when we come in."

Miguel nodded.

"I guess we're all set, Miguel."

"I have question, Nicolas. I think about this . . ." He paused and looked out the front window, reluctant to bring it up.

"Yes? What is it?"

"Is OK if I carry gun when I go there?"

Though it was reasonable, it surprised Hayden. He had come to think of Miguel as being almost fearless and above such practical considerations.

"No, I can't let you have a gun. Why? Do you have one in the car?"

"If you go in there like me, would you have gun?" Miguel asked the question with no bitterness, just curiosity.

"Yeah, I would, but I've got a badge. We never let informants carry weapons. It's policy, but I don't blame you for asking."

"Is OK," said Miguel, turning to face Hayden. "I no think you let me."

"We'll cover for you."

"I not worried. The Lord protect me . . . gun or no gun."

They sat in silence for a few moments.

"I go now?" inquired Miguel.

"Let me turn the recorder on. Lean forward a little." Hayden felt for the lever beneath Miguel's jacket and locked it into the ON position. "We know Rico and the others are in there, so there shouldn't be any delays."

"OK," said Miguel, opening the passenger door. He had one foot on the gravel and one inside the car when he turned to Hayden. "Thank you, Nicolas. No worry. Whatever happen now is God's will."

"Right," Hayden said. There was a moment of awkward silence. "Remember, you're being recorded."

Miguel shut the door and returned to his car. Hayden could hear his breathing and the rubbing of the microphone against his shirt through the receiver. It sounded like a scuba diver under water. Hayden picked up the mic.

"We're on our way. I'll let you know when he's out of his car." A series of ten-fours came back.

Hayden followed Miguel east on Belmont Avenue. Mexican music came from Miguel's car radio through the receiver on the backseat, a lively tune featuring a singer wailing about the woman who had left him, though Miguel's microphone was cutting in and out—fuzzy snaps followed by brief silences. Hayden found it unnerving. He'd tested the equipment with Floyd Baker and everything seemed to be working fine, though Baker had warned it could be temperamental.

The pace of Hayden's thoughts accelerated. He thought again of the surveillance units, their distance from the bar. He grabbed the mic. "Tom, if Nieto isn't still out there watching, maybe you can get closer."

He knew Kane wouldn't appreciate the suggestion. The silence went on for at least ten seconds.

"You read, five-eleven?" said Hayden finally.

"We can't start moving around now," said Kane coldly. "It'll draw attention."

Nick let the statement linger without a response. Kane was right—again. Hayden sat rigidly at the wheel. Everything that had happened that morning sharpened a sense of looming disaster: the receiver connection to Miguel breaking up, the other agents being too far away, Nieto's nervousness, even Miguel's request for a gun. An image came racing through his mind: *Rico tearing Miguel's shirt off, exposing the network of wires, and throwing Miguel against the wall . . .*

The transmitter cut out again, and Hayden looked up to see the Fairlane turning north on Western Avenue. Nick swung into the passing lane, pressed his foot to the floor, and made a squealing left turn just after the light turned red. The scratchy sound of the microphone and music from Miguel's radio again came through the receiver and then, moments later, another dreamlike image arose: *Rico pulling out a semiautomatic and rapid-firing several rounds into Miguel's chest . . .*

They turned east on Irving Park Road. Though it was cool, Hayden had begun sweating. He concentrated on gripping the wheel firmly to prevent his mind from drifting. In a few minutes, Miguel would enter El Palacio. It was out of his hands. Just let it happen, he told himself, but yet another vision flashed through his mind: *Carmen and the children gathered around a crude memorial—photos of Miguel, a cross, and soft-glowing candles . . .*

Kane's voice seemed to shout through the speaker. "Nick, we have an ETA?"

Hayden felt like he was sliding in and out of a dream. He could see the Fairlane passing a cemetery in the distance. "He should be there in less than five minutes," he said, surprised at how calm his voice sounded.

They went past the cemetery into a mixed commercial and residential area. Miguel turned south onto Sheridan Road, passed under the elevated tracks, and slowed to find a parking spot across from El Palacio, which was on the other side of the street. Moments later Hayden turned onto Sheridan and pulled over where he couldn't be seen from the bar. He watched as Miguel began squeezing the Fairlane into a vacated spot.

Suddenly the receiver made a fuzzy snap and the sound of Miguel's breathing stopped. There was a low hum from the receiver that hadn't been there before, as though the connection had been severed. Nick stretched over the seat to check the dials and settings. The needle was in the red zone, meaning no signal. Perhaps the microphone had worked its way loose, though he had been careful to fasten it securely. But it was too late to intercept Miguel to check the equipment without being seen by somebody at the bar. Hayden grabbed the radio mic.

"Our guy is parking on Sheridan, but there's a problem with the transmitter."

"It's normal for it to cut out here and there," said Kane dismissively. "It'll come back."

Hayden watched as Miguel stood next to his car, waiting for the traffic to clear so he could cross the street. He knew there were only a few seconds to decide what to do. He desperately hoped that Miguel's microphone would come alive, but it remained silent.

Then, in a moment of absolute clarity, he knew that it was irresponsible to leave Miguel's fate in the hands of Salvador Rico, especially with no way to monitor the deal. He couldn't let that happen.

"The transmitter isn't working," said Hayden into his microphone. "We're gonna have to take 'em down right now. I'm going in."

A moment later, Rick Meadows called out over the radio: "Hayden's out of his vehicle—running toward the bar! What should we do, Tom?"

Miguel had crossed the street and was twenty feet from the bar when Hayden grabbed his shoulder and spun him around.

"Get the hell out of here, Miguel. Go back to the meet site!" he shouted. He looked at the window of El Palacio. The curtains had been pulled back, and he could see faces and somebody, possibly Nieto, waving his arm frantically in a warning. He had to get inside before they destroyed evidence or tried to escape.

Hayden pushed on the solid wood door, but it opened only a few inches and then hit against something at the bottom. He could hear the shuffling of feet and somebody shouting. Stepping back, he lowered his right shoulder and drove it into the door, feeling bodies being pushed away as his momentum carried him inside. Two young men moved aside, grinning as though blocking the door had been a joke. Chacon, standing behind the bar, looked terrified and didn't move.

Hayden, pulling his .357 revolver from the shoulder holster, ran toward the beaded curtain in front of Rico's office. The door, a few feet to the right behind the curtain, was slightly ajar, and there was light coming from inside, but as he pushed through the beads, the light went off. He swung the door open and turned to face Rico's desk, but the darkness stopped him. The only meager light came through the open door behind him. He could barely make out a figure—he assumed it was Rico—sitting behind a large desk at the far end of the room.

"Federal officer," Hayden shouted and pointed his gun toward the figure at the desk. "Get your hands up against the wall."

The room was silent as Hayden struggled to see through the darkness. There was a shadowy figure standing against the wall on his left, next to the sofa, and another figure against the wall to the right. They stood motionless, facing him, trying to assess what they were dealing with and, perhaps, waiting for orders. He knew they could see him much better than he could see them, as he was silhouetted by the light behind him.

A calm voice came from behind the desk. "*Federales* no do things alone. Who are you?"

"I've got a shield on my belt. Turn on a light, and you'll see it," shouted Hayden, trying to fill the darkness with his voice. But his command was met with silence.

"I said get your hands up against the damn wall!" Hayden bellowed. As his eyes slowly adjusted, he could see the large figure to his left had his arms folded across his chest: Nieto. And then he could see Rico's head nodding toward Nieto. Hayden instinctively pivoted toward the Bolivian and fell into a crouch. Nieto was moving, his arms rising. Hayden began to squeeze his trigger slowly, not yet committed, aiming at the center of the man, and then an orange muzzle flash lit up the room, and Hayden completed the squeeze of the trigger, firing twice in quick succession toward the gun, and he felt the heat of a bullet searing his left shoulder, and there was a hollow moan and the metallic sound of a gun bouncing off the tile floor, and before he could swing toward Rico, another shot rang in his

ears, its reverberations so loud that he thought for a moment
he'd been shot in the head.

Some force had stopped Rico, who was motionless in the
chair, his elbows pinned awkwardly inside the chair's arms.

The man to Hayden's right had turned around, placed his
hands against the wall and was looking back over his shoulder.

"No shoot, please no shoot," the man cried.

Hayden could feel a presence behind him and glanced over
his shoulder. Miguel stood with his arms lowered, his hands
gripping a blue-steel revolver.

"Miguel, what the hell!" he gasped. "See if you can find
a light switch."

Miguel found the switch for the overhead light and flipped
it on. Hayden looked back at the motionless figure of Salvador
Rico and a black semiautomatic pistol that lay on the desk.

"Get Rico's gun, Miguel," said Hayden, as he kicked Nieto's
pistol under the desk and out of reach. Nieto was lying curled
on his side, his hands pressed into his abdomen, making soft
moaning sounds. There was a pool of blood on the floor next
to him.

Nick turned toward the other man. "Get on your knees
and put your hands behind your head," he shouted at the
shaking man, who he could see was Felix Pinal. The man
instantly complied.

Hayden felt alternating sensations of pain and numbness
in his shoulder. "Watch him, Miguel," said Hayden, nodding
toward Pinal. Nick stepped around the desk to get a better
look at Rico.

Salvador Rico had been pushed so far into the chair that
his feet dangled, not quite reaching the floor, his head tilted
back. There was a fresh bullet hole through his left eye. The
bullet had pushed the pupil inside his head, and blood flowed

from the hollowed socket, across the side of his nose and into his mouth. He had died instantly.

Kane and the team of agents charged noisily into the room, guns drawn. Four agents surrounded Miguel Chavez, grabbed the two pistols he was holding, and threw him against the wall, gamely sticking to the original plan.

"The semiauto is Rico's," Hayden called out. "There's a gun under the desk, and that guy needs to be searched."

Three agents stepped around a pool of urine near Felix Pinal, who was still on his knees. They did a thorough frisk, finding a semiautomatic pistol wedged into the small of his back, and placed him in handcuffs.

Several agents surrounded the curled figure of Rosario Nieto, and one of them grabbed Nieto's gun from under the desk. Moments later, Nieto let out a high-pitched moan and went limp.

Hayden sat down on the sofa next to where Nieto lay. His shoulder had gone numb, and he was sweating profusely. Kane used his walkie-talkie to call for an ambulance and had Stark call the police.

"Looks like both of these guys are dead," somebody called out.

Kane helped Hayden remove his leather jacket and could see that the bleeding was steady but not gushing. He yelled for Meadows to get a towel from the bar. "It may not be too bad," Kane said hopefully.

Meadows returned and handed a small towel to Kane, who wrapped it around Hayden's shoulder. The other agents padded nervously around the room, frustrated that the action had occurred before their arrival.

A bluish haze of smoke had drifted toward the ceiling, and the smell of gunpowder filled the air. The room had quieted, the agents trying to absorb what had happened and unsure about what to do next.

Hayden, though woozy, summoned the strength to jolt them into action. "We better leave the bodies where they are so the cops can take photos. Somebody needs to talk to Pinal about where the documents are located." His voice sounded uncharacteristically loose and slack. The other agents looked at Kane for direction. Hayden became angry at their hesitation and shouted, "Somebody get those cuffs off Miguel! He just saved my life, for chrissakes!"

Finally Kane spoke. "Yeah, let's see what we can find. I'll talk to him," he said, motioning toward Pinal. "Meadows—take a couple of guys and serve the search warrant on the bartender and look around out there. The rest of you can search this room."

Kane called over to Miguel, who was standing against the wall. Miguel walked over, and Kane used a key to undo the cuffs. Kane winked at Miguel. "Just sit here a minute, amigo."

Kane sidled up next to Hayden. "Who the hell shot who here?"

"I shot Nieto," said Hayden. "Miguel got Rico. They were ready for us." He nodded toward Felix Pinal. "If this guy hadn't frozen, we would have been in deep shit. And thank God Miguel disobeyed me."

"Where'd he get the gun?"

"Must have had it in his car." There was a brief pause before Hayden said, "Tom, I had no choice when the transmitter went down. I couldn't let Miguel go in like that."

"I know. You did what you thought you had to," said Kane. "Anyway, we have to get you to the hospital. I'll take care of things from here."

Hayden was very weak and felt he was about to lose consciousness.

17

Hernan Garza had moved swiftly since his return to Chicago—reclaiming his basement utility room, and then discreetly following Salvador Rico in an old Buick Regal he'd borrowed from a Peruvian friend. To prevent easy recognition by Rico or the Colombians, Garza now concealed his layers of tattered garb beneath a blue nylon jacket that fell almost to his knees. A navy baseball cap and oversized sunglasses completed the makeover.

Garza had discovered that Rico was living in a modest apartment building on Paulina Street. He'd twice seen Rico park his car in the lot behind the building and then walk to a small garage across the alley, briefcase in hand. Rico would spend a few minutes in the garage before heading back to his apartment building. Garza suspected that Rico was storing contraband there. It could be nothing at all, but he couldn't resist making at least one attempt to have a look inside the garage before providing information to the feds that would blow the lid off Salvador Rico's lucrative document empire.

At eleven o'clock in the morning on September 27, Garza drove down the alley and saw that Rico's car was gone, so he parked and jumped out of the car. Seeing nobody around, he tried to lift the garage door, but it wouldn't budge. On the side of the garage he found a window protected by iron bars and, nearby, a narrow wooden door. He tried opening the door, but it, too, was locked. Going back to the window, he peered between the bars and could make out an assortment of shovels and rakes, a stepladder, and stacks of old newspapers in the corner. The center of the garage was empty, the cement floor covered with oil spots. In the far corner he could see a large metal trunk, the kind that might be used to store tools, its lid fastened with a heavy padlock. The trunk was intriguing. He would come back after he figured out how to get into the garage.

Garza drove off, hopscotching through side streets, and stopped at a liquor store just off Diversey Parkway. Behind the counter an old man with pale skin that hung in folds beneath his chin was sitting on a stool, sleepily watching a small television.

Garza's hands were shaking as he stood at the counter and struggled to remove a ten-dollar bill from his wallet. "Give me pint Old Crow," he demanded. As the man went to retrieve the bottle, the flashing red lights on the television screen caught Garza's attention. They had interrupted the regular program for a live news report, and he recognized buildings along Sheridan Road. There was a shot of ambulances on the street, and a reporter was talking excitedly about the shooting deaths of two men at El Palacio. Garza thrust his head forward and leaned over the counter to catch every word.

The men were purported to be involved in the sale and distribution of counterfeit documents. Two suspects, Salvador Rico and Rosario Nieto, were dead, and another man was under arrest. An INS agent had been wounded. There was a brief shot of paramedics carrying a covered corpse on a stretcher.

Garza grabbed the bottle of whiskey, twisted the cap off, and guzzled the flaming liquid so eagerly that some dripped down his chin and onto the floor.

"Hey, this isn't a tavern," said the old man disgustedly. "Go outside if you can't wait."

Garza stumbled out, dazed, and piled into the Regal. He took another pull from the pint, felt the biting heat through his chest, and let the news settle in his mind. His plans were now destroyed. *He* had wanted to take Rico down. He took another swallow of whiskey, wiped his lips with the back of his hand, and let out a warm belch. Well, it was good that Rico was gone, he reasoned, even if it upset his plans for revenge. He considered that for a moment, and then remembered—the metal trunk! It might be too late. The agents might already be on their way to Rico's apartment and the garage. He would need the bolt cutters he'd seen among the janitor's tools in his basement hideout.

It was a quiet working-class neighborhood, most of the homes unpretentious brick two-flats. Maple trees filled with maroon leaves lined the street.

Marvin Johnson, clad in overalls and a gray sweatshirt, was kneeling down, spreading mulch into a flowerbed when he heard something behind him. He turned and looked up at Hernan Garza.

"Hello, sir," said Garza, bowing respectfully.

Garza's appearance—the purplish nose, furtive eyes, and smell of alcohol—set Johnson off balance. He waited for Garza to state his business.

"My cousin, Salvador Rico . . . he die today," Garza said, struggling to produce his best English. "I come . . . to get properties."

Johnson, a tall, elderly man with a long face, rose from his knees and, towering over Garza, looked down suspiciously. "Died? He was a young man. How did he die?"

Garza's heart leapt. The old man knew Rico!

"He shot today," said Garza, who quickly crossed himself. "The police shoot him dead. Is on the TV."

Johnson had always been wary of Salvador Rico, ever since Rico had approached him six months earlier to ask about renting space in his garage. Rico had offered him fifty dollars a month just to use Johnson's metal trunk to store tools. It was easy money.

"How do I know you're his cousin?" asked Johnson, noting the absence of any resemblance between this man and Salvador Rico.

"Here—I have letter from Salvador," said Garza, pulling a folded piece of paper from the pocket of his jacket and handing it to Johnson.

Marvin Johnson held the paper out as far as his arm would extend, his eyes straining to make it out. He read aloud in a plodding, deliberate manner, "I hereby give my cusin, Hernan Garza, all my properties when I die." An unreadable signature was scratched at the bottom.

"Well, you're a pretty lucky guy, aren't you?" said Johnson with a wry smile. As he looked down at Garza, he noticed something hard protruding above the belt at Garza's waist, concealed under the blue jacket. This was the sort of guy you would expect to carry a gun, Johnson thought. He assumed the note Hernan Garza had presented was phony. But somehow the man knew Rico well enough to know about the

tools in the garage. Or whatever was in there. When Johnson
had parked his truck in the garage ten minutes earlier, he'd
noticed cars with red lights flashing in front of Rico's apartment building. Perhaps Rico *had* been killed. But then another
thought came to him. What if the police found drugs in the
trunk—*his* trunk and in *his* garage? Would *he* be a suspect,
somebody who was cooperating with Salvador Rico to hide
drugs or other contraband? He suddenly pictured reporters
with TV cameras swarming over his garage, wanting to talk
to him. And what would this small but dangerous-looking
man do if he refused to let him recover whatever was in
the trunk? Johnson's most fervent wish was to rid himself of
any connection to Salvador Rico, preferably before anything
damning could be found on his property. He had heard of
homes being seized if they were used for illegal purposes, and
envisioned federal agents brusquely taking over his property.

"He put a lock on my trunk. Do you have the key?" asked
Johnson.

The trunk! "No, no have key," he said. "They take Salvador
away. But I have tool to cut."

Johnson studied Garza, his eyes shifting between Garza's
face and hip. It now seemed clear what Garza was up to. He
was probably Rico's partner in crime. And Johnson had a sense
that for all his attempts to appear congenial, this little gangster
was determined to get whatever Rico had in the trunk, with
or without his cooperation. He didn't *need* to know what was
there. If he could get rid of whatever was in the trunk and
sever any connection to Salvador Rico, so much the better.

"Let's go take a look," said Johnson cautiously.

"I bring car in alley," said Garza.

By the time Garza pulled in front of the garage, Marvin
Johnson had lifted up the garage door. But now something

else was bothering the old man. What if Rico wasn't dead, as Garza claimed? Rico would no doubt blame Johnson if the trunk had been emptied, and Rico was probably even more dangerous than this character. If he could only verify that part of Garza's story, he would feel better.

"Just wait here a minute," said Johnson to Garza, who stood peering anxiously into the interior of the dark garage.

Garza's face fell into an angry scowl. "Why? What is wrong?"

"I'll be right back," said Johnson, who trudged off in the direction of the rotating lights.

For an instant Garza thought of pulling the .38 and forcing him back, but instead he froze. There might be nothing in the trunk. Things could get ugly, and there were cops nearby. There was no way to stop the old man. Garza looked nervously up and down the alley and back into the garage. Perhaps there was time to get it open before the man returned. Garza opened the passenger door of the Regal and pulled out the bolt cutters. He looked back across the alley, but there was no sign of the man. The filthy bastard was going to turn him in—perhaps tell them about the trunk!

Garza walked over to the trunk, heaved the bolt cutters into place, and, leaning his full weight into it, cut through the padlock. Flinging the trunk's cover open, he stared in disbelief at what he saw inside: an innocuous collection of tools strewn over a canvas lining.

"Hey, I thought you were going to wait," snapped Johnson, stepping into the garage and around his pickup truck. He saw Garza kneeling alongside the opened trunk, his head hanging over the edge as though he were ill.

"Well, go ahead and empty it out," said Johnson huffily, "but you can't stay parked in the alley too long. There's an agent out there who says you'll need to move your car. I said you were picking something up and would be gone in a minute. You were right about Rico. They told me he was killed today. I guess he was involved in counterfeit documents or something like that."

Johnson walked out, leaving the crestfallen Garza alone in the garage. He'd been pinning his hopes on finding something useful in that trunk. Now what would he do? He suddenly didn't care if INS came charging into the garage to arrest him. What difference did it make? Rico was dead. He might as well return to Peru. There, at least he didn't have an unreasonable hope for riches, a sort of disease that infected everybody in this country.

Garza decided to take the tools that appeared to have some value—a large crescent wrench and a power drill. As he removed them, he spotted something curious. The sharp corner of a piece of paper was barely visible along the edge of the canvas liner. Then he noticed that the liner appeared to be about four inches higher than the bottom of the trunk. He pulled back the corner of the liner for a better look and gasped. It was a crisp hundred-dollar bill. His hands shaking, Garza removed the few remaining tools and pulled the liner away. There in front of him was a thick layer of bills that nearly took his breath away. They were stacked carefully to create an even bed beneath the tools. Garza placed the tips of his fingers on the bills and pressed down to confirm they were real and not some illusion that flowed from booze and self-pity. He pushed them around and could see that they were all hundred-dollar bills, perhaps three or four thousand of them.

His heart pulsing with glee, Hernan Garza shoveled the loose bills into a large, black garbage bag he found next to the newspapers, afraid that the old man would return at any moment. He had just put the last of the bills and the bolt cutters in the bag when a voice came from behind.

"Hey, you there." The deep baritone voice filled the garage and lifted Garza to his toes as he swung around toward the alley. There, just inside the garage was a huge figure, backlit by the sunshine. It was INS agent Tim Reynolds.

"We're federal agents. Is this your car parked out here?" asked Reynolds impatiently.

"Yes, sir."

"Well, it's blocking that parking lot and we need to get in there," said Reynolds, stepping out from the garage and into the sunlight.

Garza didn't hesitate. He threw the heavy bag over his shoulder and walked boldly toward the officer, leaving the tools behind.

The agent watched Garza, who brushed against him with the loaded bag as he marched quickly to his car. Reynolds could smell alcohol even before Garza spoke.

"I move car, sir," said Garza with a shaky smile.

Reynolds peered curiously into the garage and back at Garza, who quickly threw the bag into the backseat and fired up the Regal. Something about the little fellow struck Reynolds as suspicious. He not only had a thick Spanish accent and had been drinking but also was a bit too eager to leave the area. Garza drove slowly forward toward Reynolds, who was standing in front of him in the middle of the alley. Reynolds held up a huge arm for Garza to stop.

"Hold up a minute," he called out, and Garza rolled to a stop.

Reynolds walked to the car window and leaned over to look inside. His eyes shifted from Garza to the plastic bag on the backseat.

"You've been drinking," said Reynolds.

Garza gave him a big smile that showed his stained and rotting teeth. "Just a little. I not drunk," he said. Garza dropped his right hand from the wheel to his hip, feeling the gun with the inside of his wrist.

A white evidence van had entered the parking lot. Reynolds looked toward the van and then back at Garza. He thought there was a good chance this guy was illegal. Though his English was better than most, he smelled of not only liquor but also fear. Still, Reynolds knew that if he questioned the man about his immigration status, *he* would be responsible for processing him for deportation. Reynolds guessed he wasn't a Mexican, so the processing would take even longer. He was already busy collecting evidence on the Rico case. Who had time to deal with yet another illegal alien? To hell with it.

"Well, drive safely and don't stop for another drink, you hear?"

"Yes, sir. Thank you, sir."

Tim Reynolds looked on as the Regal drove slowly over dried leaves. Garza, watching Reynolds in the side-view mirror, stuck his hand out the window and offered a cheerful parting wave.

———

Nick's shoulder was throbbing, though he also felt a lingering euphoria from whatever narcotic had been administered, and it infused everything with the hazy texture of a dream. Not yet fully awake, he peered out the window at stars shimmering in an ebony sky. Puffs of gray clouds passed through the sky like sheep moving in the night.

He finally turned away and glanced around the room, lit only by a small nightlight next to his bed. The door out to the hallway was partly open, and he could hear the soft padding of feet and murmur of conversations among the nurses down the hall. Though warm, the room had a cool antiseptic feel and odor.

A nurse stopped by and told him the surgery had gone well. The bullet had caught the outside of the shoulder and exited cleanly. No major arteries had been severed. He should feel lucky, she told him. His arm and shoulder would be placed in a soft cast and sling. Anxious to regain clarity of thought, he refused more pain medication.

Tom Kane arrived at the hospital at about eleven thirty. He let out a grateful sigh as he let his weary body collapse in a chair next to Nick's bed.

"I had to badge my way in because it's past visiting hours," said Kane with a weak grin. There was an awkward silence as Kane stared gloomily at Hayden's shoulder, swollen with bandages.

"I wish we hadn't been parked so far away," said Kane. "We had to break down the front door of the bar. Somebody locked it after you and Miguel got inside."

Hayden was expecting Kane to be miffed. Nick was open to charges that his actions were rash—an emotional response that placed the other agents and Miguel at greater risk. No doubt Kane considered it a misguided and unprofessional concern for the safety of an informant who knew well enough the risks involved. Then there was the matter of Miguel having a gun. Nick recalled that Miguel never answered his question about having a gun. He should have swept the vehicle. Then again, if he had, he'd probably be dead now.

"I think I'm awake enough," said Hayden. "What happened after I got carted away?"

Kane poured some water from a pitcher on the nightstand into a plastic cup, drank half of it, and paused to organize his thoughts.

"Well, Pinal helped us out and that made things a lot easier."

Kane reported that Felix Pinal, just happy to be alive, had chosen to cooperate fully. Like many inexperienced criminals, he'd assumed the government knew a great deal more than it did and that he had no leverage.

After the counterfeit documents earmarked for Miguel were found in a briefcase under the sofa, Pinal led agents to a removable ceiling panel, and behind it were over ten thousand more documents. He then opened Rico's small safe, located behind a wood panel on the wall, where Rico kept his operating cash, and agents seized $81,000, most of it in hundred-dollar bills, along with two hundred bogus Puerto Rican birth certificates. Pinal said they sold the birth certificates for a thousand dollars apiece and that this part of the business was growing rapidly.

Though minutes earlier Kane had appeared exhausted, he was now revived. "You're not gonna believe what else he came up with," he said.

Pinal had produced a key to a storage locker Rico was renting under another phony name, and there they found dozens of packages of blank counterfeit green cards and social security cards. There hadn't been time to do a complete count, but the initial estimate was staggering: 140,000 green cards and 100,000 social security cards. Street value: several million dollars.

"We ended up arresting about twenty-two vendors around the city and seizing a bunch of manufacturing equipment. The arraignments will be tomorrow."

Stark was handling press inquiries at the office and had issued a brief press release. Two suspects were dead and one officer had been wounded. That was all. Once the dust settled and official identification of Rico was received, Stark would hold a press conference and get the word out that Salvador Rico was one and the same as Liriano Solis, wanted in Panama for murder. That revelation would help divert attention from the embarrassing fact that an informant carrying an unauthorized weapon had been the one to kill Rico.

"I told Stark that what you did was justified. If Miguel had gone in there, gun or no gun, there was a good chance he wasn't coming out alive, especially with the wire down. Pinal said they had decided to search Miguel again and that Rico would have killed him, destroyed the tape, and tried to make a run for it. It looked like some kind of rip-off when you came in alone—that maybe you were a dirty cop."

"And what did Stark say?"

"Not much, but I could tell he wasn't happy about what you did. You better watch out. I have a feeling he might come after you. He's going to have to explain about Miguel having the gun. It's not as clean as he'd like it to be."

Kane sat silently for a moment, reviewing a day crammed with innumerable details. Then his eyes lit up.

"Oh, I almost forgot," said Kane, leaning closer. "Pinal says Rico has a stash of several hundred grand in cash hidden somewhere—maybe more. He would always clear out the safe if there was a substantial amount in there. He says Rico was very careful about not letting anyone know where it was kept. He doesn't think it's in a bank because Rico didn't want to draw attention with large cash deposits. But it's out there somewhere. We searched his apartment and vehicle and came up with nothing except a few guns."

Neither of them said anything for a few moments, and then Hayden lifted his eyes toward Kane. "Sorry it all fell on you."

"Don't worry about it. It worked out well except for what happened to you. This thing has turned out to be a lot bigger than we expected. We got lucky, first with Miguel and then with Pinal."

"Yeah, Miguel was the key. He should get a lot of the credit."

Kane finished the water and stood up to leave. "Well, I'm gonna grab a beer and get some sleep. Tomorrow will be busy with all the arraignments." He patted Hayden's outstretched leg.

"Thanks for coming over, Tom."

"I'm just glad you seem to be doing OK. But I'm going to need your help finding Rico's stash of money, so get out of here as soon as you can," said Kane as he trudged wearily toward the door. "I'll keep you posted."

As the narcotic effect wore off, Hayden began to review the day's events. Tomorrow he would check on Miguel—make sure he was holding up OK after a bizarre and bloody day. He realized his own problems were minor compared to Miguel's, whose fate now rested precariously in the hands of Richard Stark—hardly a comforting thought.

Nick shifted his position, which shot a bolt of pain through his shoulder, and he rang for the nurse. Then he felt a powerful wave of fatigue and closed his eyes. There were ways to keep Miguel here, even if he could no longer be an informant. Maybe Stark could be reasoned with.

By the time the nurse arrived he'd fallen into a deep sleep.

18

The sun, deceptively pale and white, blazed through a cloud-less sky. The road curved west from the Everglades into a vast, desolate landscape of sand, wetland scrub grass, and gnarled cypress trees—no sign of anything man-made aside from the road and a line of telephone poles that looked like weathered crucifixes.

After exiting the interstate, Nick had seen only one vehicle, a pickup truck heading in the opposite direction. The driver, an old man wearing a straw cowboy hat, had waved and seemed to be laughing, as though amused by what lay ahead for Hayden.

The rental car was letting out an occasional gasp, as if it was running out of gas or the engine was misfiring. Nick checked the fuel gauge and saw that he had well over half a tank. Thinking it might be the strain of the air conditioner, he turned it off, rolled down the windows, and was instantly engulfed in hot, steamy air—the heat magnified by the soft cast and sling wrapped around his shoulder. Within minutes, his T-shirt was soaked with sweat.

Nick felt fortunate to find somebody at the only business in Hollins, a general store and gas station. The owner, a middle-aged man with a handlebar mustache and a Panama hat, confirmed that Tatum was still living in the area. "Nobody knows him. Keeps to himself," he said. He gave Hayden directions to Tatum's property and then added: "You wanna be careful if he's not expecting you. Some folks around here don't take kindly to strangers."

About four miles from the store, Hayden spotted what appeared to be the sandy road the man had described. There was a carved wooden sign off to the side that read, NO TRES-PASSING! THIS MEANS YOU! He turned cautiously onto the road. On each side were pools of water covered with swirls of bright green algae. The terrain was flat, dotted with low-lying brush and an occasional willow or cypress tree. Off to the right an egret stood poised at the edge of a lagoon—its white plumage, long neck, and yellow bill etched sharply against a sea of green.

After a few minutes of slow driving, Nick saw a cluster of trees on a rise, several feet above the surrounding grasses. An old white trailer home came into view beneath the trees—a faded red pickup parked off to the side. He'd reached the end of the road, and there were no other buildings in sight. About fifty feet beyond the trailer was a small lake of perhaps twelve acres, rimmed by an endless savanna of tall wetland grasses. There was a pungent though not unpleasant smell of moist vegetation. Everything was still, the silence accentuating the landscape's desolate beauty.

The trailer was short and squat, resting on cement blocks that lifted it about two feet off the ground. Two small windows were covered with old, yellowed newspaper. Moss-covered branches of a cypress tree hung over the roof, offering a bit of shade and holding moisture that had gradually dripped brown streaks down the metal siding.

Hayden shut off the engine, got out of the car, and scanned the area. The door to the trailer had to be on the other side, facing the lake. He waited a few moments for Tatum to acknowledge his presence, but it remained quiet.

"Mr. Tatum," he called out. "I'm Michael Landau's son." He waited for a response but heard only the sound of a small animal scurrying beneath the pickup.

A well-worn path led to the front of the trailer. He followed it, noticing that the area beyond the trailer sloped down to the lake and a weathered dock. A few steps more and he came alongside a screened porch that had been built onto the trailer. Looking up, Nick froze. A large man was sitting heavily in a captain's chair on the porch, a shotgun resting on his lap.

After a brief hesitation, Nick spoke. "Mr. Tatum? I'm Nick Landau . . . Michael Landau's son."

The man didn't move, just glared suspiciously at his unexpected visitor.

"Now I go by Nick Hayden."

"Step closer, if ya don't mind," said the man with a raspy twang. Hayden turned the corner of the rough-hewn porch and paused at the steps up to the screen door. The man furrowed his eyebrows as he scrutinized his visitor, and gradually the taut facial muscles relaxed. He lifted the barrel of the shotgun away.

"Come on in," he said, standing and setting the shotgun down against the side of the trailer. Nick went up the steps and inside. Tatum thrust a hand forward. "I'm Buck Tatum. I guess you knew that." After shaking hands, there was a moment of stiff silence as they sized each other up.

Buck Tatum could have made a convincing department-store Santa Claus were it not for the palpable air of sadness that enveloped him. White hair fell to his shoulders, and there was a sunburned bald spot on the top of his head. A snowy beard flowed abundantly beneath his chin. His ruddy cheeks gave his face a cherubic glow, which seemed to evaporate beneath the brooding countenance of deep-set, owlish eyes.

He was wearing faded blue-jean overalls with straps over his bare shoulders and a pair of knee-high waders. Though large-boned, Tatum was no longer robust. Only his large, thick-fingered hands and muscular forearms projected strength. He appeared deeply exhausted—every movement an effort.

"You can use that chair," said Tatum, gesturing toward a metal folding chair leaning against the trailer. "I'll get some water."

Everything in Tatum's body language suggested that he was prepared for a serious discussion, as though he was not at all surprised that Nick had tracked him down. He stepped heavily through an open door into the trailer and returned with a pitcher of ice water and two coffee mugs, which he set between them on a small table. They sat facing the lake, their chairs angled toward each other. Hayden filled his mug and looked out at the lake while Tatum stared distractedly at the floor.

"Gators give you any trouble, Mr. Tatum?" asked Hayden.

"I've had to shoot a couple, but they generally stay clear of the trailer." Hayden noticed that the right corner of Tatum's mouth was slightly palsied, not moving in sync with the left side, but it didn't seem to affect his speech.

Tatum reached behind his chair and picked up a canteen off the porch. He unscrewed the top and poured the amber liquid into his ice water. "Want some Jack Daniel's?"

"No, thanks."

"If you change yer mind, just help yerself. What happened to yer arm?"

"A little mishap. It's better now."

There was a pause before Tatum spoke. "I know why you're here, son. Nobody told me you were comin', but I'm not surprised . . . you wantin' to know."

"I'm sorry to ask you about something like this after so many years," said Nick. He paused for a moment. "I've actually been working for INS in Chicago for the last four years." He then explained how he'd dug into the shooting as best he could, but still didn't have the full picture. Tatum listened, but seemed distracted and uneasy, which made Hayden feel vulnerable with the shotgun leaning against the trailer.

"I just wanted to hear from you what really happened . . . the night of the shooting. Do you mind if I call you Buck?" Nick asked gently.

Tatum pulled a wrinkled white handkerchief from a side pocket of his overalls and wiped it over his face. His hands were shaking. "Sure, you can call me Buck. I reckon you got a right to call me anything you want, seein' as how I was responsible for yer pa's death." Tatum let the statement hang in the air. He picked up his cup and took a swallow before continuing. "It was bad enough I caused Kelso's death."

Though taken aback, Hayden was uncertain about Tatum's mental state and the reliability of his statements. He waited a moment, hoping Tatum would continue on his own, but he'd gone silent again, so Hayden pushed ahead. "Maybe we can go back to the shooting itself."

Tatum blinked his eyes and shifted in his chair.

"I talked to people and read the shooting report," said Nick. "It didn't say much about what happened when my father tried to help Kelso with the arrest—no specifics."

"No, a'course not." Tatum's eyes narrowed, and a bitter smile lifted the left side of his mouth. He reached into a front pocket of his overalls, pulled out a hand-rolled cigarette, and gestured with it to Hayden, who shook his head. Tatum fished a wooden matchstick from the same pocket and scraped it on the porch. He lit the cigarette and released a cloud of bluish smoke.

"Yer pa was in a tough situation, havin' to work with a bunch of guys from the Patrol. They didn't take kindly to the idea of hirin' people off the street, an' he was one of the first. They sized him up real quick—guys like Willard Smith. He did the investigation."

"Yes, I know."

"They knew he'd been a social worker, had a college degree—wasn't one of the good ol' boys. I rode with yer father for a few days. Then he was Kelso's partner. He wasn't tryin' to be somebody else or change to fit in. I liked that about him. He didn't go drinkin' with the others or try to impress 'em . . . wouldn't play the game. They thought he was aloof an' arrogant.

"But yer pa wasn't givin' 'em anything to justify firin' him at the end of his probationary year. He was smart, an' he knew how to handle himself. Then it happened, an' Smith had what he was lookin' for. But he needed me to make it stick."

Tatum took a deep breath, as though girding himself for what lay ahead.

"It looked like any other arrest at the start," he continued. "We were on North Clark Street. I was followin' yer father an' Kelso. When I pulled up, Kelso was already havin' trouble with the guy—yer dad was runnin' over to help. Kelso was wearin' his holster backwards on his left hip. He shoulda known better, a'course—made it real easy for Cano to grab the gun. That's probably what gave Cano the idea; it was just too easy. So Cano got hold of the gun, an' it went from a routine arrest into somethin' a lot worse. The gun was already out when your pa got there. They were strugglin' for control of the gun, an' it was pointed at Kelso. Your pa jumped right in and tried to push the gun away."

Tatum paused to flick ashes from the cigarette.

"But Cano was strong an' got a round off, even with yer pa an' Kelso tryin' to push it away. By that time, I was close enough to get a clear shot. Once Cano had the gun, if yer father had pulled his hand away to reach for his own gun, Cano probably woulda been able to fire off more than one round into Kelso. Tryin' to push the gun away was the only thing yer father could do at that moment to save Kelso. He needed both hands to try an' throw off Cano's aim. If yer pa hadn't done that, Cano might have gotten all three of us."

Tatum took a final drag on the cigarette and crushed the butt on the porch with his boot.

"Yer father did nothin' wrong. In fact, he did everything right. He got screwed because Smith was lookin' for an excuse to get rid of him. They were lookin' for a scapegoat because one of their Patrol buddies was dead. In their eyes it was proof that they shouldn'a been hirin' guys off the street. The fact he never fired his weapon looked suspicious to anybody who wasn't there an' had doubts about him in the first place. I could have stopped all that, but then Smith showed up."

Tatum's eyes shifted toward the lake.

"How soon after the shooting did Smith show up?" Hayden asked.

"The next day. Smelled blood in the water."

Nick waited, but Tatum seemed reluctant to continue. He'd come to the really difficult part, thought Hayden.

"So Smith talked to you about it?"

"Wasn't much of an investigator, Smith—wasn't into details. But when he found the file, he figured he had me . . . had the pressure he needed."

"What file?"

"Cano's file," said Tatum.

"Where did he find Cano's file?"

"My file cabinet. Been there for almost two years," Tatum said, his voice wavering. "It was assigned to me. Then I knew why the guy's face looked familiar, from the photo in his file. There was a warrant for deportation on Cano. He just had to be picked up. He was walkin' around Chicago the whole time I had the file. His rap sheet was in the file so we knew he was a bad guy, had a criminal record, including an armed robbery. It was easy to forget about those cases with all that was goin' on in area control. But that's no excuse. Because of my negligence, Kelso lost his life. An' yer pa—"

Hayden cut in: "Those cases probably weren't considered that important. They still aren't. If they were, your supervisor would have intervened." In reality Hayden suspected that even with low-priority cases, two years was not tolerated—not with call-ups every three months to review case status. But even if Tatum *had* been negligent, it didn't make him responsible for Kelso's death.

"Connelly was my supervisor," Tatum continued. "He hadn't done the case reviews like he was supposed to. Would have messed up his career if they found out. But he an' Smith were buddies—had been at the same station in the Patrol."

"So what did Smith say about it?"

"That he would bury the information about our negligence if I cooperated. I told him straight what happened with the shooting, but he didn't like how that sounded. He was convinced that the fact that I had to shoot Cano meant yer father wasn't able to pull the trigger, even after I explained it. He didn't wanna hear the truth. He said there was no reason why it had to come out about the Cano case—that he wouldn't put it in his report, an' there'd be no record I ever had the file."

"Sounds like he had all the bases covered," said Nick.

"An' I let him write his report like he wanted. He said yer pa wasn't right for the job. He would have to go, an' the shootin' incident would convince the probationary review panel. He knew that if any question came up about an agent's willingness to use deadly force, the agent wouldn't be retained. I knew what he wanted. He was obsessed with keepin' the 'old Patrol' in charge. Yer father had no chance without me to clear things up. I stayed quiet because I woulda been tainted in everybody's eyes—the guy whose negligence caused Kelso's death."

"Did Smith tape your conversation?" asked Hayden.

"Yeah, but he cut it short when he didn't like what I was sayin' about how it went down. I'm pretty sure he destroyed that tape an' the one with yer father. It woulda contradicted what he wanted in his report."

"There's an envelope for the tapes in the shooting file," said Nick. "But they aren't there, and it looks like they never were."

"No, Smith couldn't risk somebody hearin' them tapes. An' he was determined to get rid of yer pa. So I asked myself: Why should I go down with him? There woulda been disciplinary action against me an' Connelly for how we handled the case."

"Did my father ever come to you to talk about it?"

Tatum took a sip of Jack Daniel's before answering. "Yeah, he came to me. I said that I'd told Smith the truth, but I never told yer pa he'd done nothin' wrong. Never gave him that peace of mind. He probably took that to mean I thought he screwed up. Smith's version became gospel, maybe even to yer father. The truth is yer father wasn't quite sure he *hadn't* done somethin' wrong. There was part of him that felt guilty, like maybe he coulda done somethin' different to save Kelso."

There were a few moments of silence before Tatum continued. "It was a terrible thing I did—lettin' Smith railroad your pa. It was cowardly. I screwed up an' ended up wreckin' other people's lives just to save myself . . . my goddamn reputation. I know it isn't much consolation, but I'm sorry, son. Real sorry."

It was now clear: the resistance to change personified by Smith and the pressure to reject anybody who didn't fit the mold. For Tatum, it was the fear of being judged by his peers that made him believe he had to choose between his own reputation and that of Michael Landau. And it was obvious that Tatum had already paid an enormous emotional price.

Tatum wiped his eyes with the handkerchief. "I told myself that he was a smart guy an' was better off leavin'—gettin' away from INS an' guys like Smith. That's how I lived with it. Later I heard about what happened when your pa went to Portland. That's when I retired. I couldn't be there anymore . . . had no right to carry the badge . . . an' couldn't deny it."

"Deny what?"

"That I managed to kill three guys: Cano, Kelso, *an'* yer pa." He paused and searched Hayden's eyes. "Nobody knew, except Smith an' Connelly. An' now *you* know." Tatum stared at Hayden warily—fear in his eyes.

It would take very little to send Buck Tatum even deeper into the web of guilt he'd been trapped in for almost two decades. Tatum's pain was so acute, so debilitating, that Hayden could muster no anger, only pity.

"By shooting Cano, you probably saved my father's life," said Hayden. "What happened later was the system—the pressures built into it. It wasn't you, Buck." He leaned over and patted Tatum on the knee.

Tatum began weeping, tears rolling down his cheeks.

Nick, too, felt a rush of emotion—and a profound sadness. But he also felt a deep sense of relief in finally knowing the truth—a long overdue vindication of his father.

Tatum took a couple of deep breaths, wiped the moisture off his face, and stuffed his handkerchief into a front pocket. They sat quietly for a minute.

"Want to walk down to the dock, Buck?" asked Nick.

"OK," said Tatum softly. Standing and moving seemed to relax both of them. As they descended the sandy slope, Tatum noticed Hayden scouring the shoreline. "Don't worry. The gators won't bother us."

"Do any fishing from the dock?"

"Yeah, there's a lot of bass an' sunfish."

They were standing at the foot of the narrow dock—the wood planks sun-dried and cracked. "Will this support both of us?" asked Hayden.

"Yeah," said Tatum, brightening. "It's stronger than it looks."

19

The dismantling of Rico's document empire sparked extensive news coverage, plaudits from headquarters, and even a congratulatory nod from the Justice Department. Stark, Farber, and the entire Chicago office were widely hailed. The fact that an informant had killed Rico with an unauthorized weapon was considered rather minor in light of what had been accomplished. The prosecutor hadn't yet decided what to do about Chacon but was considering seizing the bar in addition to filing criminal charges. Felix Pinal was facing a long prison sentence.

The whole affair was a boon for McGinty's, which instantly became a command post for gossip and rumor. Cops from other agencies, envious of any high-profile criminal case that wasn't theirs, now packed the saloon and vented their theories and opinions about how the deal had gone down, most of it based on pure speculation. It was an irony Charlie McCloud had noted on many occasions: those who earned their living collecting hard evidence were often the ones most inclined, when not on the job, to arrive at hasty conclusions tainted by cynicism and ego.

During his three weeks of doctor-ordered convalescence, Nick kept in close touch with Kane. He also contacted Joe Willis, as promised, to fill him in on details that hadn't appeared in news stories, and it seemed to lift Joe's spirits a bit.

When Hayden returned to the office, now without the need of a sling, several agents expressed concern about his shoulder, but there were few congratulations. Considering the success of the case, the reception was rather cool—apparently the result of lingering suspicion about his conduct during the operation.

Meanwhile, Richard Stark was avoiding Hayden as if he were radioactive; all communication suddenly went through Kane. That was how Nick found out that they'd been given another month in fraud, into the middle of November, to clean up loose ends. They'd be informed within the next few weeks about their permanent assignments—whether they would continue in fraud or be moved back to area control. Hayden thought there was the possibility of disciplinary action, if only for negligence in the matter of Miguel's having a gun, but he hoped that the overall success of the case would give him a chance at remaining in fraud.

Though Nick had a clear conscience about shooting down Nieto, he still felt a sense of loss—a heaviness that was only gradually diminishing. He quietly resumed his duties but noticed the same questioning eyes his father must have seen—evoking a sort of surreal camaraderie with his father.

Over beers at McGinty's, Nick told McCloud what he'd learned from Buck Tatum.

"It must be a relief to finally know the truth," said McCloud.

"Yeah, like a weight has been lifted off me."

"The whole thing shows how important reputation is in this business. Even good, experienced guys like Tatum will do anything to avoid being tagged by their colleagues."

They sipped their beers quietly for a minute.

"So, have you told your mother what you found out?" asked McCloud.

"No. I thought about it. Part of me wants to tell her, but it would only churn up the past and make her feel guilty. She's moved on and dealt with it in her own way."

"Too bad that lizard Smith isn't alive," said McCloud. "That was a crime, what he did, literally a fucking crime. An investigation should be done to clear the record."

But Hayden knew it was time to let it go. He'd learned the truth about the shooting and the circumstances that led his father to such an acute state of guilt and despair. And Tatum had been through enough.

McCloud reported that he'd spotted Alderman Francisco Campos outside Farber's office a few days earlier.

"You guys took care of Campos's problem with the merchants on Cermak and Twenty-Sixth Street," said McCloud. "My guess is he's persuaded Farber to back off again. If you guys keep going after vendors, prices will stay high, and Campos's people won't be happy—the wets *or* their employers. He wants to go back to the good old days—plenty of supply but no visible presence to annoy the business owners. Sweep it under the rug. In return he'll hold off on bashing INS in press conferences for a time. That should be enough for Farber."

"The vendors will come back," said Hayden.

"All this publicity has changed things. The cops can't just ignore these guys anymore. Campos might be able to have the cops keep them off the street with vagrancy laws or something, but the cops still won't be able to work directly with INS. The document trade will keep going, of course, but in the shadows."

"So the vendors go underground," said Hayden disgustedly. "And nothing changes except appearances."

"You think they care about anything *but* appearances? They're politicians, for chrissakes! Appearance is *everything*. By the way, a couple of regional headhunters are in town," said McCloud with an impish grin. "They're going beyond the shooting, looking into the money angle—Rico's money. Like maybe you and Miguel have it stashed somewhere. Stark's directing them."

"So Tom and I are just *pretending* to look for it?"

"They're trying to understand what you did, and greed makes more sense to them than a concern for Miguel's safety. They don't trust what they don't understand. Anyway, Stark doesn't figure he can trust you, even though it was your case that's going to make him the next director of investigations. Just make sure you don't give him anything else he can use against you."

———

The internal investigators from the regional office, derisively referred to as "headhunters," made everybody in the office a little nervous. They spent two weeks in Chicago reconstructing the shooting scene and taking statements, and leaned heavily on Miguel, implying that if he "came clean" about Hayden, they could get him permanent legal status. To their chagrin he offered nothing but praise for the agent's conduct. Responding to questions about his ability to shoot down Rico in the dimly lit office at El Palacio, Miguel explained that he had grown up on a ranch where guns were everywhere, and he had learned as a boy to fire accurately. It wasn't as difficult a shot as they seemed to think. He assured them that

Hayden knew nothing about the gun he'd retrieved from his car after Nick entered El Palacio.

The tape recorder fastened to Miguel's body was downloaded and, to their disappointment, confirmed Hayden's version of events. Baker checked the equipment and found that a damaged wire inside the receiver had cut off audible reception from Miguel. The regional investigators did perfunctory interviews with Kane and Hayden, who had already furnished detailed memos. The investigators informed Stark that Hayden had been negligent in not searching Miguel's vehicle for weapons, but they found no other impropriety. They left Chicago on a cold, dreary day in November.

The next morning word swiftly circulated through the office about Joe Willis. The night before, Willis, alone in his apartment, had shoved his beloved .357 Smith & Wesson revolver into his mouth and blown off the back of his head. He was found outfitted in his old, dark green Border Patrol uniform. There was a collection of newspaper articles about the Rico case on a table next to Willis's body. It was only two months since he had been forced to retire at age fifty-seven. Some were shocked, but others had seen it coming. The decibel level in the office dropped to a low hum for the rest of the week.

———

Richard Stark cleared out his inbox and half-listened to the morning radio traffic through the walkie-talkie behind his desk. He lit a cigarette, peered through the floor-to-ceiling window overlooking the plaza, and tried to prepare himself for what promised to be an uncomfortable meeting.

For a ruthlessly ambitious man, Stark had a surprisingly difficult time executing decisions on personnel matters. It was one of the reasons he longed for higher office; let his subordinates handle the dirty work. He'd hoped the regional investigators would unearth something damning enough on Hayden to make it simple, but they had found nothing to warrant more than a slap on the wrist. Useless bastards! Connelly, still ostensibly in charge of the investigations branch, was now taking sick leave for weeks at a time without even the pretense of illness. He had made it clear that he wanted nothing to do with it and had named Stark the acting director of investigations in his absence. This was useful to Stark, as District Director Farber would get used to him occupying the post.

Stark had his secretary call Hayden and Kane into his office. As the two agents took seats in front of his desk, Stark had the somber look of a man preparing to deliver a funeral oration.

"Well, you guys have done a hell of a job," said Stark, forcing a weak smile. He glanced momentarily at Hayden and then fastened his gaze on Kane. "Even with a few unexpected problems, we did a good job of upsetting the flow of documents." He paused, waiting for some agreement or expression of gratitude, but they remained silent, and this made him even more nervous.

Stark cleared his throat. "I want to tell you both what is going to happen as far as your permanent assignments, now that your detail is at an end. I've given this some serious thought," he said gravely. He paused and ran a hand over his teal-colored silk tie. "Kane, you're going to stay down here in fraud. Hayden, you're going back to area control. I think it's best for everyone concerned."

Nick had prepared himself. He knew what it meant for his career. It wasn't likely he would get another opportunity, certainly as long as Stark was in charge.

"Sir, why should Nick have to go back?" asked Kane. "He was more responsible than anybody for this case."

"It's a management decision, Kane," he said acidly. "It's not your concern."

"With all due respect, it *is* my concern. He almost lost his life over this case, and now he's sent back to area control? That's not fair."

"The last time I checked, Kane, nobody had appointed you director of investigations," said Stark, his eyes smoldering with anger. There was dead silence for a few moments before he continued. "Anyway, it's not like being in area control is some kind of punishment."

Hayden began to feel like an object being argued over in a divorce proceeding. If Kane continued his noble defense, they might both be sent back to area control. Besides, he knew there was no way Stark would change his mind during this meeting.

"It's OK, Tom," said Hayden evenly. "I don't mind going back."

"It doesn't mean he won't be back at some point in the future," said Stark, glaring at Kane. He let that concession hang in the air, where it soon fizzled.

"What about the task force, sir?" asked Hayden. "Will Tom and others still be working counterfeit documents?"

"Task forces are generally set up to resolve a specific issue," Stark said, leaning back in his chair. He was starting to relax, thinking the worst was over. "You guys accomplished what we wanted. So, no, for now there won't be anybody working documents. Kane will be working other things in fraud."

With two sets of disbelieving eyes staring back at him, Stark looked out the window and nervously fiddled with his tie.

So, it was true about Campos, thought Hayden. McCloud had guessed right. The alderman, who regularly trashed Farber and the INS, had gotten his way. They had made a conscious decision to again ignore the problem, so long as business was conducted behind the scenes. And there would be no second-guessing from the regional office or headquarters. They were all quite comfortable with the way things were, taking their lead from a Congress that secretly applauded the ineffectiveness of the very laws it had passed. Hayden's detachment began to dissolve. The absurdity of the policy—and its being openly defended—made him slightly nauseous.

"Let me get this straight," said Hayden. "We just proved that the sale and manufacture of counterfeit documents is a multimillion-dollar industry, that the counterfeits are necessary so tens of thousands of illegal aliens in Chicago alone can circumvent the law, and you're telling us nobody is going to do anything about it?"

"We have a lot of priorities around here, Hayden, and we don't have unlimited manpower. You know that as well as anybody."

"But, sir," Kane protested, "if we don't keep the pressure on in some way, it's going to be completely out of control. There'll be fights over turf. The media will want to know what we've done about it, or why we've done nothing."

Stark didn't like being on the defensive, especially with two novices who didn't understand the obscure wisdom and logic of the INS bureaucracy.

"*We'll* worry about the media impact," he said, his voice rising. "I'm not going to debate this any further."

"It's all right," Hayden quickly offered. "We know you aren't calling the shots on this." As soon as the words left his mouth, he realized that Stark's ego could not handle that sort of candor.

"No, you're wrong, Hayden," Stark declared. "I *am* calling the shots on this. It's *my* decision!"

"I didn't mean to suggest you aren't in charge," said Hayden. Stark searched Hayden's face vainly for any hint of sarcasm.

After taking a deep breath, Stark tried to regain his footing by again praising what they had done on the task force, assuring Hayden that it was all but official that his shooting of Nieto would be declared justified. There might be some minor reprimand for not thoroughly checking Miguel for weapons, but it was "nothing to worry about." Calm was momentarily restored. But there was one final matter.

"Oh, by the way, Hayden," said Stark casually, "about Miguel Chavez . . . we obviously can't use him as an informant anymore. You'd better take care of the paperwork."

Stark had blundered headlong into a very sensitive area.

"I thought we might use him for intelligence purposes," said Hayden calmly. "Not on undercover operations, but it would allow us to keep him on as an informant."

"No. He's damaged goods. If he does something unpredictable again, whether it's undercover or not, we'll look bad. We can't take that chance."

"Even if he's no longer an informant, I assume we can keep him on a schedule of voluntary departure periods," said Hayden, "so he and his family can stay here—for all he's done for us."

"No, we'll have to move him," Stark said, waving his hand dismissively.

"Yes, out of the Chicago area," said Hayden hopefully. "That might not be a bad idea."

"No, Hayden," Stark replied, exasperated. "I mean out of the *country*! He's an illegal alien, remember?"

Hayden felt a dangerous stirring.

Stark, aware he had struck a nerve, tried to soften it. "Of course, he won't have to leave this week or anything. We need to keep him here until we have pleas from all our defendants. That should happen within a few weeks. Then we can give him a month or so to get his affairs cleaned up." Stark's eyes shifted nervously between Hayden and Kane.

Hayden spoke very softly, trying to check his anger. "Sir, this guy just put his life on the line and saved mine. This is how we take care of those who do heroic things—throw them on a bus to Juárez?"

"He's an outlaw, Hayden, sort of like you," bellowed Stark, now raging mad. "We can't tolerate that kind of behavior, and we sure as hell aren't going to reward it! He's just another wet, as far as I'm concerned."

By now Stark was leaning over the desk, his head thrust forward. With his eyebrows angled sharply to a point above the bridge of his nose, he looked like an enraged gargoyle. His silk tie was hanging down on the desk invitingly, within easy reach of Hayden, who grabbed the tie and jerked it firmly, pulling Stark from his chair, his forehead striking the glass desktop. Seized by a euphoric release of adrenaline, Nick leaned over the desk, pulled Stark upright by the loose folds of his shirt and was winding up with clenched fist to deliver a blow to the center of Stark's face when Kane pulled Hayden by the shoulders and sent him spinning into the window blinds.

Wheezing and standing shakily on bended knees, Stark slowly righted himself, loosened the tie around his neck, and fell heavily back into his chair, gasping for air. A trickle of blood curved around his right eyebrow where he had come down on the glass.

Hayden disentangled himself from the blinds and was sitting on the radiator against the window, his hair askew, breathing heavily. Tom Kane stood between them with his arms spread out like a boxing referee, looking back and forth to be sure neither would initiate further contact.

Nick stared at the floor. Lashing out at Stark, the personification of everything wrong with INS and immigration policy in general, had felt good for a moment, but he already regretted it. He knew he had now blown any chance of getting Stark to alter his decision about Miguel, however unlikely that might have been. He also realized he was facing an eventual thirty- or sixty-day suspension.

Stark pulled a handkerchief from his desk drawer and was dabbing the cut over his eyebrow. For several moments there was only the sound of Hayden and Stark breathing heavily. Finally, Stark spoke. "You're a fucking lunatic, Hayden," he croaked. "And we can't afford to have lunatics around here."

Hayden thought of Willard Smith . . . of Joe Willis. Their brand of lunacy had always been tolerated. Then his mind shifted to Miguel, who'd been pulled into this mess, performed heroically, and was now being betrayed. Nick knew he had to do something creative—and be damn quick about it.

———

Connie Salinas took the bus into the Loop, walked to the INS office, and asked to speak to Special Agent Tom Kane, who had been mentioned in newspaper stories about the investigation that led to the shootings at El Palacio. She now felt a compelling need to tell the truth about her deceased former husband, Marcos Ortega.

The receptionist immediately phoned Kane, who was at his desk in the fraud unit. "There's a woman here who says she has information about a guy named Marcos Ortega," she said.

Kane pulled Ortega's file, went to the reception area, and introduced himself. Connie was wearing a black leather coat over a beige pantsuit. She was now thin and pale, her hair cut short and combed back in a masculine style. Kane led her down the hallway to one of the windowless interview rooms. The small room, with only a table and two chairs, was lit by an overhead fluorescent light.

Once they were seated, it was Connie who asked the first question. "Are you Catholic, Mr. Kane?"

"Yeah, I'm Catholic. Why?"

"I was told a few weeks ago that I have cancer . . . pancreatic cancer," she said softly. "I have maybe six months to live. That's what they say, anyways. I don't want the radiation treatments or chemotherapy."

"I'm sorry," said Kane.

Connie pulled a tissue from the purse on her lap and dabbed her nose with it. She suddenly seemed very far away.

"I *am* sorry about your illness, Ms. Salinas, but what did you want to tell us about Marcos Ortega? Did you know he was involved in selling counterfeit documents?"

"No, I didn't know anything about that until I read the stories in the newspaper," she said.

"So what's the connection between you two?"

"We were married, me and Marcos. That's how he got his immigration papers."

As Kane started leafing through the file in search of a marriage certificate, Connie reached into her purse, casually pulled out a revolver, and placed it on the table.

Startled, Kane grabbed the gun and her purse. The gun was an old, blue-steel Smith & Wesson .38-caliber snub nose. With a flick of his wrist, Kane rolled out the cylinder to find it was not loaded.

"What the hell else do you have in here?" he growled, as he rifled through the purse. He found nothing but tissues and a wallet.

"I'm sorry," she said. "I didn't mean to frighten you."

He had her stand up with her hands against the wall, opened the door, and called out to a secretary to get a female agent who could do a pat-down. Connie patiently cooperated with the search before resuming her seat.

"So, why'd you bring the pistol?" asked Kane, still a bit rattled.

"That's the gun that shot Marcos Ortega," she said.

"Yeah? And who pulled the trigger?"

"Me. I killed Marcos."

Though she didn't seem like a violent person, she exuded a grim, take-it-or-leave-it attitude that he found credible. She didn't care whether he believed her or not. He left the interview room to search out an evidence envelope and tape recorder. For a moment he considered cuffing her to the chair but decided it was unnecessary. She *wanted* to be there. He came back, slipped the gun into the envelope, and placed the recorder in the middle of the table. Kane read the Miranda rights to her, and she signed the waiver. Her story tumbled out with a minimum of questions.

"I was stupid and thought I loved him, but he left me before we even lived together. I figured I'd have him deported, but the officer said they can't. That shocked me. My father woulda killed Marcos if I told him. But I was ashamed to even admit how stupid I was, and I didn't want my father to go to jail for something that was my fault. I just wanted to keep it all a secret, so I didn't fight it and I let Marcos pay for a divorce."

"Where did you get the gun?"

"Some guy outside a gun show on Randolph. He had some guns in his trunk."

"Had you ever fired a gun before?"

"My father owns lots of guns. He used to take us out to his cousin Eloy's place in Calumet where we would have family picnics, and we all shot at targets on hay bales. I remember my dad saying if you ever really wanted to kill a person you should shoot 'em in the face."

"I understand you being hurt, but what made you actually go through with it?" asked Kane.

"He broke my heart and made a fool outta me. So I was already mad and hated him, but when I saw him with his Mexican wife and kids on the street it really got to me, and I felt like I had to do something. You guys weren't going to do anything. So I planned it all out. I knew he liked that bowling alley on the North Side. I even went over there one Sunday night when it was closed just to see if it would work. Then I called him and said something about needing money and suggested meeting there. I knew he wouldn't tell his wife he was meeting me. He was secretive that way."

Though her voice was steady, she'd begun crying and took a moment to wipe the tears away.

"It was a perfect night because the wind was making a lot of noise, and there was nobody around. I got there early and parked in back of the building. I waited a few minutes after he got there and then walked out toward him, and he was standing there, and the light behind him made him stand out real clear, like a big target. The shot wasn't loud because of the wind."

Connie dabbed her nose with the tissue.

"At first, I didn't feel badly, just sort of numb. I figured he had it coming. But later I started thinking about his wife and kids. I saw them a couple times on the street, and I knew that what I did was a terrible sin, so I started going to church again. Then I got sick."

"Have you told anybody else about this?" asked Kane.

"Only the priest. I told him last week at confession. He said it wasn't enough—that to make it right with God, I needed to tell somebody official."

"Why come to us instead of the police?"

"It was all an immigration thing. That's what started it. I don't mean any disrespect, but you shouldn't let guys take advantage—like Marcos did. It doesn't make it right, what I did, but you shouldn't let it happen."

"You're right about that, but the law is so weak that it invites scams like the one Marcos pulled on you."

Kane left her alone for a minute and called the homicide cops to see what they wanted to do with Connie. The detective seemed annoyed that Kane had taken the confession and said he would be right over to take her into custody. When Kane returned to the interview room, Connie was looking absently at the wall. Her legs were stretched out alongside the table, and Kane noticed she was wearing black cowboy boots with silver tips.

"Thanks for listening, Mr. Kane," said Connie softly. "I feel better now."

———

Kane, alone in the office, answered the phone at six o'clock in the evening.

"Investigations, Kane speaking."

"*¿Habla español, Señor Kane?*"

"*Sí.*"

The man continued in Spanish: "You are the one who was in the paper . . . the story about the fake documents?"

"Yes."

"I wanted to tell you—there is a man who took over for Salvador Rico."

Kane bolted upright in his chair and grabbed a notepad. "What's his name?"

"His real name I don't know. They call him 'the Little Umpire' because he wears a blue jacket and baseball cap. He is from Peru. He comes back from California with thousands of the green cards and social security cards." The caller spoke Spanish slowly and distinctly so that Kane had no trouble understanding him.

"Where does he live?"

"This I don't know. But he drives a new Chevrolet Impala. Most nights you can find him at the Little Lima Bar on Ashland. He always carries a gun—a revolver."

"How old is he?"

The man laughed. "He could be thirty-five or fifty-five. You can't tell."

"What does he look like?"

"He is short . . . his teeth are bad."

"How do you know about his new business?"

There was silence at the other end.

"It would be held in confidence," said Kane. "You can talk freely."

There was only the sound of breathing. Afraid the man would hang up, Kane continued. "What else do you know about him?"

"The Colombians thought he was a government informant. But then they heard that Salvador Rico was the informant, so they are no longer after him. One other thing—'the Little Umpire' suddenly had all this money when Rico died. Before, he had nothing. It is odd, don't you think?"

"Yes, it is very odd," said Kane. "We should meet to discuss this further."

"I must go now," the man said, and the line went dead.

Kane smiled as he set down the receiver.

———

All was quiet on Francis Street. Though the rain had stopped, gray clouds were still thick overhead. Inside the car, condensation clouded the windshield. Nick cleared it with his hand and scanned the street.

If you come through, we'll take care of you. You can trust us to do that. Those were the words he'd spoken to Miguel. He'd said it because he believed it was true—and Miguel had counted on him, trusted him.

As Nick climbed the steps to the porch, Miguel swung the door open.

"Paco sees you from window," he said, smiling warmly. "Please, come in."

"Let's talk out here on the steps, if that's OK with you," said Nick.

"*Claro.* Yes, of course."

The porch was damp, so Miguel picked up a rug from inside and spread it over the top step. Hayden noticed that

Miguel was wearing a jacket, the same one he had worn the day of the shooting. "Were you headed out somewhere?"

"No. Is cold inside." Miguel pulled the collar of his jacket around his neck. "How is arm?"

"It's better. I can move it pretty well now," Nick said, rotating his shoulder.

Neither of them spoke for a few moments.

"Something is wrong?" Miguel asked.

Nick had to force the words out. "They want you to go back to Mexico. I tried to stop it . . . you have to believe that."

"Yes, I believe, Nicolas."

"But I have a plan for you and your family." He reached inside his leather jacket, pulled out a thick envelope, and handed it to Miguel. "With these you'll be able to stay in this country as long as you want—all four of you. You'll have different names, but you'll be as good as US citizens. I can get you a job in California, and you wouldn't have to do anything for INS anymore."

Miguel opened the envelope and pulled out the folded documents. There were four official-looking birth certificates that appeared to have been issued by the State of California. The stamps and seals looked genuine. Miguel's name would be Miguel Fernandez. He examined them carefully.

"You get to keep your first name," said Hayden. "Those are genuine California forms and seals. They're on file. The social security numbers are good. That was a family that died in a car crash a couple of years ago. Your birth dates will be different, but not by more than a year each."

"Where you get these?"

"It's better if you don't know about that."

Miguel looked down at the papers. Carmen would have to change her name to Luz Fernandez. Paco would be Luis Fernandez. He considered them for several moments and then carefully folded them together, slid them into the envelope, and handed it back to Hayden.

"No, thank you, Nicolas."

"What do you mean? Why not?"

"I no can do this."

"Sure you can. Don't let them push you around like a piece of garbage. With these you control your destiny."

Miguel spoke evenly. "I no think we control destiny. You risk much and I am grateful, but we no can do this . . . changing our names. I no can ask them to live false life."

Hayden hadn't considered that he might refuse the documents. Miguel had already saved his life; now he was saving him from crossing a line into criminal activity.

"Is great country here," said Miguel, "but we go back now. Is no good to be where you not wanted. I thought they want us here. That is why I think is all right to come."

"You *are* wanted, Miguel."

Miguel smiled. "Is OK, Nicolas. We have many family there. Carmen miss them very much. My parents . . . they old and soon they need us. They be happy we come back."

Nick stuffed the envelope back into his leather jacket. They sat quietly for a few moments before Nick spoke. "They want you to leave when the criminal case is over . . . probably about six weeks. Maybe I can get you more time."

"Thank you, but we no need more time." Miguel turned to Hayden. "What about you, Nicolas? After all that happen, you are OK?"

Hayden was taken aback. How could Miguel possibly think about *him* at a time like this? It took a moment to shift focus. "Yeah, I'm fine," he said, smiling appreciatively.

"Good. Still, I pray for you."

The clouds were beginning to break up on the horizon and the retreating sun crowned the rooftops with a stream of pale gold light.

"I going to miss this street," said Miguel wistfully. "I remember when I come here and see the street name."

"Francis Street?"

"St. Francis Xavier—he is patron saint for immigrants. He watch over us."

Though he didn't share Miguel's Catholic faith, Nick knew there had been a subtle yet dramatic shift in his own consciousness. He wasn't sure where it was leading him, but he was gradually becoming aware of a higher dimension—a dimension that in some mysterious way binds us all together.

"You're a good man, Miguel. You've helped me more than you know."

"We help each other same, Nicolas," said Miguel. "What you do at the bar—I not forget this. We always be friends."

As they rose from the steps, they shook hands and Hayden said they would talk again soon.

———

Nick turned off Francis Street into brisk traffic on Eighteenth Street. He called in to the radio operator and asked her to check for messages, but she had nothing for him.

Heading north on Western Avenue, he came to a stop at a red light. On the corner was a metal drum factory where many area control operations had been conducted over the years. It could always be counted on if a few extra bodies were needed for the day's quota. Nick watched the Mexican workers as they stacked fifty-five-gallon drums on pallets, and realized that he now felt differently about them. Though he didn't condone their illegal status, their mere presence was no longer a source of personal frustration. That burden had been lifted. The last vestiges of the ego-driven gladiator syndrome seemed to have faded away.

His thoughts were interrupted by the squawk of the radio and the voice of Richard Stark.

"Base to Hayden, do you read?" said the voice, still raspy from their encounter in Stark's office. It was unusual for Stark to be in the office this late and had to be something important. Nick picked up the mic but did not speak.

After several moments of silence, Stark repeated: "Base to Hayden." Another pause and then a demand: "Answer the damn radio, Hayden. I just heard you check in a few minutes ago."

Nick placed the microphone in its holder, turned the switch off, and watched the red light of the receiver flicker and fade. Stark was saying something, but his voice was too small to make out and disintegrated into nothing.

The traffic light turned green, and Nick pulled through the intersection. He would drive north to the Chinese restaurant with the happy cooks and waitresses.